Snow Kissed

RaeAnne Thayne

CANARY STREET PRESS

**CANARY
STREET
PRESS™**

Recycling programs
for this product may
not exist in your area.

ISBN-13: 978-1-335-00107-8

Snow Kissed

For questions and comments about the quality of this book, please contact us at CustomerService@Harlequin.com.

Canary Street Press
22 Adelaide St. West, 41st Floor
Toronto, Ontario M5H 4E3, Canada
CanaryStPress.com

HarperCollins Publishers
Macken House, 39/40 Mayor Street Upper,
Dublin 1, D01 C9W8, Ireland
www.HarperCollins.com

Printed in U.S.A.

To everyone missing a child, a parent, a partner or a friend this Christmas. You're not alone. Love can stretch across miles, silence and time. Hold on.

CHAPTER ONE

—

"ONE OF THESE DAYS, YOU NEED TO LEARN HOW TO SAY THE word *no*."

Holly Moore sighed as her twin sister's words seemed to ring through her little florist shop, resounding with truth.

Hannah was almost always right. Her sister was one of the smartest women she knew and Holly couldn't disagree with her about this. She had a problem with trying to please everyone and she *did* need to learn how to say no.

Most of the time, anyway.

"I can't. Not in this case."

"Your former sister-in-law will survive if she doesn't have Lydia as her flower girl. She can find someone else. I'm sure there will be plenty of people who don't think she should do it anyway."

Holly fought a sharp ache at the words, even as she didn't necessarily agree with her sister's harsh words.

Her ex-husband's family loved Lydia and did their best to embrace and include her. She couldn't deny that there were plenty of other people in society who would prefer her daughter and others with similar developmental disabilities stayed in the background, where their presence wouldn't make anyone uncomfortable.

"Kristine is a fantastic aunt to Lydia. They have a close relationship. It might not be as close as the one you have with Lydia, but Kris tries hard to be inclusive. Which is why I can't refuse."

Holly tucked a few more stems of greenery into the arrangement she was working on. "Unfortunately, all the plans have been made," she went on. "Kristine has already talked to

Lydia about it and showed her the dress she bought for her to wear. There's no turning back now."

Hannah frowned. "She should have asked you first before talking to Lydia."

"You can't unscatter dandelion fluff. It's done now. Lydia is all excited, even though she doesn't have any idea what being a flower girl involves. I mean, the dress is gorgeous. Velvet, red, with a little white faux-fur collar. You and I would have loved to own a dress like that when we were flower-girl age."

"I suppose you can't break her heart." Hannah gave her a sympathetic look. "If our Lydi wants to be a flower girl, she won't easily budge. That girl is as stubborn as a mule on a mountain trail."

"You don't have to tell me."

Her daughter might only be five but Lydia had amply demonstrated her iron will in that handful of years. She had learned to walk before any of the doctors and specialists expected it, she had basically potty trained herself, she could write her name and she could pick out sight words.

Most of the time, her determination filled Holly with pride. With all of her daughter's challenges, Lydia would need to be fierce as she confronted the world. But in certain circumstances, it could be tough for a mother with her child's best interests at heart to convince that child something she wanted might not be the best thing for her.

Being Lydia's mother was a complete joy most of the time. Still, pitting her own will against that of a determined five-year-old girl who didn't always understand subtext or subtle nuances of meaning could sometimes be exhausting.

Any five-year-old would probably be the same.

"Don't listen to me. I'm sure everything will be fine," Hannah assured her. "Lydia will have a great time and look fabulous in her red velvet dress with the fake-fur collar. And I have no doubt the flowers you're doing for the wedding will be amazing, as always."

The thought of it all, along with everything else she had to do this month, left Holly exhausted.

Her sister was absolutely right. She needed to learn how to say no. She should never have agreed to provide the floral decorations for her former sister-in-law's upcoming wedding and reception, especially when she'd already had two weddings booked for the month of December before Kristine and Matt decided on a holiday ceremony.

Beyond her wedding responsibilities, December was one of her busiest months of the year, when people loved to buy wreaths, flowers for hostess gifts or centerpieces for their holiday decorations.

If she managed to get any sleep this month, it would be a true holiday miracle.

"I'll help you," Hannah assured her. "You know I'm here to do anything you need. And all of us can pitch in to help you with Lydia. Mom and Dad love having her and I'm sure we could talk the boys into helping, too."

The boys were their older brothers, Asher and Micah Goodwin, who also were helpless to resist Lydia when she put her mind to something.

Her daughter was beloved by nearly everyone she met, which left Holly deeply grateful.

Impulsively, she leaned over and hugged her sister, careful not to poke her with the stems of the white heath aster in her hand that she was using to fill in between the pink gerbera daisies and baby roses.

"I know. Thank you. I don't know what I would have done the past two years without all of you."

Since her divorce, her family had rallied around her, helping her take over her aunt's florist shop, move into Rose

Cottage, raise a special-needs child. She would have been lost without them.

Hannah hugged her in return. "We've got you," she assured her. She stepped away and looked at the elaborate arrangement. "This is really pretty. Who is the mom? Anyone I know?"

Holly stuck in the spray of aster before looking at the name on the order form. "Dana Harris. I don't know her. Do you?"

There was a time when she had been certain she knew every single person in their small Idaho town of Shelter Springs.

Hannah frowned. "Never heard of her. What's her husband's name?"

She looked at the form again. "I don't know. I didn't have a chance to speak with him. Ginger took the order before she left to make deliveries. She didn't write his name down, only the words *hot dad*."

Hannah laughed. "Well, that's super helpful. Sounds like our Ginger."

"Right?"

Ginger Martineau, one of four staff members at Evergreen & Ivy, might be scattered and easily distracted but she was also creative, loyal and hardworking. More importantly, her sunny attitude and whimsical sense of humor made Holly laugh in a world that sometimes didn't feel all that funny.

Holly and her sister were chatting about Hannah's work as a music therapist when the bells on her front door chimed and in walked the most gorgeous man Holly had ever seen in real life.

He was tall, muscular, with a hard jawline, short dark hair and stunning green eyes.

She was aware of a completely inappropriate flutter of awareness.

This must be the hot dad who had ordered the new baby flower arrangement, though how Ginger had managed to deduce he was gorgeous simply over the phone, Holly had no idea.

She did know she had never seen this man before in her life or she absolutely would have remembered him.

He looked around at her shop, bedecked for the holidays with three live trees, garlands, wreaths and fairy lights.

Somehow the inherently feminine surroundings, flowery and cheerful, only served to make him look more gorgeously masculine in contrast.

She gave him a bright smile. "Hi. You're right on time! I just finished your order. Congratulations!"

She walked around the corner of the worktable holding out the lush arrangement in a pink container shaped like a large building block with the words *It's a Girl* on the front.

He looked at it as if she had held out a live barracuda.

"Um, what's this?"

She tried not to bristle at his blatant rejection of something she had considered lovely, perfect for the situation.

"This is what you wanted for your wife, who just had a baby girl this morning. Congratulations again. The holidays are such a fun time to have a new baby. You must be so thrilled. What's her name?"

"I think there's been some kind of mistake."

She gazed down at her lovely creation then back at him, dismayed. "Oh no. Was it a boy? I'm so sorry."

She seriously needed to have a long chat with Ginger about paying more attention to details. This wasn't the first order the other woman had typed wrong into the system. Or even the first one this week.

"Don't worry at all. I can change it. Give me five minutes.

I've got some pale blue roses and some yellow aster that came in this morning. I can swap them out. And we can put everything in a different container."

She hurried back behind her counter but before she could start undoing all her hard work, he followed her.

"No. I think you've mistaken me for someone else. I don't have a wife. Or, God forbid, a newborn baby, girl or boy."

Good heavens. How many hot strangers had moved into town when she wasn't looking? And why did they all suddenly need flowers?

She winced. "I'm sorry. I jumped to conclusions. I assumed you were here to pick this up. How can I help you?"

"I'm looking for my niece. I was told to meet her here."

"Your niece?" Holly exchanged a look with her sister, who had been following the interchange with interest. "Why would she be here?"

He shrugged, wide shoulders rippling inside his black jacket. "I have no idea. I only know she texted me and said she was picking up somebody named Lydia and would meet me here."

All the pieces suddenly clicked into place. "Oh! You're talking about Audrey! You must be Audrey's uncle. Ryan, isn't it? I had no idea you were coming today. Audrey didn't mention it. In fact, Kim said you wouldn't be able to make it to town until next week."

"I was able to rearrange some things back in San Diego. I texted Audrey this morning to tell her I was on my way."

Why hadn't Kim ever mentioned that her brother looked like he should be on the cover of some sexy military guy calendar?

"You're Kim's little brother?"

He turned his attention to Hannah when she spoke and Holly could see him do a double-take.

As for Hannah, she looked at him with an appreciative look

that left Holly feeling oddly territorial, like when they were kids and Hannah wanted to play with one of Holly's brand-new toys.

"Yes. Hi. Ryan Caldwell. You're twins."

"Have been all our lives. I'm Hannah Goodwin."

Her sister beamed at him and held out her hand. After a beat, he shook it, looking bemused.

Not for the first time, Holly wished she wasn't always the quiet sister, the serious, bookish one. Sometimes she wanted to be the fun, flirty twin who was comfortable talking to anyone.

"How kind of you to drop everything in San Diego and come out to help Kim with Audrey during the holidays," Hannah went on.

He shrugged. "We're family. Isn't that the kind of thing family does for each other?"

"Definitely, though I would have thought Audrey could stay with your dad over in Haven Point."

Something hard flashed across his expression but it was there and gone so quickly Holly thought she must have been mistaken.

"The colonel is busy taking care of Diane after the accident as well as running Caldwell Aviation. He doesn't have time to run Audrey back and forth to school here in Shelter Springs."

"How is Diane?" Holly asked, feeling great sympathy for the other woman. She couldn't imagine being laid up over the holidays, with broken bones sustained in an accident a week earlier.

"She came home from the hospital a few days ago, apparently. I talked to her this morning while I was driving and she assured me she's fine. I haven't seen her yet. I was thinking I could take Audrey there this evening, after we pick up her things from your place. She has been staying with you, right?"

Audrey, Kim's thirteen-year-old daughter, had been sleeping in Holly's spare room since Sunday.

"She has. It's been no problem."

"Thank you for that. I know my sister is grateful."

"There is nothing to thank me for. Audrey is a delight. I enjoy her company and she's wonderful with my daughter. I was grateful her mother trusted me enough to let her stay with me while Kim gets the help she needs."

His mouth tightened again and he gave a short nod. She had only spoken briefly with her friend and employee since Kim checked herself into an addiction treatment facility in Boise the morning after the accident, the one that had injured Kim's stepmother, Diane.

"I didn't mind at all," she said again. "In fact, she could have stayed with me the whole time Kim expects to be in Boise. I told your sister that. You really didn't have to come out here."

"I wish I could have made it earlier, but it took me a few days to arrange leave."

Kim talked often about her younger brother while she and Holly were working together at the shop. Holly almost felt like she knew him. She likely knew far more about him than he did about her.

She was aware that Ryan Caldwell was a naval pilot who flew helicopters—a pilot who had been relegated to a desk job the past two months while healing from a knee injury sustained in the line of duty.

It was one thing to know information about a man in the abstract. It was entirely different when the same man was standing in her floral shop, looking rough and masculine and gorgeous.

"I'm sure Audrey will be happy to see you," she said.

Before he could answer, the bells on the door heralded a new arrival. A young man rushed in, clearly in a hurry. He was good-looking in a clean-cut way but not at all in the same league as Ryan Caldwell.

Happiness also beamed out of him so brightly it probably could power all the Christmas lights in town.

"Hi. I'm Austin Harris. I'm here to pick up a bouquet for my wife. She just had a baby this morning."

He brimmed with excitement and pride, as if no other couple on earth had ever been clever enough to bring a child into the world.

"I ordered it about an hour ago and the person I spoke with said it would be ready at three p.m."

Holly quickly turned away from Ryan, switching back into business mode. "Congratulations to both of you," she said warmly. "Is this your first?"

"Yes. That is, she had a miscarriage around this time last year, so technically our second."

His words and the hint of sorrow on his expression made her like him that much more, though she couldn't help but remember her own miscarriage, the year after Lydia was born. That dark time had been the beginning of the end of her marriage.

Her now-ex-husband hadn't been at all thrilled to find out she was unexpectedly pregnant, as if she had found herself in that condition all by herself. When she lost the baby at ten weeks, Troy hadn't bothered to hide his relief and Holly had never been able to forgive him for it.

Of course, now he and Brittany, the woman he had married only two months after their divorce was final, had a child together. Hudson was a healthy, adorable baby boy, and the man who had claimed he didn't want more children couldn't be more thrilled.

She pushed away the lingering hint of bitterness she had no right to. She did not regret their divorce at all. She had accepted the inevitability of it a long time ago and knew both she and Lydia were much happier now.

When she presented the arrangement to Austin Harris, his already bright face lit up even more. "It's perfect! Gorgeous."

As she processed the order, he went on gushing about how brave his wife had been, how thrilled they both were at the healthy delivery, how adorably perfect their baby girl was.

His sheer delight made Holly smile as she handed him the receipt to sign.

He was still beaming as he grabbed the bouquet and hurried out of the store. Before the door closed behind him, Holly saw a light snow had begun to fall.

"I've got to run too," Hannah said, gathering up her coat, hat and scarf. "I'm meeting with Reverend Ashford to go over the final music selections for the Christmas Eve service."

"Thank you for lunch. I wouldn't have had time to grab anything if you hadn't taken pity on me and picked up a sandwich," Holly said.

"What are twins for?" Hannah said, then turned a flirtatious look on the other man in the shop, who had been standing to the side, waiting for her to finish the interaction with the new father.

"Nice to meet you, Ryan. I hope you enjoy your stay in Shelter Springs."

"Thanks," he said.

After she left, he glanced at the sleek watch on his wrist. "What time do you expect Audrey and your daughter?"

"It should be any minute, though sometimes Lydia likes to dawdle," she admitted.

The words were barely out when the door burst open and

her beautiful girl rushed through as if she were chasing a pack of wild puppies.

"Mommy! Mommy!"

She dropped her backpack just inside the door and lunged for Holly's outstretched arms.

"There's my girl." She hugged her close. "Hi Lydi-bug. Did you have a good day?"

Lydia nodded. "We drew pictures and heard a story and played at the sand table and sang songs. And we had pizza for lunch. I love pizza."

"I know you do."

Holly was deeply grateful for the teacher and aides at her child's special education kindergarten class, as well as the regular ed teacher where Lydia was mainstreamed for half of her day.

They were all angels, as far as Holly was concerned.

Smoothing her flyaway hair away from her face, Lydia gave Kim's brother her wide, generous smile. "Hi. I'm Lydia."

Ryan Caldwell looked nonplussed for an instant then gave her a slow smile in return that Holly somehow found even more devastating.

"Hello. Nice to meet you, Lydia. My name is Ryan."

"Uncle Ry!"

Even as he spoke, the door opened and Audrey came in looking breathless, as if she had run after Lydia the whole way from the elementary school, which was just down the street from the middle school Audrey attended.

"You're here already! I didn't think you would be here for a few hours! I'm so glad you were able to come early."

Audrey hurried toward him and gave him a hug, which he returned. Holly found the clear affection between them reassuring.

"I'm sorry it took me so long to make the arrangements," he said.

"Totally fine." Audrey gave him an apologetic look. "I can't leave with you yet, though. I'm sorry! I promised to watch Lydia until the store closes."

When Ryan shifted his attention to Holly again, she tried not to feel guilty.

"She's been babysitting Lydia after school for me. Usually I try to work my schedule around Lydia's so I'm done here by the time school is over. It's a little more, um, challenging now that I'm short-staffed."

While her best employee, Kim, was absolutely where she needed to be, her absence created a scheduling nightmare this time of year, especially when the season also inevitably brought more sick days for her staff.

"Audrey has been so great to help out."

"I love Audrey," Lydia announced. "She's my friend."

The older girl tousled her hair. "And you're mine. We're besties."

"Besties," Lydia repeated with a giggle. She truly did adore Audrey, which warmed Holly's heart. She was grateful all over again for the older girl's kindness and willingness to take a job babysitting for her.

"Why don't we skip today and start up again Monday?" Holly suggested.

She was still overwhelmed, especially with the first of her three seasonal weddings the next day, but she was sure she could figure out how to work around Lydia's presence. With luck, Holly might even be able to get her to take a nap in the break room, where she and Audrey usually hung out.

"I'm sure your uncle could use your help getting settled in at your place," she went on.

"But what about my bestie here?" Audrey asked.

"We'll be fine," Holly assured her. "We've finished all the deliveries for the day and I don't expect the afternoon to be too busy. I'm only going to be working on wedding decorations and Lydia can help me with that. Isn't that right?"

"I'm a good helper," Lydia declared. It wasn't precisely true but Holly would never dispute her daughter's claim.

"Are you sure?" Audrey looked worried.

"Positive."

"I was thinking we could head over to Haven Point to check on your Grandma Diane this afternoon," Ryan said to Audrey before turning to Holly. "I would hate to put you in a bind by stealing away your babysitter though. We don't have to go this afternoon. There's no rush."

"It's no problem," she said. "Go."

"What about my stuff?" Audrey asked. "My suitcase is still at Rose Cottage with my phone charger and everything."

"I can gather your things and your suitcase and take them to you later tonight."

"You don't need to go to any trouble," Ryan said with that stiff politeness again. "I don't want to put you out further, especially when it looks like you have your hands full. If it works for you, we can stop by later this evening to grab them."

"We have a Christmas tree," Lydia announced. "Audrey doesn't have a Christmas tree."

"We'll have to do something about that, won't we?" Ryan said.

Lydia nodded with a vigor that made him smile.

"While I'm here, do you have some kind of bouquet I could take to my stepmom?" he asked Holly.

"We have a few premade arrangements." She pointed to the large refrigerator with the clear door. "You can take a look and see if you like any of them. If not, I can throw something else together for you."

"I'm sure we can find something that works. I don't know anything about flowers. Can you help me choose, Audrey?"

The two of them made their way to the display and quickly came to the counter with one of her favorites, a lovely spray of red roses, white Asiatic lilies and red-and-white carnations. It was accented with pine cones and seasonal greenery along with a small balloon pick that read Get Well Soon.

"This is a nice one," she said as she rang it up and gave him the total.

"Yes. It's lovely," he said, swiping his credit card.

"I suppose we'll see you later tonight, then," he said, after she gave him the receipt.

"Sounds good," she answered, trying her best to ignore the little quiver of anticipation she didn't want to feel.

Something told her Ryan Caldwell was trouble, something she definitely didn't need this year.

She had endured enough trouble because of a man who wasn't good for her. She didn't need to go looking for more.

—

CHAPTER TWO

HOW HAD HIS LIFE COME TO THIS?

As Ryan drove through a lightly falling snow toward the home of the father he usually did his best to avoid, he tried to figure out what the hell he was doing here.

His leg hurt like the devil from the long day of travel. He didn't want to be here. But what else could he have done? Kim needed him.

He still reeled when he thought of her tearful phone call a week ago, the day after Thanksgiving.

He had been stretched out in his condo with his knee on ice, settling in to watch a bowl game, when Kim called, her voice panicked and tearful.

"Diane's been hurt. There's been an accident. She's in the hospital. I was arrested. Dad bailed me out."

The barrage of information hit him like the spray from a .50-caliber machine gun and he could do nothing but stare, certain he must have misheard something.

"Arrested? For what?"

She made a tiny noise, almost a whimper. "DUI," she finally said. "I was under the influence of pain meds. I should never have been driving. I could have killed all of us. Diane. Audrey. Me. The other driver. Oh, Ry. I screwed up so bad."

At that, the whimper became a full-on sob, followed by another and another.

"Slow down. Deep breaths, Kim."

His own words reminded him painfully of how she tried to comfort him during those dark weeks after their mother died. He had been thirteen, trying to tell himself to man up and not be such a mess. Kim had been two years older, forced to step into a caregiving role long before their mother died, when Laura Caldwell had barely been able to get out of bed from the effects of chemotherapy and radiation.

Kim had been the one who comforted Ryan, who hugged him even when he insisted he didn't need to be hugged, who sat quietly without judgment when he cried.

Their father certainly hadn't been there for his two grieving children.

Kim had held the fractured pieces of their family together. Now she was the one who sounded fractured.

"First of all, how is Diane?" he had asked her. Ryan actually liked his father's second wife, whom the colonel had married about ten years earlier.

"Not good." Kim's voice hitched. "They were worried about internal injuries but didn't find anything. Thank God. She has a broken arm and a broken leg. She's having surgery this afternoon on her arm. She also needed about eighteen stitches in her face. I don't know how she'll ever be able to forgive me."

"I'm sure she understands it was an accident."

"An accident that might not have happened if I had been more aware of my surroundings. I should have seen the other driver wasn't stopping at the red light. Instead, I was distracted by something else and turned right in front of him."

"So you were T-boned?"

"Yes." She hitched out another sob and fought for control. "By a high school student who only had his license for three weeks. That's not the point, though. I should never have been driving. I knew I shouldn't have been behind the wheel. But Audrey and Diane wanted to hit some Black Friday sales and Diane asked me to drive. I thought I would be fine. I only took one pain pill but I . . . chased it with bourbon."

He had no idea what to say. He knew his sister had struggled with substance use when she was younger, after she ran away from the boarding school their father had sent her to. But that had been years ago. Since she had her daughter, Kim had worked hard to turn her life around and had stepped up to raise her on her own after Audrey's slimeball father had died in prison.

"I . . . I think I need to go into rehab. Dad's found a place in Boise that can take me. I hate to leave Audrey, especially this time of year, but if I can check in now, I might make it home for Christmas. By New Year's at the latest. Dad thinks if I can prove to the court I've sought help on my own, I might be able to avoid jail time."

Apparently Colonel Douglas Caldwell had his daughter's life all figured out. Like always.

"Was anyone else injured in the accident?"

"Audrey and I have a few cuts and scrapes. The other driver only had minor injuries, thank heavens."

"I'm so sorry this happened. Thanks for keeping me in the loop."

Kim paused for a long time. He was about to ask if she was still there when she finally spoke, her voice small. "Ry. Can you come here?"

He should have instinctively said *Hell yeah*. If his sister needed him, he should be willing to drop everything and go to her.

Instead, he had said nothing while he tried to figure out the logistics. Apparently his silence spoke volumes.

"Forget I said anything. It was a silly thing to ask. It's just . . . there's Audrey. I would normally have her stay with Dad and Diane but they live in Haven Point, eight miles from her school, and Dad will be busy caring for Diane after she gets out of the hospital. She doesn't need a thirteen-year-old girl underfoot while she recovers."

"I could maybe move some things around and put in for emergency leave," he said. "Let me see what I can do."

He wasn't exactly out there saving the world anyway. He couldn't fly until he was medically cleared from the injuries he sustained in a hard landing after a malfunction.

The staph infection he had acquired had nearly taken his leg and his recovery had been far longer than he or anyone else expected.

"It might be a few days before I can get there. Do you have somewhere else for her to stay while I see what I can do?"

"Yes. If you can't, it should be okay. My boss, Holly, has already said she can take her in. I've told you about her, I think. She's great but she's so busy. I don't want to burden her with one more thing."

He could understand that now, as he drove along the lake toward his father's place. He didn't know everything Holly Moore might have going on right now, but he had seen the smudges under her eyes, the subtle fragility.

"Plus, it's Christmas," Kim had said. "Audrey should be in her own bed in her own house with her own family, if at all possible."

"I'll see what I can do," he had said.

"That's all I can ask. You are the best brother in the world, Ryan, in case I haven't told you that lately."

He was far from that. If he had been a better brother, he might have seen the signs earlier that his sister was struggling. He should have been paying more attention and identified that she was on the edge, instead of being consumed with his own injury and his uncertain future.

He looked at his niece now, who was scrolling on her phone.

"I think we're about a mile from your grandpa's house,"

he commented to Audrey, more as a conversation starter than anything else.

What did one say to a thirteen-year-old girl, anyway? He hadn't been great at speaking to girls her age when he'd actually been a teenager himself.

She looked out at the dark trees lining the road here on both sides as they drove around the lake. "Yeah. It's not much further."

"Sorry about taking you from your babysitting gig."

She shrugged. "Holly and Lydia will be okay. Lydia's pretty good most of the time. She's cute, isn't she?"

He pictured the girl with her blue eyes and wide smile. "She seems really sweet."

"And she's smart, too. She struggles with her words sometimes but there's a lot going on in her head."

"Do you babysit her every day?"

"No. Just when Holly needs me. Lydia's grandma or her aunt sometimes pick her up after school."

"Ah."

She put down her phone and angled toward him. "You didn't have to come all the way to Idaho to stay with me. I know Mom asked you to but I would have been fine staying with Holly and Lydia. Holly's super nice and I think she was happy to have my help in the evenings with Lydia, especially this time of year when she's so busy."

He shouldn't ask more but Ryan had to admit he was curious about the woman who was Kim's boss and her friend, a woman who had somehow seemed both independent and vulnerable.

"Is Lydia's dad in the picture?"

"They're divorced. I've never met him. He lives in Oregon and his name is Troy. He's coming home for Christmas, though.

I heard Holly talking to her sister about it. They're twins. Did you know that?"

"Yeah. Her sister was in the store when I got there. It's kind of hard to miss."

"Don't you think it would be cool to be a twin?"

"I've never thought of it."

"I have. I wish I had a twin sister. It would be like having a constant sleepover, right?"

"I suppose. As long as you get along."

"Anyway, Holly was talking about Lydia's dad coming for Christmas with Hannah. She seems super stressed about it."

Had it been a hard divorce? He supposed there was no such thing as an easy one. Even when both parties wanted out, untangling the threads of lives that had been woven together by time and experiences must be tough.

It wasn't any of his business. He couldn't imagine his path would cross Holly Moore's much in the few short weeks he planned to stay in Shelter Springs with Audrey.

"Do you have homework tonight?" he asked as they neared his father's house, which had once been Diane's childhood home. The two of them had purchased it, added on and made a forever home out of it after Doug retired from the air force.

"Only a math worksheet. It won't take me long. I can even do it in home room in the morning."

"We can work on it later. Have you been by to see Diane since the accident?"

"I spent the first night here with Grandpa after Mom was arrested. That was rough. We went to the hospital to see Diane the next day. And then Holly brought me over here to visit her a few nights ago after Diane got home from the hospital, which was super nice of her since she doesn't even really know Diane. We took her flowers then, too."

Ryan had been here only once before, after Kim and Audrey moved to the area to be closer to the colonel and his wife.

He was not surprised to see that at least from the outside the house was neat and orderly. Not a trace of snow covered the driveway or sidewalk, as if the weather wouldn't dare sully Colonel Douglas Caldwell's property.

Ryan couldn't deny it was a lovely house, on the shore of Lake Haven, with its stunning mountain backdrop.

It still seemed odd to him that his father would choose to retire here to this quiet Idaho tourist town, especially after a lifetime spent in positions of authority at various military bases around the world.

Diane probably had a huge role in that decision. She had grown up in Haven Point and had inherited the house after her mother died a few years earlier.

Audrey jumped out as soon as he turned off the engine.

"Here. You take the flowers," he told her.

"You bought them."

"They can be from both of us."

She rolled her eyes but grabbed them and carried them toward the house. She rang the doorbell when Ryan was still only halfway up the sidewalk. As he walked up the steps, his leg aching with every movement, the door opened. His father stood silhouetted in the doorway.

"Audrey, my dear," he exclaimed. "What a nice surprise."

"Hi, Grandpa. Look who's here! Uncle Ryan!"

His father looked up and some hint of emotion Ryan couldn't identity flashed across his features but disappeared quickly.

"Son. Good to see you." Doug smiled and held out a hand. After a pause, Ryan reached out and shook it briefly.

"How's Diane?" he asked. While his relationship with his

father was strained, he was fond of his stepmother. She was as warm and friendly as Doug was stiff and remote.

"Better but still in a great deal of pain. She's being stubborn about taking her meds on a schedule."

He could relate. He was the same. He rarely wanted to take more than the occasional ibuprofen now, even when he had a bad day, and hadn't been thrilled at round after round of antibiotics.

"Is she up for visitors?" he asked.

"She will love it," his father assured him. "She's in the family room. We were watching a movie. Come through."

Ryan scanned his memory but couldn't remember a single time his father had relaxed enough to settle into the family room and watch a show with them.

Maybe he had blocked it out, though. Douglas hadn't always been working. He could remember his father coming to the occasional soccer game or swimming together with the whole family at the base recreation center.

Ryan freely acknowledged that most of his memories of his father were tinged with bitterness for the hard, emotionless automaton he had become after Laura's death.

The family room was spacious yet cozy, with a wide flat screen TV above a gas fireplace, plump, comfortable-looking furniture and floor-to-ceiling windows overlooking the lake.

In a deep leather recliner, his stepmother stretched out with her leg up on a pillow. She looked as elegant and lovely as ever, though she had a wide bandage across her forehead and another across one cheek.

Still, she smiled when they walked into the room. "Oh, what a lovely surprise," she exclaimed, her voice warm with welcome. "Hello!"

"Hi, Grandma Di." Audrey leaned over and hugged her grandmother, careful of her arm in the sling.

Diane hugged her back with unfeigned affection. Whenever he talked to his stepmother, Ryan was struck by how different she was from the colonel. Warm where he was rigid, gentle where he was forceful.

Oddly, she reminded him of his own mother, whom he remembered as always laughing and smiling, even as cancer slowly stole away her life.

It baffled Ryan how a man as cheerless and cold as Doug somehow managed to convince two bright, bubbly women to marry him.

"These are for you," Audrey said.

"More flowers? They're beautiful. I would have known they were from Evergreen and Ivy without even looking at the card. Holly Moore does lovely work. Thank you so much."

"They're really from Uncle Ryan. I just helped him pick them out."

Diane smiled at him. "Thank you. Doug, dear, will you set them on the table over there, where I can admire them?"

As his father stepped forward to take the flowers over to join several other arrangements on the table, Ryan leaned forward to kiss his stepmother's unbandaged cheek.

"How are you?"

She made a face. "I'm fine. This is all a bunch of fuss over nothing."

"It's not nothing," Doug said with a grunt. "You have a broken leg and a broken arm."

"But other than that, I'm having a great week," she said, grinning at Audrey and Ryan.

When his father married her a decade earlier, Ryan had been prepared to dislike her. Diane made that impossible.

"I'm sorry you were hurt," he said.

"So am I. We had some lovely plans for the holidays but accidents happen."

"Is there anything I can do for you?"

"Having you here with Audrey is enough. I was so touched when I found out you were coming to stay with her, though she is always welcome to stay here, of course. We would have loved having her."

His sister was right. His father had his hands full helping Diane recover. They didn't need the additional responsibility of taking a middle schooler back and forth to another town for school.

"I had plenty of leave coming to me. It worked out."

"How are you feeling since your own hard landing?" his father asked.

Tension tightened his shoulders but he forced himself to relax. The colonel wasn't being critical. He was only asking.

"Fine. Still on desk duty."

"How are the other crew members?"

"Everybody is recovering."

He didn't like thinking about the incident, when an engine malfunction during a training mission had forced an emergency landing in the southern California mountains.

The quick thinking of his crew and the fact he was able to call for help promptly had prevented a bad situation from becoming catastrophic, though Ryan and one other member of his four-person crew were still sidelined from flying, awaiting medical clearance.

He didn't want to talk about the crash, especially not with his father, who probably thought Ryan should have been able to prevent it.

"How's Caldwell Aviation?" he asked instead. "Are you able to take off the time you need so you can be here for Diane?"

The irony of the question didn't escape him.

"It's a slow time of year," his father said. "We usually have a few sightseeing flights, maybe some heli-ski tours, but it's not as busy as the summertime."

After moving to Idaho, his father had purchased two small prop engine planes and a helicopter and rented a hangar at the small county airport, creating Caldwell Aviation.

Ryan knew he flew small private commuter trips around the area, and sometimes took tourists and hunters on trips into remote areas of northern Idaho.

"I've got a good staff who are handling everything in my absence. We've had to cancel a few things and rescheduled others so I can focus on Diane for now."

"That's good," Ryan said, instead of what he *wanted* to say.

Where was this performative show of spousal concern when the mother of your children was dying of cancer?

"You know, son, I can always use more help. If you'd like to take up a few flights while you're in the area, we can set you up. It wouldn't take you long to learn the ropes on either of our planes or the helicopter."

While he wanted to get back up in the air with a fierce ache and knew it was only strict military guidelines, not capability, keeping him sidelined, he had zero interest in helping out his father.

"Audrey is my priority while I'm here."

"Totally get that. But she's in school, plus she's got that babysitting thing after school for Kim's boss, from what I understand. That will leave you with a big chunk of free time on your hands."

Yeah. He had thought of that, wondering how he would fill his time over the next three weeks. He wasn't good at sitting still, something his father probably knew about him.

"I'll have to see once the dust settles."

Audrey giggled suddenly and he looked over to see she was

showing Diane something on her phone. He heard a song clip and guessed it was a social media video of some kind.

The two of them both laughed at the same time, though Diane's laugh turned into a wince.

"Oh!" she exclaimed, holding her arm closer to her body. "It hurts to laugh."

Audrey immediately looked stricken and lowered her phone "I'm sorry. I should have thought."

"Don't apologize, honey. It's hilarious. I'm glad you showed me. People are so creative, aren't they?"

"Yeah. My friends and I want to take the Secret Elf challenge."

"What's that one?"

"You take video of yourself secretly dropping off cookies or a little Christmas gift at the house of someone who might need a lift."

"That sounds very nice."

"Anonymously, of course. You're not supposed to give away any identifying details, like address numbers or what the house looks like."

"Naturally," Diane said.

"I even know whose house I want to take it to. My friend Megan. Her parents are in the middle of an ugly divorce, which sucks at Christmas."

"That is tough," Diane said.

They visited for a few more moments but Ryan could tell Diane was tiring. She made the occasional grimace he doubted she was even aware of and occasionally lost the thread of the conversation, staring off into space instead.

He stood up. "We should go. We still have to pick up Audrey's things from her neighbor."

Diane smiled, though he saw the lines of pain bracketing her mouth. "Thank you for coming. You've lifted my day."

"Is there anything we can help you with before we go?"

He expected polite denials. Instead, his father stood also.

"Diane should be back in her bed. It's the most comfortable place for her, but she insists on getting up and coming out here as much as she can."

"I like it out here. And I'm not very good at laying around in bed for hours at a time." She nodded toward the screen. "What about the movie?"

"We can finish watching another day. Or we can always catch the ending on the TV in the bedroom," Doug answered, before turning back to Ryan.

"Since you're here, I could use help getting her back into our room. I can handle it on my own but as you're here, it's probably safer to have two of us for her to lean on."

That was also something new, his father actually asking for help. "Absolutely."

Audrey pushed over a folding wheelchair from the corner of the room while Diane worked the controls of her recliner, which Ryan noticed had a lift function.

"That's handy," he said.

"Isn't it?" Diane said, with a smile that turned into another grimace. "We were able to rent it from a medical supply company, with help from the hospital social workers. I feel ancient using it, though I must admit it's convenient."

"We also rented a hospital bed and moved it into our bedroom, since we have plenty of space in there. When she needs a different position, it's adjustable and also height adjustable so it's much easier for her to get in and out."

"I would rather sleep in my own bed, but your father's right. For now, the hospital bed makes sense."

Not sure of his role, Ryan stood by as his father guided Diane into the wheelchair then pushed her down a short hallway to their bedroom, a large space that contained a large king-size bed as well as a sitting area near the stone fire-place.

The bed had been pushed to one side and the sofa removed. In its place was a hospital bed covered with pillows and a co-ordinating quilt.

"How can I help?" he finally asked as his father moved his wife's wheelchair next to the bed.

"This is the tricky part. She has to pivot a little and I'm always worried she'll fall. Just stand close to provide support if she needs it."

Diane seemed perfectly capable of making the transfer with-out his help, though she was pale, her mouth pinched, by the time she settled into the hospital bed.

"Thank you," Doug said.

Ryan hadn't really done anything but it was nice to feel useful. "No problem. Anything else?"

"We should be good. Think about what I suggested, taking a few flights for Caldwell Aviation while you're here."

"I will," he said, not seeing the point in telling his father that while he would think about it, he had no intention of doing it.

As he and Audrey walked outside and headed for his truck, Ryan accepted the unpleasant reality that he was going to be in the same county with his father at least until Christmas. They were going to have to interact, whether he wanted to or not.

He could do his best to avoid the man, but that wouldn't be fair to Audrey, who clearly loved her grandfather and step-grandmother.

Ryan would simply have to figure out a way to be polite to the colonel. Fortunately, he had plenty of practice from those years after his mother died, when he had been expected to pretend everything was fine.

CHAPTER THREE

———

"I DON'T LIKE MATH. IT'S TOO HARD."

Holly smiled down at her daughter, who was scowling at the worksheet on their kitchen table.

While she wanted to say *you and me both, kiddo,* she didn't want to skew Lydia's perception of mathematics or give her the message that she couldn't handle any task set before her.

"Math can be hard. But it can also be fun. It's like solving little puzzles. You love puzzles, right?"

Lydia nodded. "Puzzles are hard, too."

"But don't you feel good when you put the last piece in? That's how math is. And it's useful, too. We need math to show us how to build things, how to count cookies and how to go shopping. I use math every day when I'm cooking or driving somewhere or even figuring out how many flowers I need to order for the store."

Lydia didn't look convinced. "Why is it hard?"

"That is an excellent question. I guess the best things in life are always hard."

Definitely true. Being a mom was the hardest job she could imagine but it was also the most important thing in her life.

While Lydia finished her worksheet, Holly set the table and made final preparations for their dinner while her stomach rumbled. In the end, she hadn't eaten much of the sandwich her sister brought her, as the last hour of business at the store had been slammed. She was more than ready for dinner.

She was finishing the tossed salad when the doorbell rang.

"I'll get it!" Lydia jumped up from the table, apparently eager for any distraction from her homework.

"I need to see who's here first," Holly reminded her, following to make sure Lydia didn't open the door to a serial killer.

She couldn't open the door to anyone, serial killer or not, since Lydia had yet to figure out how to work the childproof lock, much to Holly's relief.

Home security only made common sense. She was a single woman living alone with a vulnerable child. Shelter Springs had a relatively low crime rate but it wasn't wholly idyllic.

Beyond the usual reasons, she locked the door for Lydia's safety. Holly had heard from others in her online support group for parents of children with Down syndrome about harrowing circumstances where their children had wandered outside. Sometimes it was harder for children with developmental disabilities to understand the potential dangers that awaited them out in the world.

She peered through the door and caught her breath.

Not a serial killer, then. At least she didn't think so. Only an extremely attractive man and his thirteen-year-old niece.

Lydia peered through the window next to the door. "It's Audrey! My friend. Hi, Audrey!"

"She can't hear you, Lydi-bug. Not until we open the door."

She worked the deadbolt and the childproof lock before pulling open the door.

Oh, Ryan Caldwell was gorgeous. Why hadn't Kim warned her? It would have been the decent thing to do.

My brother is coming to stay with Audrey and in case I forgot to tell you, he's hot. Be prepared.

"Hi. We're here to grab Audrey's things," he said after an awkward moment when she stood on the threshold, ridiculously tongue-tied suddenly.

Good grief. She couldn't stand here gawking at the man. She cleared her throat. "Of course. Come in."

He and Audrey walked into her house, with Lydia talking eagerly with her friend.

"It smells like Christmas in here," Ryan said, looking around at her festive living room.

She couldn't tell if he meant the words as a compliment but she decided to take them as such.

"Thanks. We have a particularly fragrant Christmas tree this year. It's a Scotch pine. My brothers went up into the mountains before Thanksgiving and brought enough trees back for everyone in the family, plus two for the store."

"It's very . . . bushy."

She couldn't argue with that. "This one was a little bigger than I was expecting. It was originally intended for Evergreen & Ivy but I decided it would take up too much room so we swapped trees with a smaller one for the store and brought this one here instead."

"I helped decorate the whole house a few days ago," Audrey said with an unmistakable note of pride in her voice. "Holly did the lights then Lydia and I put on all the ornaments."

"Impressive."

Holly had loved putting her own personal touch on Rose Cottage. Her decorating style tended toward lush, dramatic, feminine, with bold colors and plenty of flowers.

Somehow, as she had thought earlier in the day at the store, the surroundings only served to emphasize Ryan Caldwell's inescapable . . . maleness. She told herself it was only her constant fatigue that left her feeling slightly breathless.

"It smells delicious in here," Audrey said.

She forced her attention away from the man to his niece. "That's the chili you helped me put together last night, remember? It's been in the slow cooker all day."

"Oh man. I bet it's delicious."

"I can put some in a container for you two to take home."

"That's not necessary," Ryan said stiffly. "We're planning to go to the grocery store after this."

"But I'm hungry now," Audrey said.

"Okay. In that case, we can pick up takeout before we head home and then go shopping later tonight or tomorrow."

"I'd rather have chili than takeout." Audrey had that stubborn look Holly had come to recognize, mostly because Lydia so often wore the same expression. A certain set to the jaw, a firmness of lips, a determined look in her eyes.

"Why don't you stay and eat with us? It's ready now, which means it's even quicker than running somewhere for fast food."

As soon as the words were out, she regretted them. Why had she issued the invitation? She wasn't at all sure she liked Ryan Caldwell. She did know she wasn't eager to spend more time with him than she had to, especially given this sudden and unexpected attraction.

On the other hand, her heart squeezed with compassion for Audrey. Despite her brave face, the girl was struggling with the sudden tumult in her life, with her mother gone for the weeks leading up to the holidays and her grandfather and his wife preoccupied and unable to care for her.

Audrey was doing her best in the middle of a tough situation and Holly could not help but admire her for it. And Audrey *had* helped her prep everything the night before. It seemed only fair that she have the chance to enjoy the fruits of her labor.

"I have fresh corn bread with honey butter, if that makes a difference in your decision."

Ryan arched an eyebrow. "Well, why didn't you say so. How can I say no to fresh corn bread?"

His dry tone almost made her smile, the first sign of levity from a man who seemed as tough as a granite cliff.

"Excellent. Lydia, can you set a few more places at the table for our guests?"

"Yep." Her daughter beamed happily at all of them, clearly thrilled at the chance to spend more time with Audrey.

"I'll help you reach the plates," Audrey said and led the girl into the kitchen, leaving Holly alone with Ryan.

She had a sudden wild wish that he was more ordinary looking, which annoyed her. It was silly to feel so tongue-tied around him and even more ridiculous that she had this vague sense of resentment.

She had allowed good looks to influence her decision-making once. Troy had been charismatic and charming, the kind of guy who could treat a woman like she was the most important thing in his life, until she wasn't.

She, who had never had a boyfriend in high school, had been completely seduced by his attention.

"Sorry to force your hand, if you really didn't want chili and corn bread for dinner," she said.

"I have nothing against chili. Or corn bread, for that matter. I love them both. But you have already done enough to help Audrey and Kim. Our family seems to be sliding further and further into your debt."

She guessed Ryan Caldwell was not a man who accepted help easily. Why was it so important for him not to find himself beholden to anyone?

"That's silly. No one is in anyone's debt. Audrey basically threw the whole chili together for me. By that logic, I'm in her debt, actually. We wouldn't be having this delicious dinner tonight if not for her. The only thing I did was make the corn bread after work, and that was only from a mix, with a few tweaks. You're more than welcome to join us."

"It's very kind of you," he said, his voice stiff.

"People in Shelter Springs like to help each other out. I expect when word gets out you took military leave to come out here and stay with Audrey, you will have people knocking down the door with casseroles and soups."

Especially women, once they caught sight of the town's newest temporary resident. She decided to keep that particular opinion to herself.

"Thanks for the warning."

His dry tone again made her smile as she led the way down the hall toward her kitchen.

He looked around as they made their way through Rose Cottage. "This is nice."

She loved this house, with its exposed beams, the stone fireplace, the original wood moldings. She couldn't wait for her first Christmas with Lydia here. From the moment she bought the house, she had dreamed of holiday traditions she could create with her child.

Rose Cottage was on the small side and had some old-fashioned elements and more than a few quirks, like the drafty windows and the uneven flooring in the kitchen.

Still, it was hers. Well, hers and the bank's, anyway.

She pushed away her ever-present financial worries as they entered the kitchen, where she found Audrey and Lydia pouring glasses of water from the filtered pitcher out of the refrigerator.

"We're a little tight in here but I'm afraid my dining room is currently crammed full of supplies for my shop."

"Why do you keep them here and not at your shop?" he asked as he took a seat.

"Convenience, mostly. I'm doing the flowers for three weddings this month, two with some artificial floral elements, and it's easier to have some supplies here at my house so I can work on things after Lydia is in bed."

Childcare was her biggest challenge as a single mother. She couldn't hire a sitter every night in order to head back to the store so she tried to arrange her time and resources to work on as many projects as she could in those precious hours that her child slept.

It meant long hours and considerable fatigue but she was willing to pay the price if it meant more time with her child.

When had her kitchen shrunk? Somehow Ryan seemed to fill all the space. What was already a room on the small side now felt cramped and airless.

She did her best to ignore her reaction to him as she dished bowls of chili for everyone and cut pieces of corn bread.

Lydia insisted on saying grace as she loved to do. Some of her words were a little hard to follow, as usual, but not her enthusiastic "Amen."

She added some cheese to Lydia's chili and a couple of ice cubes to help cool it.

"Yum, Mommy," Lydia said as she ate her first bite.

"This is soooo good," Audrey added. "I was starving."

"It really is," Ryan said.

Fortunately, Lydia and Audrey chattered throughout the meal, talking about school, their friends and the upcoming holidays.

"That really was delicious," Ryan said when everyone seemed to be finishing up. "I'm glad we stayed. Thank you."

She had a feeling that wasn't an easy admission for him. "You're welcome," she said.

Audrey pushed her chair away from the table. "I guess I had better go pack up my stuff."

"Do you need my help?" Holly rose from her chair.

Audrey gestured for her to sit back down. "No. I don't have that much. Only my clothes and chargers and stuff. It will take me five minutes, maybe."

"I can help, Auddy."

Lydia jumped up and followed the older girl she adored out of the room.

Holly felt on edge, suddenly, at finding herself alone with him again. She rose quickly and began clearing away their dinner dishes.

"Your daughter seems very sweet," Ryan said as he stood to assist.

"She is. And smart, too. She is only five but can already read a few basic words."

"You must work with her a lot."

His words sparked more than a little guilt. In a perfect world, she would be able to devote as much time as needed to work on speech, occupational and physical therapy with Lydia. Her job was to give her child the best possible chance at a good future.

Juggling everything so that she could continue providing a roof over their heads meant she had to do her best with the time she had.

"I would love to do more, enroll her in every possible therapy. But I also feel it's important for her to be a child first."

He nodded as he rinsed off a dish and added it to the dishwasher. "I can't imagine what a huge responsibility it must be, trying to prepare a child with challenges to face a world that might not always be accepting of them."

To her dismay, she felt her throat close up. "I struggle with that every day. I can only keep trying to do my best."

"Is Lydia's dad a big part of her life?"

She avoided his gaze as she continued scooping the leftover chili into a storage container.

"We divorced two years ago, when she was three." She tried to keep any inflection out of her voice. "Troy moved to

Portland after our divorce. He comes back to visit when he can but it hasn't been that often."

"In other words, he's not really in the picture."

"I didn't say that."

"No. You didn't. I said it."

Of all the choices she had made in her life, the one she regretted most was not making a better choice of man to be her child's father.

Troy wasn't a bad person. He had plenty of good qualities, but he had struggled with that serious responsibility Ryan had been talking about. Lydia and her early challenges had overwhelmed and exhausted him.

"Actually, he's coming out for a few weeks over the holidays with his wife and their baby. His sister's wedding is one of the three I have this month. Hers is the weekend before Christmas."

He raised an eyebrow. "Seriously? You're handling the flowers for the wedding of your ex-sister-in-law?"

She shrugged. "Yes. Why not?"

"It's not awkward and uncomfortable?"

"Kristine is still my friend, even though her brother and I are no longer together. She will always be Lydia's aunt and her parents will always be my child's grandparents. Troy and I divorced but there's no reason I can't still maintain a good relationship with his family."

"I suppose that's true. You make it sound easy but I'm guessing there's more to it than that."

His insight surprised her more than it probably should. "To be honest, I was hoping I could participate from behind the scenes. You know. Sit in the back of the church during the ceremony, duck out of the reception early, skip the wedding rehearsal. That kind of thing. But now Kristine has asked Lydia to be her flower girl."

"So much for staying behind the scenes."

"Exactly. I wish I could pull Lydia out of the wedding party but she's so excited about it. I can't be that cruel, to her or to Kristine."

"That's a tough situation."

Her whole life felt like one tough situation after another.

She shrugged. "We'll be fine. It's only one day. A few hours, really. I can survive a few hours of discomfort for the sake of people I care about."

At least she hoped she could.

CHAPTER FOUR

———

RYAN WASN'T AT ALL SURE WHAT TO THINK ABOUT HOLLY Moore. She was lovely, yes, as pretty as sunlight dancing on the waves of his favorite San Diego beach. And she obviously made one hell of a good chili.

She was also clearly too nice for her own good.

If he had been in her shoes, he probably would have told the former sister-in-law to take a hike, instead of stepping up to help with the wedding decorations *and* allowing her daughter to be included in the wedding party.

The point was moot, though, since he never planned to marry, which meant he would never find himself with a sister-in-law, former or otherwise.

"I understand you were in some kind of accident yourself," Holly said with a sideways look. "Kim said you messed up your knee. Kim and Audrey flew out to help you right after it happened this summer, right?"

Tension stiffened his shoulders, hardened his jaw. Why did everyone want to talk about the hard landing? First his father, now this woman he had only met a few hours ago.

Yes, he had messed up his knee and ended up with a nasty infection that complicated the situation. He was lucky, though. The other pilot, a rookie who had been at the controls at the time, had sustained much worse injuries and would likely never fly again.

"They came out and stayed for a week, even though I told Kim over and over it wasn't necessary."

He hadn't even told his family about the accident but somehow Kim had found out anyway. She had dropped everything to come out to California and help him.

His sister had always had his back, watching out for him at every new school they moved to, hanging out with him and playing video games in that invariably awkward phase right after a military move when they had not yet established any friendships.

He owed her more than he could ever repay, which was the main reason he was here in this small Idaho town for the holidays.

"Siblings can be a pain," Holly went on. "You met my twin sister today. We also have two older brothers who never listen to anything I say. Technically I'm the baby since Hannah was born first. She never lets me forget it, either."

He couldn't imagine a big family, filled with noise and chaos. Even before his mother died, his and Kim's childhood home had never been chaotic. His father wouldn't have allowed it.

"Do they all live close?"

"Yes. Hannah works as a music therapist in town and my two brothers own a security company together."

"It must be nice having everyone nearby during the holidays," he said, even though it sounded far too complicated for him.

He went out of his way to avoid being with his family during Christmas. Beyond the constant tension between him and his father, the memories of losing their mother only a few days before Christmas were still too painful, despite the two decades that had passed.

"I do love it. Most of the time, anyway. They've all been amazing since the divorce to help me with Lydia. I really couldn't have done the single-mom thing without them all."

She washed the final dish and set it in the rack. "I have to tell you what a lifesaver Audrey has been, too. I've been so happy to have her help with Lydia after school and on the occasional Saturday. Lyd loves her. As you can probably tell, she's wonderful with her. They have a great time together. I hope you don't mind letting her continue through the holidays."

What was he supposed to say to that? To him, Audrey was still the little girl in braids who used to love going with him to the beach at whatever naval base he currently called home. He had fond memories of walking with her in the sand, looking for sea glass and agates. It still astounded him that she was now a teenager, old enough to be trusted with the responsibility of caring for a child with special needs.

If Kim had approved the gig, he didn't feel right about second-guessing his sister, though.

"It should be okay, as long as she doesn't get behind on her schoolwork."

"I'm not taking advantage of her, I promise. I pay her above the usual babysitter rate, since Lydia's needs are somewhat unique compared to other children her age."

"That sounds fair."

"And I try not to take up too much of Audrey's time. She needs a chance to hang out with her friends and chill. She's only thirteen, with plenty of time ahead of her to rise and grind for the rest of her life."

Is that what Holly felt like she was doing?

Before he could answer, he heard the click of rolling suitcase wheels and a moment later Audrey came into the kitchen pulling a carry-on bag, with Lydia close on her heels.

"Thanks again for letting me stay with you, Holly. You're the best."

"Ha. You are." Holly smiled at his niece and wrapped her in a tight, generous hug that somehow touched him. "Be good for your uncle, okay?"

"Sure. Uncle Ry and I are buds," Audrey said.

"You're always welcome here, though I'm sure you can't wait to go back to your own bed."

Audrey shrugged. "Yeah, but it won't be the same without Mom there. Especially at Christmastime."

"She'll be back as soon as she can."

"I know." Audrey turned to Lydia. "I'll see you later, Lyd."

In answer, the little girl threw her arms around Audrey's waist and sniffled loudly. "Love you, Auddy."

She smiled. "Love you too, Lyd-Lyd."

The snow had picked up while they were inside and it took a moment to clear off the few inches from his truck. Audrey helped him, reaching on tiptoe with the scraper he had been wise enough to pick up at a gas station on his drive here.

When the vehicle windows were clear, the two of them headed toward Kim's house, which he knew was only a few streets over from Holly Moore's.

As he pulled into the driveway, the small ranch-style house looked dark and cheerless compared to all the festively lit houses in the neighborhood.

"Your mom told me I could find a spare key she keeps in a fake rock. Any clue which is the right rock so I don't have to dig through the snow for all of them?"

Audrey rolled her eyes. "We don't have to dig through the snow of Mom's flower garden. We can use the garage code. You might as well park there too, since Mom's car was totaled in the accident."

She slid out of his truck and went to the keypad on the garage, where she punched in the code. The garage opened and he drove inside.

Once parked, he picked Audrey's rolling suitcase and his own duffel from the backseat and carried them to the door that led into the house, trying not to limp.

After driving for two days and spending the afternoon and evening on the go since pulling into Shelter Springs, his knee throbbed and burned. He should probably elevate it with some ice, if he could find some.

"It's freezing in here!" Audrey exclaimed as soon as she walked from the garage into the open plan kitchen and living area.

She hurried to the wall and flipped a switch to turn on a gas fireplace and then made her way to the hallway, where she fiddled with the thermostat for a moment, undoubtedly turning up the furnace.

It was cold enough in the house, he might not need to put ice on his knee. He could only hope his sister's pipes hadn't frozen in the week since she had been here.

"I'll take your bag to your room. Second door on the right, yes?"

"That's right. You can stay in Mom's room across the hall or you can stay in the guest room."

After setting Audrey's suitcase in her room, he decided to head to his sister's room. He had experience in the guest room/office that held a small daybed with trundle. He had stayed here once when Kim moved here and had spent the first night with his legs dangling over the edge, until he had ended up on a camp bed on the floor.

As embarrassing as it was to admit to himself, Ryan wasn't at all certain he would be able to get up off the floor right now, with his bad knee.

"If you think she won't mind, I'll stay in your mom's room for now."

"She won't mind. She would want you to."

"Okay. Point me to clean sheets."

After she found them for him, he made the bed. When he returned to the living room, he found Audrey on the sofa, scrolling through her phone with her legs tucked under her.

He took a seat on the adjacent armchair. "How are you doing, Audrey? Really doing?"

Thanks to his dad's example, Ryan did not like talking about emotions. And what he knew about the emotional journey of a teenage girl would fit in a headphone jack. But being here for his niece didn't only mean showing up physically to feed her dinner and pick her up from school.

Audrey looked up from her phone, her eyes deep and troubled briefly before she blinked and forced a smile.

His instincts were right. Despite her casual air, Audrey was stressed out by the situation.

"I'm fine."

He studied her, head cocked. "You know I'm a highly trained officer in the United States military, right? I've been trained in techniques to extract information from people who don't want to talk."

She snorted. "Ha. Are you going to torture me until I spill all my deepest feelings?"

"I hope it doesn't have to come to that." He smiled. "You need to know, though, that you can talk to me about anything that might be bothering or worrying you. I can't guarantee I will always know the right thing to say but I'll do my best."

His and Kim's father's attitude after their mother died had been the exact opposite. He hadn't allowed them to talk about her, had acted like they should go on with their lives as if nothing had happened, as if her loss had not left a gaping hole.

Kim had pushed everything down. Was it any wonder she had turned to self-medicating to cope, when their father had turned their home into a cold place with plenty of rules but very little love?

"Thanks, Uncle Ryan."

She looked down at her phone for a moment then set it in her lap.

"I miss Mom," she finally said after a long pause. "It's only been a week but I really, really miss her. She's my best friend, you know? We talk about everything. Don't get me wrong. Holly is great and everything and I really love little Lydia but it's not the same as being with my own mom."

"It's not," he agreed. "Do you know that I was exactly your age when my own mom died? Thirteen."

Kim and Audrey could both have been hurt far worse in that accident. What if Audrey had permanently lost her mother, like Ryan had at her age? The loss would have haunted her the rest of her life.

She hadn't, though. Kim was alive and on the road to recovery. In a few short weeks, she would be back with her daughter, hopefully in a much better place.

Audrey's features, so much like her mother's, softened with sadness. "Mom was fifteen, right? She talks about Grandma Caldwell a lot. She said she was the kindest person she ever knew. I wish I'd had the chance to meet her."

"So do I. She would have loved being a grandma. She would have spoiled you rotten."

She grinned briefly before her mouth drooped with sadness again.

"Mom still really misses her. A few months ago, I was doing homework in my room while she was in here washing dishes. I came in for a drink of water and found her crying at the sink. She told me it was her mom's birthday and she always misses her extra hard on that day."

Laura Caldwell had been the glue holding his family together. Kind, giving, funny, she had seemed the exact opposite of their father. Wherever Doug's military career had taken him across the world, Laura had worked hard to make their home a warm and welcoming space for her children and their friends. Her softness provided a counterpoint to Doug's dogged ambition.

Despite their differences, they seemed to have had a happy marriage, though Ryan had only been a kid. What did he know?

Regardless, Laura should have had decades more to bring light to the world instead of being taken far too early.

"I'm not sure you ever stop missing your parents when they're gone, no matter how old you are."

"I don't really miss my dad," Audrey said, almost as if she were confessing a guilty secret.

He wanted to tell her that Zachary Barnes was not someone who deserved to be missed but somehow he managed to restrain himself.

Kim's ex-husband had been an enlisted man on base who had taken advantage of a grieving, lonely teenage girl rebelling against her father.

Zachary Barnes had dragged Kim into a life of partying and hard drugs. After she became pregnant, he had married her reluctantly and had been dishonorably discharged a year later for selling drugs to others on base.

In the three short years of their marriage, he had walked out on her several times and been arrested several more before he was ultimately killed in jail by another inmate while awaiting trial on drug charges.

Still, one amazing thing had come out of his sister's short-lived relationship and he was looking at her.

"You were little when he died. You probably don't remember much about him." He could only hope.

"Not much. Mom hardly ever mentions him." She paused. "Do you remember much about him? "

He absolutely didn't want to talk about Zachary Barnes. "I was at military school for much of their marriage and she was living in the Las Vegas area so I didn't have much chance to spend time with him."

"I don't really miss *him*, you know, though I do miss having a dad," she admitted. "But Grandpa is really good about doing all the dad kind of stuff with me now that we live closer to him and Diane. He even let me practice driving his car. We only went around an empty parking lot a few times but it was still cool."

Funny. He couldn't remember his father taking him to practice driving when he was a kid, even as he was preparing to take his own driver's test. One of his friends' fathers had done it.

"It's good that you have him close by," he said, hoping his voice didn't sound as stiff as he felt.

"And Diane is really great, too. It's kind of fun to have a grandma."

"Right. Well, remember that if you need to talk, I'm here. I might not be as good as your mom or Diane but I'll do my best."

"Thanks."

"Did you say you have homework?"

"Only a quick math worksheet. It won't take me long. I have all weekend, anyway. I can do it Sunday afternoon."

Right. He had forgotten it was Friday.

Audrey yawned suddenly. "I should probably head to bed. I need to work tomorrow at Evergreen and Ivy to help with Lydia since Holly has that wedding in the afternoon."

She looked around the house, which had at least started to heat up thanks to the fireplace and the furnace.

"Do you think we could put up some Christmas decorations? Mom and I were going to do it last weekend after Thanksgiving but obviously we didn't get the chance."

He knew less about decorating a house for Christmas than he did about teenagers. He had never seen the point in bothering much about the holidays while living in base housing.

Still, he had promised to be here for his niece during the holidays. If that meant decking the freaking halls, he would do his best.

"Sure thing. Why don't we plan on doing that this weekend? Maybe we could take care of it Sunday afternoon."

"That would be great, Uncle Ryan." To his surprise, she hugged him. "I'm really glad you're here," she said.

"So am I," he said, suddenly grateful he had been able to arrange his life to free up time for his niece.

She needed him, whether she wanted to admit it or not.

CHAPTER FIVE

—

"THANK YOU FOR HELPING ME OUT THIS MORNING FOR A FEW hours with Lydia. My mom and sister both had other obligations this morning or they would have taken her. My sister's going to pick her up this afternoon, though."

"Not a problem," Audrey assured Holly. "We love hanging out together, don't we, Lyd?"

"I love Auddy," her daughter said, smiling brightly at the older girl.

"We're going to do some crafts then I told her maybe we could watch a Christmas movie," the older girl said.

"Sounds perfect. You should be able to find something on one of the various streaming services we have."

Though she had set up a comfortable media area in the break room of Evergreen & Ivy, she tried not to use screen time as a babysitter for her child too often.

"Don't worry about us. We're fine. Take care of what you need to. We'll find plenty to do, won't we, Lydia? Maybe we can bundle up and take a walk through the park."

"Yes! I want to take a walk."

"Thanks again, Audrey."

She hurried out to the shop floor, where she planned to wrap up the fresh flower centerpieces for the Myers-Balboa wedding later that day.

She had approximately three hours to finish before she had to head to the wedding venue, a lovely primitive barn that had been renovated into a reception space, with a huge wall of windows overlooking Lake Haven.

In between the occasional customer coming in for get-well flowers, party centerpieces or birthday bouquets, she was able to finish in plenty of time. She was setting the final centerpiece in the box she would use to transport everything to the venue when the bell on the door rang as Lydia came out of the break room.

"Grandma!" Lydia's voice rang out and she ran toward the door with Audrey close behind.

Holly looked up in time to see Lydia hugging a slim woman with dark hair and trendy glasses, followed by a younger woman who looked a great deal like her.

Not her own mother, she saw at once. Troy's mother. Her former mother-in-law, along with the bride-to-be.

"Hello, darling." Susan gave Lydia a warm squeeze and so did Kristine.

Holly looked between mother and daughter. "I'm sorry. Did we have a meeting set up today?"

Her packed schedule loomed as large as the mountains outside. She knew from experience her former mother-in-law could quickly swallow up every available minute of her day if she let her.

Susan shook her head with a reassuring smile. "Not officially, no. But we were in town picking up some little gifts for the bridesmaids and wanted to stop in and check to see if everything is on track with flowers."

Kristine's wedding was still two weeks away. She had two others to worry about first.

"It's all going to plan. I've ordered everything and should be able to set aside plenty of time right before the wedding to create the arrangements, so everything can be as fresh as possible."

Susan adjusted her glasses and moved closer to Holly. "I hate to be a pain, but is it too late to make any changes?"

Yes, she wanted to yell. *For the love of all things holy, the wedding is only two weeks away and we've been over and over this.*

Instead, she forced a calm smile. "What sort of changes?"

"I'm having second thoughts about the calla lilies. They're so beautiful and elegant but my friend Barbara told me lilies are considered bad luck for a wedding. What if we went with white roses instead?"

She fought the urge to close her eyes and pray for patience.

Kristine was the baby of her family and the last one to be married and Holly knew Susan wanted every detail to be perfect. She could understand that. Still, everything had already been ordered weeks ago. If she had to change the plan now, there was no guarantee she would be able to get the new supplies in time and Evergreen & Ivy might be stuck with four dozen calla lilies that would be tough to unload right before Christmas.

"The lilies will be gorgeous, I promise. Just like the inspiration board pictures you brought in, only better."

"Are lilies considered bad luck at weddings? We've had enough divorce in our family. We don't need to invite more trouble."

Then maybe you should have taught your son not to cheat on his wife with his personal assistant. Again, she bit back the tart words. It was only stress and fatigue lending a sharp, waspish edge to her thoughts. She didn't need to turn those thoughts into words she couldn't take back.

"It is true that some cultures associate certain kinds of lilies with funerals, but calla lilies are different. They're elegant and demure. Kristine will look so beautiful carrying a bouquet with two or three lilies as part of the whole package. As we have red roses planned for the bouquet, I think the contrast of the white lilies will be nothing less than striking."

Susan looked conflicted. "I want everything to be perfect."

"It will be absolutely perfect," Kristine said, sending Holly an apologetic look. "I love the calla lilies, Mom. They're the flowers we picked. As I told you on the way here, I don't think it's fair to mess everything up for Holly when we're only two weeks away from the wedding."

Her expression twisted into sudden panic. "Oh man. I'm getting married in two weeks. I'm not ready!"

Maybe Susan ought to focus on allaying her daughter's panic instead of trying to mess up all the plans they had agreed upon weeks earlier.

"I'm ready," Lydia informed her grandmother and aunt. "I have a new dress. I look like a princess."

Her words did the trick of distracting Kristine. She swallowed hard and hugged Lydia again. "I know you do. You're going to have so much fun being a flower girl. Thank you again for helping me."

"Welcome. This is Auddy. She's my friend."

Kristine smiled at the teenager. "Hi. Any friend of Lydia's is a friend of mine."

They visited for a few moments about other details for the wedding. As Holly was trying to think of a tactful way to excuse herself so she could return to her lengthy to-do list, Susan glanced at her watch and winced.

"We should go. We still have to go check on the catering to see if they can add a different vegetarian option, since my cousin's son is allergic to onions."

Holly truly pitied the catering company handling the wedding. She suspected Susan had already changed menu items multiple times.

"Thanks for stopping by. As I told you, everything has been ordered and is either already here or on the way."

"And you're still coming to the bridal shower, right?"

She nodded, though fitting one more social engagement in her packed schedule was about the last thing she had time for.

"Wouldn't miss it," she said, giving Kristine a hug.

Troy's family had always been warm and friendly to her throughout the years she dated him and after their marriage. She considered his mother and sisters to be close friends and she adored his aunts. Those relationships were still important to her and she worked hard to maintain them, for her own sake as well as Lydia's.

"I made a Christmas tree. Want to see?" Lydia asked, slipping her hand into her grandmother's.

"Of course I do. I'll take a quick look, then we really have to go." Susan smiled as Lydia tugged her into the break room, leaving Kristine and Holly alone.

"I'm so sorry about the whole calla lily thing," Kristine said in an undertone. "She's driving me crazy. She wants to change everything. You'd think she hasn't done this before."

"You're her baby and she wants everything to be perfect for you."

"I know she does. And I'm grateful, believe me. But at this point I keep asking myself why Matt and I didn't simply fly down to Vegas and get it all over with."

Holly remembered that vague feeling of panic all through her wedding preparations. In her case, she suspected some part of her psyche was telling her not to go through with the wedding.

She should have listened to it, but then she wouldn't have Lydia.

"Enough about me," Kristine said. "I promise, I'm trying hard not to be a bridezilla, completely focused on myself. Have you found a date yet?"

"I have a date," she answered calmly. "Lydia."

Kristine frowned. "As amazing as she is, you know that's not what I meant. You need a date-date. Someone you can dance with to the kickin' band we've hired."

"Are you kidding? I love dancing with Lydia. We have lots of dance parties at our house."

"I'm sure you do. But I would love to see you dancing with a great guy. Matt has a couple of single friends who work with him at his tech company. They're cute and smart and make great money. I would love to set you up with one of them."

She forced a smile. Over the past two years, she had found that one of the hardest things about being divorced was the well-meaning but misguided efforts of those who cared about her constantly trying to set her up.

"I appreciate that, but it's not necessary."

"I want you to be happy, Holly. You're the nicest person I know and you deserve better than what my stupid brother did to you."

"Don't worry about me. I'm fine."

She could tell by Kristine's concerned expression that the other woman didn't believe her. Later, when she was kicking herself for opening her big mouth, she had no idea what made her say it, other than she didn't like the pity in Kristine's eyes.

"I'm fine because I already have a date," she blurted out without thinking it through. "I think you'll like him."

Kristine squealed. "Oh, I'm so glad! Who is it? Anyone I know?"

What had she done? Holly tried to figure out a way to backpedal but nothing came to her. She didn't want to lie or make up a name so she quickly improvised.

"Um, he's still not sure if he can make it so I would rather not name any names. It's early days yet."

"Is he nice? What am I saying? Of course he's nice. You wouldn't be going out with him if he wasn't great."

Holly didn't bother pointing out that she had not only dated Kristine's brother but she had been married to him. And look how great that had turned out.

"I can't wait to meet him! I'm so glad. I was worried every-thing would be awkward with Troy and Brittany coming with their new baby. But if you have someone too, it won't be weird at all."

Oh, she was so stupid. What had she gotten herself into? And where was she going to find a date willing to go with her—and her daughter, since she couldn't very well leave Lydia home—to a wedding five days before Christmas?

She should blurt out the truth now, before she dug a deeper hole for herself.

Instead, words spilled out as if on their own accord.

"It won't be weird at all," she lied. "Everything will be great. I totally have someone, too. You're going to love him."

"I can't wait!" Kristine hugged her again, any trace of wed-ding nerves gone, at least for now.

Holly was still trying to figure out how to extricate herself from the ridiculous lie when her former mother-in-law re-turned with Lydia and Audrey.

"Thank you for showing me your picture, my dear," Susan said to Lydia.

Lydia beamed. "You can have it, Grandma," she said. "It's for you."

Susan looked touched as she hugged her granddaughter. "Thank you. I will hang it right on my fridge."

When she released Lydia, Susan rose and hugged Holly in turn. "Thank you for putting up with me," she said. "I know I'm a mess. I've been all over the place with this wedding."

"It's totally fine. Don't worry. Everything will be perfect, I promise. I'll see you both at the shower."

"Great. Until then."

At least she would have a few days to come up with a plan to avoid any more questions about her nonexistent date.

SHE WAS STILL asking herself how she could have created such a mess for herself an hour later as she loaded the last of the wedding flowers into the back of her SUV.

Her sister's shock when she told her what she had done didn't help anything.

"What were you thinking?" Hannah asked, incredulous.

"I lied, okay? I don't know why I did it, the words spilled out before I had a chance to think them through. Kris was so worried that things would be awkward with Troy and Brittany and was trying to set me up with one of Matt's friends and before I knew it, I was telling her I had a date. So now I have to figure out who that is."

Hannah grinned. "The fake-relationship trope is my absolute favorite."

She made a face. "Only in all those romance novels, the fake relationship always morphs into a real one. That's not going to happen to me."

"You never know. We just have to find the perfect guy willing to pretend he's crazy about you."

"Any suggestions?"

"What about Justin Sanchez, the new soccer coach at the high school? He's super cute. He has a longtime girlfriend but Troy's family members don't have to know that. I'm sure he would be willing to help us out."

"I don't think that would work. It's a small community. What if somebody at the wedding knows Justin or his girlfriend?"

"Hmm. Good point. What about the new guy who moved into my condo building? I think he's an electrician or something. He's a little hairy but I've seen him in the condo gym and he's super ripped."

"Does he have a girlfriend? Or a boyfriend, for that matter?"

"Not sure. I haven't seen him with anyone, but he might have a long-distance thing. I can ask him."

Hannah made a face. "On a negative note, he sweats a *lot* and he never wipes off his machines at the gym."

"Gross."

"I mean, nobody's perfect."

"True enough."

Hannah appeared lost in thought for a moment before her features brightened. "What about Kim's brother?"

Holly almost dropped the last box of wedding flowers as nerves suddenly jumped through her.

"Ryan? I can't ask him! I barely know the man."

"Why not? He's perfect!" Hannah held up her fingers to enumerate the advantages. "He's gorgeous, he's a stranger in town nobody knows and better yet, he's only going to be here through Christmas. No messy questions. After he goes back to California, you can tell Troy and his family you're having a long-distance relationship with him."

Holly frowned as she considered the suggestion. Okay. The idea might actually have merit after all. A fake boyfriend would be useful in myriad ways.

She would love not having to endure pitying looks from Troy's family, the awkwardness of being alone when everyone else seemed to have a partner. Maybe they would even stop trying to set her up with random people. She could focus on her daughter, not on trying to fend off well-meaning but mis-guided matchmaking efforts on her behalf.

If she had to pretend to have a fake relationship, why not with Ryan Caldwell? He was a great candidate for the role. Hannah was right. He was gorgeous. More than that, he was only here temporarily, which would mean she wouldn't have to keep up the pretense for an extended period. Only through the holidays.

On the other hand, she shuddered to think about actu-ally having that kind of humiliating conversation with Ryan Caldwell.

Hey, do you mind pretending to be my boyfriend and going with me and my daughter to a wedding with two hundred people you don't know?

She could only imagine how that would go.

"It's a brilliant idea, if I do say so myself," Hannah pressed. "If you have to find a pretend boyfriend, why not make him a hot, mysterious stranger?"

Holly could think of a hundred different pitfalls to the plan, not least of which was trying to convince Ryan to actually go along with it. Why would he agree to something so ridiculous, when she could think of no actual benefit to him?

"I'll think about it. That's the best I can do."

Hannah made a face. "You think too much. That's your whole problem, Hol. Sometimes you need to follow your impulses. Seize the day and all that. Or in this case, seize the gorgeous helicopter pilot and don't let go."

Holly decided it was probably not a good idea to mention to her twin sister exactly how appealing she found that idea.

CHAPTER SIX

—

RYAN HAD NO CONCEPT OF HOW EXHAUSTING HE WOULD find the prospect of trying to figure out how and what to feed a thirteen-year-old girl on the regular.

Three meals a day, every single day, until she moved out of the house. He was overwhelmed just thinking about it. How did Kim do it?

At least his niece didn't seem to be a particularly picky eater, other than she didn't like anything with onions or mushrooms. He couldn't blame her for the latter.

Plus, he would be able to get a little bit of a break when she ate school lunch during the week, so that took a few meals off his plate, at least until Christmas break. He could only hope his sister would be home by then and the responsibility could once more fall on her no-doubt much more capable shoulders.

"Do you have a favorite kind of cereal?" he asked, scanning the offerings on the shelves of the grocery store.

"I don't usually eat a lot of cereal," Audrey admitted, looking up from the phone that seemed glued to her hand. "I used to like it more when I was little but now if I have time for breakfast I usually have toast with maybe some peanut butter on it."

Ryan had a sudden memory of Kim often fixing that for him when she had become his de facto caregiver during their mom's illness and after her death.

"Not a bad breakfast. It's how I survived flight school."

"We have plenty of peanut butter at home but we're almost out of bread. I can show you the kind Mom always gets."

"Sounds good."

They headed in the direction of the bakery. She shoved her

phone in her pocket and focused on helping him with the shopping. As they worked their way through the store, Audrey was full of funny commentary about items she liked and didn't like, something she ate a friend's house, a brand of cookies she wanted to try.

He had discovered since he arrived in Shelter Springs that he liked being with his niece, much to his surprise. She was funny and insightful, with a unique way of looking at the world.

Ryan had always told himself having a family of his own wasn't in the cards. He wasn't cut out to be a husband, a partner, a father. Besides the poor example his own father had set for him, Ryan had been in a few relationships with women earlier in his adult life who had basically told him he was closed off emotionally.

They complained he was too focused on his military career and didn't make enough room in his life for softness and connection.

Spending all this time with Audrey, seeing her sense of humor and her compassion and her kindness, was almost enough to make him wonder about all the what-ifs he had closed the door to a long time ago.

They were nearly finished shopping after making their way through nearly every section of the store when a woman with wavy blond hair and familiar features turned into their aisle. Holly's twin sister. Hannah, he remembered.

She moved in their direction, focusing on the shelves. When her attention shifted to them, she froze, blue eyes going wide as if they were the last people she expected to find in the store.

"Hi, Hannah," Audrey said.

She smiled at his niece. "Audrey. Hello. And Ryan, isn't it?"

"Hello."

"Uncle Ry, you remember Hannah Goodwin, right? Holly's twin sister. I think you met her the other day."

"Yes. I remember."

"It's great to bump into you. If I didn't know better, I might almost call it fate."

Hannah looked delighted and something in her expression immediately set him on edge. He didn't believe in fate or kismet or anything of the sort, but somehow he still had a premonition of impending danger.

She scanned their cart. "How's the shopping going?"

"Good," Audrey answered. "We're almost done. We only have to grab some, um, feminine hygiene products for me. I had my first period last month and Mom and I were going to pick up some other stuff before the next one but didn't have the chance before she had to go."

Holly's sister gave him an amused look, as if expecting him to be uncomfortable. He raised an eyebrow, completely unfazed. Menstruation was a normal part of life, right? Okay, he hadn't much experience in shopping for supplies but he was always willing to learn.

"Do you know what you're looking for?" Hannah asked her.

"Not really. Mom bought everything last time."

The older woman studied her. "Would you like me to go with you to that particular aisle and help you choose?"

Audrey looked relieved. "Yeah, actually. That would be great. Thanks a lot."

Ryan followed them to the feminine hygiene aisle and was instantly overwhelmed at all the options.

To his relief, Hannah took charge, discussing the pros and cons with Audrey of the various products.

After they finally made a couple different selections and added them to the cart, Audrey looked down the aisle and her features lit up.

"Hey! There's Jenny Hernandez. We're working on a project for our English class together. Can I go talk to her for a minute?"

"Yeah. That's fine. I'll take this stuff to the checkout. Come find me when you're done talking to your friend."

"Okay."

She hurried away, leaving him with Hannah Goodwin.

"Thanks for your help," he said. "I'll admit, shopping for period products is above my pay grade."

"No problem. I remember how confusing all the different products can be. Holly and I started our periods only a week apart. That is apparently common in twins."

He expected that was probably more personal information than Holly wanted her sister to disclose to a near stranger.

"And speaking of my sister, like I said, I'm actually really glad I bumped into you."

His wariness from earlier at her strange reaction when they first encountered her returned tenfold. "Oh?"

She chewed her lip and hesitated for a moment before plunging ahead. "Holly will kill me for this but I know she will never ask you herself."

He was suddenly quite sure he did not want to hear whatever she was about to say. What would Hannah do if he suddenly whirled his cart in the other direction and hurried away from her?

He couldn't do that, especially when she had taken time from her own shopping to help out his niece.

"My sister is the most amazing, kind person I know," Hannah said. "She is a fantastic mother, a dedicated small business owner, a volunteer for various organizations around town. She takes care of everybody around her. Everyone except herself."

Somehow he didn't need Hannah to tell him that about her

twin. In their few interactions, he had already received that same impression about Holly Moore.

"Just to show you how kind she is," Hannah went on, "this month she is providing the flowers for the wedding of her former sister-in-law. Lydia has been asked to be a flower girl."

"I know. Holly told me."

He still wasn't sure what any of this had to do with him.

"I tried to talk her out of both of those things. I didn't think she should be providing the flowers or letting Lydia be in the wedding party. Holly insisted it would be the right thing to do."

"Why did you think she shouldn't participate?" he asked, genuinely curious.

"Because her ex-husband is going to be there and he is an absolute jerk. Troy walked out on his family when Lyd was only three. He left my beautiful, amazing sister for another woman, the administrative assistant at his insurance firm, and they had a baby earlier this year. Lydia's half brother, Hudson. The baby is adorable, I will give him that. He is also, to quote his and Lydia's father on one memorable occasion, a quote-unquote *normal* boy without any obvious disabilities."

Had the man actually been stupid enough to say that? Ryan disliked him already.

"Holly thinks she will be perfectly fine to go to the wedding of Troy's sister by herself, with only Lydia. I disagree. I think she should take a date. A gorgeous date."

He blinked, not sure how to respond to that. "Did you have any one in mind?" he asked, though he suspected he already knew the answer.

"We went through all the possibilities of guys in town today and nobody really felt right. Except you."

"Me."

Hannah nodded. "I think you would be the perfect person

to take her to the wedding. Troy doesn't know you at all, a mysterious naval pilot from out of town who won't be sticking around to make things complicated. Plus you're all . . . this."

She waved a hand in front of him and he again didn't quite know how to respond.

"Troy would hate seeing Holly with someone like you. Anything Troy hates, I am completely behind. I know that makes me sound petty. But you know what? I don't care."

"You want me to take your sister, whom I have met exactly twice, to the wedding of her ex-husband's sister." He couldn't seem to wrap his head around her suggestion.

"I know it's a lot to ask," Hannah acknowledged. "But when she's not overworked and overstressed, Holly is so much fun. She's creative, she's talented, she's a great dancer. I think you two would have a fantastic time together."

"Does your sister know you're, um, asking strange men to date her?"

"No. And like I said, she will kill me when she finds out. But siblings have to go to the wall for each other, right? That's the whole reason you're here. To help Kim."

"And Audrey."

"Right. Family. I would do anything for my sister and my niece, too. I'm sure you can understand."

He did understand that. She was right; that was the whole reason he was here in this grocery store, trying to figure out what to feed his niece for the next month.

Hannah sent him a sideways look. "You're not really a stranger, when you stop to think about it. Your sister is one of our dearest friends. Plus she works for Holly. If Kim knew I was asking you, I'm sure she would agree you're the perfect solution for Holly."

He gave a short laugh. He wasn't sure he had ever been

any woman's perfect solution. He instinctively wanted to tell Hannah her idea was completely irrational and he would never agree to it. What man would?

Then he remembered that sweet little Lydia, with her wide smile and her generous heart, and he felt a pang of sympathy for Holly, struggling to raise her daughter on her own and navigate a complicated relationship with the family of her ex-husband.

"Why would you ask me? And why would I ever agree?"

She looked at him with a hopeful expression that reminded him of both her sister and her niece.

"Maybe out of the goodness of your heart and because you're a nice guy?"

"Who says I have a heart? Or that I'm a nice guy?"

He didn't growl the words, even though he wanted to. Still, Hannah narrowed her gaze as she studied him, then she shook her head with an eye roll.

"You're Kim's brother. She would never ask you to stay with Audrey if you weren't a nice guy. And only a nice guy would agree to come out from California to help her out in her time of need."

He frowned, wondering what the others in his squadron would think if they heard Lieutenant Commander Ryan "Ripcord" Caldwell being called a nice guy. He had a hard-earned reputation for being tough and unflinching in a crisis, someone who wouldn't put up with bull from anybody.

"I'm afraid I don't have anything to bargain with," Hannah went on, her expression rueful. "I could offer to shovel your snow or fix you and Audrey a few meals but I'm not really much of a cook. You probably wouldn't go for either of those options, even if I were."

"Probably not."

"Is there anything I could offer in return to convince you?"

He wasn't aware Audrey had found them again until she spoke from behind him. "In return for what?"

He could feel a muscle tighten in his jaw and he had no idea what to say in response.

"A little favor," he finally answered. "It's nothing."

"What?" she pressed, looking between the two of them with curiosity.

"Holly needs a date for the wedding of Lydia's Aunt Kristine," Hannah said after a moment, sending him an apologetic yet calculating look. "She already told Kristine and Kris's mother she had one. Now we only need to find the perfect guy to make it so."

She paused. "Or I guess she can always admit to them that she lied and only pretended to have a date so they wouldn't feel sorry for her."

Audrey looked appalled. "No way. That's like peak cringe."

"Exactly," Hannah said.

Audrey tilted her head, giving Ryan a considering look. "You would be perfect, Uncle Ry. You have to do it. Holly is amazing. She's just, like, next level. She didn't even hesitate when Mom asked if I could stay with her when she went into rehab. Or when Mom asked for the whole month of December off, even though it's the busiest time of year for her shop."

Oh great. Now they were ganging up to pressure him. He was running out of maneuvering room.

"You have to say yes," Audrey insisted. "You know Mom would want you to do it."

Yeah. He was alone here with absolutely no cover. "Maybe Holly wouldn't even want to take me as her plus-one. You said yourself she thought she would be fine on her own."

"She needs a date. And she agreed that you would be perfect for the situation, though she did say she would never ask you herself."

Perversely, that left him wondering why not.

"Please, Uncle Ryan. Holly gave me a job babysitting Audrey even though I'm only thirteen because she knew I wanted to save up to buy Mom a new phone for Christmas, since hers is even older than mine. And mine is crap."

"I'll think about it. Let's leave it at that for now."

"I guess that's all I can ask," Hannah answered. "Thank you for even considering it.

Yeah. As he and Audrey said goodbye and headed for the checkout, Ryan had a feeling he would be thinking about her suggestion for a long time.

CHAPTER SEVEN

—

HOLLY LOVED LIVING IN THE MOUNTAINS OF IDAHO. SHE RE-
ally did. She loved the people, she loved the splendor of the
scenery and she loved the recreational opportunities from living next to a beautiful body of water.

She did not, however, love shoveling snow.

If she ever won the lottery—probably unlikely to happen
since she never played—the first thing she planned to do was
hire somebody to clear her driveway and sidewalks in the
winter.

"I'm helping, Mommy."

She looked at the area Lydia tramped through, her little snow
shovel dragging more snow across the section Holly had just
finished clearing. Snow that would probably melt and freeze
again into a treacherous line of ice.

No bother, she would come back after Lydi was in bed and
clear it all away again.

Raising a daughter willing to help her and one who felt
appreciated for her efforts was far more important than perfection.

It was one of the first and most enduring lessons she had
learned as Lydia's mother. Perfection wasn't always what it was
cracked up to be anyway.

"Thank you, darling," she said with a grateful smile. "I
don't know what I would do without your help."

Lydia grinned, her cheeks rosy in the moonlight and the
reflection from the nearby streetlight.

"I can help more."

Lydia headed off to "shovel" another section of sidewalk
while Holly continued working on the driveway.

She was making slow progress when she saw a black truck she didn't recognize pull up.

When the passenger door opened, Audrey hopped out, followed by Ryan coming around from the driver's side.

Her heart gave a silly little kick hat made her want to roll her eyes. She hadn't seen him in a few days. Somehow she had forgotten how gorgeous he was, all hard muscles and lean angles.

"Need a hand?" Audrey asked.

About a dozen of them, as long as they were all pushing snow shovels.

"You don't have to do that. We're almost done and I'm sure you have snow of your own to shovel. Thank you, though."

"We don't mind," Ryan said. "Do we, Audrey?"

"Not me," she answered. "I love shoveling snow."

"Do you have another shovel?" Ryan asked.

Holly knew she should argue with them. She was a strong, independent woman who could shovel her own snow.

But one of the other important lessons she had learned from her time as Lydia's mother was to accept help when it was offered. Sometimes it required her to swallow her pride, yes. That was a small price to pay for all the benefits, both to herself and to the person offering their help.

"I do, actually. Right inside the garage door, I have a few more shovels."

Ryan headed in that direction while Audrey went to praise Lydia's efforts, which made her daughter glow with pleasure.

A moment later, he came out carrying two more snow shovels. He handed one to Audrey then went to work alongside Lydia with the heavier one.

"I noticed you also have a snowblower in the garage. Any reason why you aren't using it?"

She could feel herself flush and hoped the cold air disguised it. "I can't figure it out," she admitted. "Troy bought it used right after we were married, when we were living in a rental with a long driveway that he hated shoveling. He left it with me after he moved to Portland, figuring he wouldn't need it as much as I would."

"Makes sense. Except it's sitting in the garage while you're out here with a shovel."

"I don't know how to even start it up. And yes, I've tried. I even watched a couple of videos online but couldn't make it work. I think maybe something's broken."

"I could maybe take a look at it for you while I'm in town," he said, then looked as if he regretted the offer.

"You don't have to. I've been meaning to have my dad or one of my brothers come take a look at it but I always forget to ask them until it snows."

"I guess for now we'll do this the old-fashioned way."

They worked together in silence for a few moments while the moon popped in and out from the clouds, gleaming on the ice-covered trees.

It was a beautiful night, she had to admit. Each breath puffed out in the cold, clear air. Though she was tired from working all day at the shop, she was grateful for the chance to be outside breathing in that faint metallic tang of winter.

"I met your sister the other day at the grocery store."

She looked up, surprised. Hannah hadn't mentioned it to her during their frequent text exchanges or when she had stopped in at the store earlier that day on her lunch break.

"Did you?"

"Yes. She had a lot to say. She seems very protective of you."

Oh dear. What had Hannah said to him? Maybe that's why she hadn't mentioned their encounter to Holly, because her sister knew she wouldn't like it.

"She can be. Protective, I mean. It's pretty annoying. She

thinks because she was born two minutes before me that gives her the right to boss me around for the rest of our lives."

"It's nice that she cares about you so much."

He said nothing more and she fought the urge to throw a shovel full of snow at him. He couldn't throw out a teaser like that and not follow through.

"What did she say?" she finally asked.

He seemed inordinately focused on the snow he shoveled and didn't meet her gaze.

"She, um, suggested you might be looking for a plus-one for a family wedding later this month."

"No, she did *not*." She stopped in mid-shovel as a hot tide of embarrassment washed over her.

"Afraid she did."

Oh, sweet baby Jesus.

"I am so sorry. Ignore her. Please." She wanted to bury her head in a big pile of freshly fallen snow, though she suspected even that wouldn't be enough to cool her mortification.

"Was she wrong? Are you saying you don't need a plus-one?"

"I'll be fine. I *have* a date. Lydia. She's all I need."

He studied her for a long moment then turned back to shoveling. "Okay. Probably for the best, since I didn't bring anything to wear to a wedding."

She swallowed hard, trying not to imagine Ryan Caldwell dressed up in something suitable for a wedding.

What was Hannah *thinking*? Hadn't Holly been clear that she wasn't going to ask Ryan to go with her?

She had certainly thought about it since that day in her shop but had decided her life was complicated enough without adding a fictional boyfriend into the mix. Or a real man playing a fictional boyfriend.

She would simply tell Troy's family something had come

up, plans had changed and her date hadn't been able to come after all. She could leave it at that without having to muddle the situation further.

"I'm sure you have a million things you would rather do than take a woman you barely know to the wedding of a couple of strangers."

"At least a million."

"I mean, *I* don't even want to go and I know both the bride and the groom."

"So why are you? Seems like a whole lot of unnecessary stress. If I were you, I would find any excuse I could not to put myself through it."

She didn't tell him how very tempting she found that idea of avoiding all of it.

She couldn't, though. Any more than she could avoid shoveling snow when it stormed. Some things had to be faced, like it or not.

"My ex and I might not be together anymore but he is still Lydia's father. His family will always be connected to her. I can't miss celebrating the wedding of her aunt, who happens also to be a good friend, simply because I'm uncomfortable."

"Many people would take the easier road."

Sometimes she really wished her parents had raised children who could take the easier road, instead of those who always had to choose the right one.

"If I allowed my comfort level to dictate every decision in my life, I would never leave my house. I would be inside right now on my sofa, watching Hallmark movies and eating Christmas cookies."

He was quiet as she shoveled. When he looked at her, she thought she saw a note of approval in his expression. "True enough. Too many people avoid anything in life they find hard."

"I don't want to go to Kristine's wedding. That's not a

lie. But I have every intention of going and being polite and eating substandard banquet food. Who knows? I might even dance. Because it's the right thing to do and I want to teach my daughter by example that doing the right thing is important, even when it's hard."

He gave her an inscrutable look then returned to shoveling. "Maybe having a plus-one would ease the discomfort a little. If things get awkward with your ex or his family, you can always talk to me."

She stared. Was he actually considering taking her?

"Why would you possibly agree to this? Don't get me wrong, I appreciate your willingness. I'm only trying to understand why."

After a moment, he inclined his head toward his niece. "Audrey is pretty persuasive. She is convinced I owe you for taking her in after the accident, as well as for giving Kim time off to go to rehab. She basically thinks you're a saint. I believe she said you were next level, which I assume is a compliment. She thinks that the least I can do is take you to a wedding to repay you for what you've done to help our family."

"Ha. I'm far from a saint. And I only did what any other friend would do. You're under absolutely no obligation to put yourself through this level of misery."

He set his shovel in the snow and leaned on the handle to study her, the moonlight catching silvery glints in his hair.

"What if we made a bargain?"

She rested her own shovel and gazed at him, suddenly suspicious. "What sort of bargain?"

What could she possibly have to offer a man like Lieutenant Commander Ryan Caldwell?

"You need a date to your ex-sister-in-law's wedding. I need help throwing together a decent Christmas for Audrey. I have no idea where to start."

"I thought Kim expected to be home before Christmas."

"She hopes so, but I don't know when that might be. Even if she is, I don't think it's fair to expect her to manage Christmas when she's straight out of rehab. I would like to have as much done for her as possible so she doesn't have to think about any details, and she can simply enjoy the time together with Audrey."

That was surprisingly insightful, coming from a tough, intimidating man like Ryan.

"What did you have in mind?"

"The usual. Gifts. Decorations. Cookies, maybe. I would like Kim's place to feel like yours does."

He gestured to the window where her tree gleamed. Her house did look festive, she had to admit, with lights glowing in each of the windows and the front porch adorned with greenery and branches from the red-twigged dogwoods that grew along her fence line.

"We can help each other out," Ryan said. "I'll go with you as your plus-one to the wedding. Even better, I'll pretend to be madly in love with you, to show your stupid ex-husband everything he's missing out on."

Her pulse accelerated with both awareness and alarm at the suggestion. "I don't think we need to quite go that far," she said quickly.

He grinned unexpectedly. "But only imagine much fun it could be to show everyone you've moved on."

She gripped her shovel handle, telling herself sternly that she was a business owner and a mother who had absolutely no business going weak in the knees simply because a good-looking man offered her a sexy smile.

"In return," Ryan went on, "you help me deck the freaking halls at my sister's house so I can make sure Kim and Audrey have an unforgettable Christmas together. You help me with my problem and I'll help you with yours. We both get what we need. It's perfect."

"You seem to have it all figured out, for a guy who claimed he has nothing to wear."

He shrugged. "My dad probably has a closet full of suits. We're roughly the same size. If nothing else, I can pick up a pair of dress pants and shirt and borrow a tie and a jacket from him."

"This is crazy. You don't have to do this, just because my sister was nervy enough to ask you—my sister, by the way, with whom I will be having a few strong words as soon as I'm done shoveling snow."

"Hannah was only looking out for you. I get that. And I'm looking out for my sister too, by asking for your help."

She didn't believe he really needed her guidance. He and Audrey were perfectly capable of decorating a Christmas tree without her help. Still, she found it sweet that he wanted to give Kim a memorable holiday after her rough month.

Having him as her date for the wedding really was the perfect solution. Her in-laws wouldn't have to feel awkward about having their son's ex-wife there and she wouldn't have to face the ordeal alone.

"This actually might work," she said, though she couldn't shake the feeling she was about to make a huge mistake.

She was already finding Ryan Caldwell fairly irresistible. Something told her that spending even more time with the man—especially pretending to be dating him—would only strengthen this silly crush she was developing for him.

"No *might* about it. It *will* work. We'll make sure of it."

She could only wish she shared his confidence. She shook her head and held out her mittened hand. "I guess we have ourselves a deal, Lieutenant Commander Caldwell."

He smiled and shook it with his gloved hand. As he smiled

down at her, looking big and dark and dangerous in the moonlight, she tried to ignore the little quiver of awareness.

"None of this Lieutenant Commander stuff. You're going to have to start calling me Ryan, especially since we're madly in love with each other."

She gave a short laugh. "I'm not sure pretending to be in love with each other was ever part of the bargain."

"It's in the fine print," he said with a shrug. "I've always believed that if a thing is worth doing, it's damn well worth doing right."

"Okay. I guess we're in love," she said.

Everything about this seemed wrong, she couldn't help thinking, though she had to admit it felt great to know she had a man like Ryan on her side.

It made the prospect of the upcoming wedding far less intimidating.

CHAPTER EIGHT

———

THIS PROBABLY WASN'T HIS SMARTEST IDEA EVER.

As Ryan pulled more boxes marked Christmas out of his sister's attic he had to ask himself what he had been thinking.

Why had he signed himself up for this? Bad enough that he was now committed to decorating his sister's house for her but he had also jumped into the middle of what was bound to be an uncomfortable social event. He wasn't a big fan of weddings in the first place. All that fuss over something that probably wouldn't last anyway.

A wedding for a couple of strangers, along with all the accompanying social unease, felt like the fifth circle of hell.

How could he refuse, though? He liked Holly. Something about the woman and her cute daughter stirred up all his protective instincts. Holly seemed to have been given more than her share of challenges and she was handling them with grace. He had to respect that.

He also had kind of a thing for protecting and defending the vulnerable. He didn't like the idea of Holly having to face her ex and his new family without backup.

It was only one night. He could handle that, couldn't he?

He had already talked to his dad about borrowing one of his suit jackets, though he hadn't told the colonel why.

The doorbell rang as he was setting down the last box in the living room.

"I'll get it!" Before he could react, Audrey raced from her room where she was supposed to be finishing a homework assignment before their guests arrived.

He heard her greet Holly and Lydia with enthusiasm. "Thanks so much for coming to help us," he heard Audrey say in the entryway. "We're both pretty clueless when it comes to decorating."

"Speak for yourself." Ryan moved into the small foyer to take their coats and hats. "Maybe we'll discover I have a hidden talent for this kind of thing."

"I hope so," Holly said with a smile. "Then you won't need me. And if we find that talent, I'll immediately hire you at the store while you're in town. I can use all the help I can find right now."

Yeah, working in a florist shop intimidated him far more than spending an entire day at the Christmas wedding of a couple of strangers.

"Hi, Mr. Ryan." Lydia beamed at him with her entire face and he could swear the whole world seemed to brighten.

He smiled down at her. "Hello, Miss Lydia. You are looking lovely today."

She twirled to show off a cute Christmas sweater and skirt that she wore over matching leggings. "We going to Grandma's today to take a shower."

He frowned in confusion. "Are you?"

Holly gave him a rueful smile but he noticed she didn't outright contradict her daughter; she only made a slight correction to her claim. "My ex-mother-in-law is hosting a bridal shower for Kristine this afternoon. We're heading over as soon as we're done here."

"Are you sure you have time to help us put up our tree? Sounds like your day is packed."

"We absolutely have time. We're looking forward to it, aren't we?" she asked her daughter.

Lydia clapped her hands with delight. "I love Christmas," she declared.

When you were living with so much joy, it would be hard not to love the holidays.

"Where do we start?" he asked. "I went through the attic and brought down everything I could find marked Christmas but I haven't had time to go through the boxes yet."

"That's okay. Going through boxes is one of our favorite things, isn't it, Lyd?"

Her daughter nodded vigorously. "I love presents, too."

"Who doesn't?"

Holly smiled at her daughter and something about that gentle expression, overflowing with love, left a soft ache in his chest, an unaccustomed warmth.

When she turned that smile in his direction, he felt as if the sun had come out from behind the clouds during a hard winter storm.

"Let's see what you have," she said.

He led the way to the living room, dominated now by the artificial Christmas tree he and Audrey had put up the night before.

"Oh good," Holly said. "You've already set up the tree."

"That's all we've done. We were afraid to put up any decorations. We didn't want to ruin it."

"First rule of Christmas trees, you can't ruin them. No matter what you do, if you like the results, it's perfect for you. Christmas trees don't have to be fancy. The decorations don't all have to match and they don't have to have expensive ornaments. You can use whatever you want, as long as it brings you joy."

The Christmas trees of his childhood had been elegant, with matching ornaments and ribbons, he suddenly remembered. His mother had opted for entirely new tree decorations every time they had to move to a new military base, leaving the old ornaments behind for other families.

Had that been his father's preference? Or had his mother perhaps been a little more picky about that sort of thing than he remembered?

"How does your mom usually decorate your Christmas tree?" Holly asked Audrey, as if following his train of thought. "Does she use color-coordinated ornaments or does she prefer a hodgepodge of things on the tree?"

Audrey grew thoughtful. "We always had two trees, even before we moved here. We would put the big fake one in the front room and put up a smaller real one in the family room or one of our bedrooms."

"That's nice."

She nodded. "The fake one is always fancy, with silver and blue ornaments, and the real one is decorated with all the ornaments I've made through the years or things Mom and I have made together or ornaments we've picked up on vacation."

"Since we don't have a real one this year, why don't we save most of the fancy ornaments for next year when things are back to normal for you and put all the most cherished ornaments on this one?"

"Okay."

"You and Lydia can start going through the boxes and see if you can find the ornaments you'd like to use, as well as the garland and whatever tree topper you usually have out here."

"It's an angel my mom said my grandma used to hang on the tree."

He had totally forgotten that angel. With a sudden rush of nostalgia, he remembered how much pleasure Laura used to get in taking the angel out of the box every year and setting her atop the tree.

He used to talk to the angel, he remembered, with no small amount of mortification.

"Perfect." Holly smiled at Audrey. "We'll save that job for last, since that's something you and your uncle can do without us, if we run out of time and have to leave for our shower."

"Sounds good."

"While you're looking through the boxes, set aside any other holiday decorations you are absolutely sure your mother would want you to put out."

"Okay. Lydia and I can do that."

"Great. Meanwhile, your uncle and I will head outside with that box of lights and hang them on the tree out front. As I recall, that's what your mom did last year."

Audrey nodded. "She was so happy after we moved into this house. We had always lived in apartments before we started renting this one and we never had our own yard to decorate."

"How lovely," Holly said.

"Even when we lived in apartments, Mom always decorated our balcony or patio with lights and a little Christmas tree."

Kim had loved Christmas. He should have remembered. After their mom died, when they would both come home from their respective boarding schools, she would insist the two of them decorate the house. She used to say it was her way of connecting to their mom, who had also loved the holidays.

He was suddenly grateful he had asked Holly for her help. With everything Kim was going through, his sister deserved to be able to return home to lights and decorations and holiday cheer.

"I can probably decorate the trees and shrubs outside on my own, if you want to stay here and help Audrey and Lydia."

She appeared to consider his suggestion, then shrugged. "I expect things will go faster and be less frustrating if there are two of us. In my experience, lights are easier with a team. You can string the lights while I work on keeping them untangled as much as possible."

"Good plan."

"I should have left my coat on," she said ruefully.

"Here. Let me help you."

He grabbed her coat from the rack and helped her slip her arms into the sleeves. As he did, he couldn't help noticing the sweetly seductive scent of her, vanilla and lemons and apples.

He grabbed his own coat from the rack and donned it before fishing his gloves out of his pocket.

She grabbed one box of lights and he picked up the other one and they both headed outside into the cold December day, where sunlight gleamed off the snow.

He couldn't help an instinctive shiver and she sent him a sidelong look.

"Sorry. I've been living in San Diego for two years and before that I was in Hawaii, with Guam before that."

"Must be tough."

"Well, I did spend six months deployed on a carrier in the North Atlantic, but that's been a few years. I'm still trying to get used to winter weather again."

He gestured back to the house. "Also, nicely done back there. I've had commanding officers who didn't give orders as clearly as that."

She winced. "Sorry. I stepped in and took over, didn't I?"

"I meant that as a sincere compliment. I had no idea where to start, which is probably why I haven't done anything to decorate the house since I first arrived in town. I should have. Kim loves Christmas so Audrey probably does, too."

"She does."

"I was thinking a moment ago how grateful I am that you agreed to help us."

She gave a short laugh, her cheeks going slightly pink in the cold air. "I'm coming out ahead in this deal, as we both know. I only have to help you with something I love doing anyway—decorating for Christmas—while you'll be stuck having to endure my ex-in-laws for an entire evening."

Right now, the idea of spending more time with Holly, even at a wedding, didn't seem unappealing at all.

"Don't forget we also have to persuade them we're head over heels for each other."

"Again, I'm not sure we have to go that far. Your presence will probably be enough."

"Maybe. But it will definitely be more fun."

When she opened her mouth, he picked up one of the boxes of lights to distract her. "Where do we start with these?"

As he had hoped, she allowed herself to be sidetracked. "We should probably test the lights first. It's so frustrating when you have gone to all the trouble to hang them and then find out they have a bad bulb or something."

"Right. Nothing worse than a bad bulb."

They spent considerable time checking each of the light strings, which were all in remarkably good condition, then they set to the work wrapping the lights around the branches of the small fir tree near the front porch of Kim's cottage.

She held the lights, untwisting them from the holder while he worked to wrap them around the branches.

"So tell me about your ex. How did the two of you meet?"

She flashed him a look and hesitated long enough to make him realize she did not want to answer. After a long pause she sighed.

"We both went to school in Boise. I didn't know him at all but his roommate, Josh, went to high school with me. My car broke down and was in the shop but I wanted to come home for the weekend, since it was my mom's birthday. I asked Josh if he was coming back to Shelter Springs for the weekend so I could catch a ride. He wasn't but said his roommate, who was from the nearby town of Haven Point, would be happy to give me a ride."

"Don't tell me. It was love at first sight."

She made a face. "Not even close. I disliked him at first. Maybe I should have trusted that first impression."

"Why didn't you?"

She shrugged. "Because he was charming and funny and good-looking. And I was lonely. It was my first time away from home, my first time living on my own. Hannah had gone out of state for school to a college that had a better music therapy program. I almost went with her but our parents thought we might benefit by living apart for awhile."

"Why is that? Did the two of you fight all the time?"

"Never, actually. I think that was part of the problem. Our lives were pretty entwined as we were growing up. We had the same friends, we did the same extracurricular activities, we even double-dated most of the time."

"Is that a bad thing?"

She shook her head, unspooling more lights for him as he moved to a higher branch. "Hannah is my best friend and I adore her," she said after a moment. "But without question, she has always had the stronger personality. I think Mom wanted us—particularly *me*—to not be so codependent, you know?"

"I get it. I've been in squadrons with guys who couldn't function unless they were paired up. They worked great together but struggled anytime they didn't have their battle buddy."

"I don't know if we were quite that bad, but I was always more comfortable with Hannah nearby. Going away was tough, though we texted and called each constantly."

She sighed again as she picked up another light string for him to connect to the first one. "And then I met Troy my junior year and ended up transferring all that codependence to him. We married the year after I graduated."

"How long were you together?"

"Nearly eight years. I knew he was selfish and immature

from the jump. I didn't like it, but tried to tell myself his good qualities outweighed the bad. He was a hard worker, he was nice to my friends, he treated me well. Then I had Lydia and everything changed."

"You had to grow up and he didn't."

She looked at him with a startled expression, as if she hadn't expected that kind of perceptiveness. "Exactly. He still wanted to go on like he always had, partying on the weekends, planning trips together without considering what we would do with Lydia, spending money we didn't have. I started to feel more like his mother than his wife. And I started treating him that way, unfortunately."

"I hope you don't blame yourself for the breakdown of your marriage. Your ex sounds like a real man-child."

"We were both at fault. It would be only too easy to throw all the blame on Troy. He's the one who cheated, after all. But I wasn't a very good partner to him, either, toward the end. I'm not sure if I even liked him by that point, let alone loved him."

"Sounds like he didn't make it easy." He had zero respect for any man who could pursue his own selfish desires, even knowing the devastation his actions would cause those he had vowed to honor and protect.

"No. He didn't. Regardless, he will always be Lydia's dad and I have to maintain a good relationship with him and his family, for her sake if nothing else."

"That must be tough."

"It's not the life I had envisioned when I was a girl with my head stuffed full of dreams. But I wouldn't change it for anything."

She smiled at him with no trace of bitterness or regret, cheeks flushed from the cold. He suddenly had a wild urge to stop what he was doing, step closer to her and kiss her, right here in the winter sunlight.

The impulse both shocked and unnerved him.

"So what about you, Lieutenant Commander Caldwell," she said, heedless of his inappropriate thoughts. "What's your story?"

He tried to rein in the impulse to focus on the job at hand. His instinct was to make some kind of flip remark, but Holly had revealed truths about herself that must have taken courage to share. He couldn't simply ignore her question.

"Not much to tell, really. And probably very little that you don't already know from Kim. She and I were military brats. Our dad was a pilot in the air force and we lived all over the world. The Philippines, Germany, Korea."

"And now you're also a helicopter pilot, carrying on that tradition."

He frowned. "My dad flew fighter jets in the air force. I'm a navy helicopter pilot. Totally different worlds."

She rolled her eyes. "Not to us civilians. Sorry. If you weren't following in your father's footsteps, what made you decide to become a naval pilot?"

He shrugged. "I really love flying. I always have. Maybe some of that came from growing up on bases around the world and being surrounded by aircraft but I think I would have loved it anyway. It's part of who I am. Does that sound weird?"

"Not at all. My sister, Hannah, knew she wanted to be a music therapist from the first time she ever met one, when we both had our tonsils out in Boise when we were nine. I always envied her for knowing what she wanted out of life."

"I got my pilot's license when I was sixteen and have been flying ever since."

"You didn't want to fly jets in the air force?"

"That was my dad's thing. Not mine. I *can* fly an airplane and I was a candidate to fly Tomcats. Those are navy fighter jets. But I decided I prefer helicopters. They're the Swiss Army knives of the sky."

"The Swiss Army knives?"

"Right. Fighter pilots have one job. We have dozens. Search and rescue, special ops support, cargo transport, medical evac. You name it."

"I suppose that's true."

"Besides, helicopter pilots are sexier. Fighter pilots think they're the coolest because they go fast and high but helicopter pilots know it takes skill to hover in one place. It's not how fast you get there, it's about how smoothly you make it to your destination."

Her quick flash of a smile became a full-on laugh and Ryan could only stare at her.

He had thought her pretty during the previous interactions. But right now, with her nose pink from the cold and her eyes bright with laughter, she was stunning.

The desire that rose in him took him completely by surprise.

He wanted to pull off her beanie and dig his hands in her hair, to pull her body against his, to lean down and cover her laugh with his mouth so he could savor all her sweetness and warmth.

She gazed up at him and something passed between them in that moment, a subtle awareness. She caught her breath, her lips parted slightly. He didn't stop to think it through. He probably couldn't have formed a coherent thought anyway. He only knew he wanted to kiss her. That he *had* to kiss her.

An instant before their mouths would have connected, he heard the sound of a car pulling into the driveway.

Jerked back to his senses, he eased away, reeling at what he had almost done.

He had been inches away from kissing Holly Moore, from tasting her to see if she was as soft and luscious as she looked.

That was totally unlike him. He certainly dated, but only women who wanted the same things he did. Not soft, vulnerable single mothers with tender hearts that were begging to be broken.

He turned, telling himself he was grateful for the interruption, and was astonished when his father stepped out of the late-model pickup truck, went around to the passenger side and pulled out a huge basket.

"What's this?" he asked as Doug walked up the sidewalk toward the house. The suspicion in his voice made it sound like he thought his father was hand delivering an improvised explosive device.

Doug gave him a tentative smile. "A few meals for you and Audrey. Neighbors and friends from church have been bringing meals over for Diane since the accident and our fridge is full to bursting. I also made a couple of soups Diane particularly likes. I thought you might be able to use some of this before it goes to waste. If not, you can freeze it all for Kim when she gets home."

Ryan wasn't sure what astonished him more, the idea of his father making his stepmother's favorite soup for her or that Doug could be thoughtful enough to consider that Ryan and Audrey might enjoy some of their excess.

Diane's doing, he expected.

"That is surprisingly generous of you," he said.

Doug frowned briefly at his tone but pushed it away to offer Holly a polite smile. "Mrs. Moore. How nice to see you again."

"Hello, Colonel Caldwell. How is Diane?"

"Better. She's starting to get around on her crutches."

"I'm so relieved to hear that. I've been worried about her."

"She has loved all the flowers she has been sent from your store. Other people have brought her arrangements from different florists and a few bouquets from the big box stores here in Shelter Springs, but yours are always her favorites."

"That's always lovely to hear. Thank you."

"Holly and her daughter were kind enough to help us decorate the house for the holidays," Ryan said.

"Great idea. Kim will love that when she returns."

"Can I help you with the basket?" Holly asked.

Doug shook his head. "I've got it. I'd like to check on Audrey while I'm here. See how she's doing."

Because you think I'm incapable of properly caring for her?

He thought the words but bit them back before they could spill out. Why did he revert to being a surly teenager whenever he was around his father?

"Sure. She'll be happy to see you," he replied.

Holly opened the door before Ryan could do it.

"Thank you," his father said and carried the basket inside.

He followed his father, where they found Audrey and Lydia sitting on the floor with opened boxes around them.

Audrey's features lit up and she jumped up.

"Grandpa!" She rushed to his father's side. Doug set the basket down on the coffee table and hugged her tightly.

"There's my girl. Looks like you've been busy, making the place look festive."

"We're trying. Holly and Lydia came to help us."

"That is very kind of them."

"How's Grandma Di?" she asked.

Ryan's flash of resentment annoyed him. No, Diane wasn't really Audrey's grandmother, only her grandfather's wife, but she clearly loved his niece.

Audrey never had the chance to know her grandmother. He couldn't fault her for forging a close relationship with Diane, who was a lovely, kind, generous woman.

"She is doing better every day, though a little tired of having to sit around. I think we've watched every Hallmark Christmas movie ever made."

"I don't think that's possible, unless you starting watching in July," Holly said with a smile. "Why don't I put these away for you while you visit with your father?"

She reached for the basket but Ryan picked it up instead. "I'll help," he answered. "Audrey and Lydia can entertain my father."

She sent him a swift look but didn't argue, only followed him as he headed for the kitchen.

CHAPTER NINE

—

SOMETHING ODD WAS GOING ON BETWEEN RYAN AND Douglas Caldwell.

As Holly followed Ryan to the kitchen, she turned and briefly caught a flash of something that looked like defeated resignation on his father's features before Doug quickly looked away, turning to respond to something his granddaughter said.

"If I didn't know better, I might think you were trying to avoid talking to your dad," she said in a low voice as they began transferring the containers of soup and casserole to the refrigerator.

"I don't know what you're talking about." Ryan's expression was stony, remote as Antarctica.

"Don't you?"

"My father and I get along fine," he said, his tone short, in marked contrast to the teasing and light flirtation of earlier while they were stringing lights. When he had almost kissed her.

"What makes you think otherwise?" he asked.

She chose her answer carefully. "As soon as you saw him pull up, you looked tense."

Maybe that was because he had been upset at himself for nearly kissing her. She preferred to think his sudden change in mood had more to do with his father.

"Your sister mentioned once that you and your dad aren't close. I guess that was the biggest clue."

"You talked to Kim about me?"

She shrugged, sliding a large container of soup onto a lower shelf. "When you work in a small retail shop together all day, you have plenty of time to chat about your lives. Kim loves you and worries about you."

"She should worry about herself and about Audrey. I'm fine."

Holly decided not to point out that his testy tone and stiff posture said otherwise.

Somehow she had the impression Ryan Caldwell was an inherently self-contained person who didn't let others close very often.

"Remind me to tell Kim she shouldn't be gossiping about me and my relationship with my father to a woman I had never met until a week ago."

Had it only been a week? It felt like much longer, maybe because Kim *had* talked about him often, with both concern and affection.

"Sorry I said anything. You're right. It's none of my business."

Holly knew she should keep her mouth shut but she couldn't help remembering that brief glimpse of what appeared to be raw pain on the elder Caldwell man's features.

"I don't know any of the history between you and your dad. Kim never gave me any details, for what it's worth."

"I guess I should be grateful she had a little discretion."

His clipped tone didn't invite further discussion but Holly was compelled to add one more thing.

"I do know that he and Diane have been a great support to Kim and Audrey since they moved to the Lake Haven area. She once told me the father she remembered in her youth wasn't anything like the man he had become over the past few years."

His mouth tightened but he said nothing and she decided not to add that perhaps in light of the holidays—the season of miracles, hope, reconciliation—he might try giving his father another chance.

None of this was her business. She and Ryan weren't friends.

Not really. They were polite acquaintances who were helping each other out.

Had he really almost kissed her or had she imagined that?

He placed the last container of food in the refrigerator, closed the door and carried the basket back to the living room, where they found Doug helping his granddaughter hang a garland over a door frame while Lydia watched on carefully, brow furrowed in concentration like a pint-sized project supervisor.

"Hope this is okay here," Audrey said. "I think I remember Mom hanging it here last year."

"It looks perfect," Holly assured her. "Exactly where I would have put it."

Audrey grinned as her grandfather finished hanging the garland. He stepped away and shifted his head, studying his handiwork. "Not bad."

"Thanks, Grandpa," Audrey said, giving him another hug.

"Thanks, Auddy's Grandpa," Lydia echoed.

He smiled at the girls. "You're both very welcome. I'm happy to help."

"We can always use another pair of hands, if you want to stick around a bit," Holly said brightly, though she didn't miss the glare Ryan sent her from behind his father's back.

"I would love to help but I need to go. I've got to get back to Diane. I don't like to leave her alone for long. I wanted to drop some of this food over before it goes bad. Whatever you don't think you will eat in the next day or two should probably go into the freezer."

"Thanks for thinking of us," Ryan said, the words stiff and formal. She could tell they hadn't been easy for him.

What had caused this rift between father and son? It must have been something that happened in his youth, perhaps after his mother's death from cancer when he and Kim had been teenagers.

Her heart ached with compassion for both of them.

"You're welcome. I'll see you both later. Lydia, Holly, it was nice to see you both again."

After another hug to his granddaughter, Douglas Caldwell picked up his basket and headed out the door, leaving a charged silence behind.

Doug Caldwell had a forceful personality. Not unlike his son. She had to wonder if that might be part of the reason the two of them seemed to butt heads.

Whatever might be awry between them wasn't her business, she reminded herself again. Ryan didn't strike her as an unreasonable man. He likely had good reasons to be angry with his father.

She turned her attention back to her decorating crew.

"What's next, oh mighty taskmaster?" he asked, with an exaggerated bow.

She rolled her eyes as Audrey giggled. Lydia giggled as well, though Holly was quite certain she didn't know what was funny.

"We're almost done outside. I'm sure the two of you can finish on your own, now that we've started. Why don't we decorate the tree next?"

"We need some Christmas music," Audrey declared. "I don't think you're legally allowed to decorate a Christmas tree unless you're listening to appropriate music, are you?"

Her uncle rolled his eyes but directed a smart speaker in the room to play instrumental Christmas music and a moment later, a jazzy version of "Jingle Bells" poured out.

"Much better," Audrey said with a grin as she opened another box containing ornaments.

"Where do we start?" Ryan asked, eying the tree with so much apprehension that Holly almost laughed. Had the man really never decorated a Christmas tree before?

"Since the tree is prelit, we don't have to mess with hanging lights."

"Lucky us," he answered.

"Exactly. On real trees, it can take forever to get the lights right."

"I love Christmas lights," Lydia said, her features aglow in the bright colors from Kim's artificial tree.

"So do I," Ryan told her daughter with a gentle smile that touched Holly deep at her center.

She cleared her throat. "Once the lights are on, I always start with the garland first and then hang the decorations after that."

"The garland is in the box closest to the tree," Audrey said. "Mom always used a gold shiny ribbon for a garland."

"Good to know."

She opened the box and found a roll of wide ribbon on top, coiled around what looked like a portion of a dowel.

She had to admire Kim's organizational techniques. As someone who was usually only too happy to take down her Christmas decorations—or so exhausted by all the fuss, at that point—she usually tended to store her decorations haphazardly.

"This will work nicely," she said. "Give me a few minutes to hang the garland and then the rest of you can start hanging ornaments."

"Even me?" Lydia asked, eyes wide as if afraid to hope.

"Especially you, darling." She smiled, kissing Lydia's forehead. When she lifted her head, her gaze met Ryan's and she found him watching her with an unreadable expression, one that left her feeling slightly breathless.

The next hour was surprisingly enjoyable.

Ryan headed back outside, presumably to finish hanging the few remaining light strings. Audrey seemed to relish the chance to decorate the tree, choosing where each ornament should go with care. Lydia was more haphazard, hanging most of hers in one big clump that Audrey subtly tried to redistribute more equitably.

After it was clear Audrey could handle the task without her supervision, Holly left them to the tree decorating while she went to work adorning the mantel with more greenery, ribbon and floral picks she found in the boxes of decorations.

By the time Ryan came in from outside, the house looked vastly different than when Holly and Lydia had walked in a few hours earlier.

After shrugging out of his coat, Ryan sniffed the air with an appreciation that made her smile.

"It smells good in here."

"Christmas magic," she told him. She decided not to tell him she had found some pine- and cinnamon-scented sachets in a sealed container in one of the boxes and had tucked them around the room in unobtrusive places.

Holiday cheer to her was as much about the scents and tastes as the decorations.

He looked around the room. "Everything looks great. Thanks so much for your help."

She could not disagree. The house looked warm and inviting, a haven of comfort.

"It was a team effort," Holly said.

"Mom is going to be so happy when she comes home," Audrey said with a satisfied sigh.

Holly couldn't resist hugging the girl, her throat aching a little as she thought about how cheerfully Audrey had handled the stress and disorder of this holiday season.

"You're most welcome. We were happy to help, weren't we, Lyd?"

"I'm a helper."

"You sure are," Ryan said.

Lydia giggled, clearly besotted with the man.

You and me both, kid, she wanted to say.

"Do you two want to stay for lunch? We happen to have much more to offer than we did earlier today, thanks to my dad."

"We should probably go. I have some things to do before we head over to Haven Point for the bridal shower this afternoon."

"I have to go potty," Lydia said suddenly, looking around the room as if she thought she might find a convenient toilet in a corner.

"Come on. I'll show you where the bathroom is," Audrey said, reaching for her hand.

"Thank you," Holly said as the two of them left the room, leaving her alone with Ryan.

Had he really wanted to kiss her earlier? It felt like something she must have imagined, especially since he seemed once more remote and unapproachable.

"I really am grateful for all your help. I'm pretty clueless when it comes to decorating a house in general and decorating a house for Christmas in particular."

"Yet you hung those lights like a champion. If the helicopter pilot thing doesn't work out, you could go into business hanging other people's outdoor decorations."

"Good to know. I might need to keep that in my back pocket."

"Are you looking for another career? I thought helicopter pilots were the Swiss Army knives of the sky."

"We are. Unfortunately, this one is currently a little bent."

He gestured to his leg, the one she knew he had injured in that accident that had shaken Kim so badly.

"I'm not sure if the navy will still want me in the air if this doesn't heal. And I'm sure as hell not willing to spend the rest of my career behind a desk, where I've been for the past two months."

"Kim has been really worried about you."

He looked disgruntled at that information. "I'm curious to know what else my sister might have told you about me."

She couldn't resist the urge to tease him a little.

"Hmm. Let's see. She had to sit with you on the school bus every day until you were in second grade because you were afraid of the older kids. You were something of a genius when it came to math and science, unlike her. And you don't date any woman for longer than a month, always careful to make sure she doesn't get the wrong idea and think you might be serious about her."

He frowned. "She makes me sound like a player. And like a prize ass."

"I never had that impression at all. Kim adores you and would love to see you find someone special."

"I'm afraid she's going to be waiting a long time for that."

He gave her a sly look. "Besides, I have found someone. You. I can't believe you forgot that we're madly, embarrassingly in love. That's what you want your ex-in-laws to think, right?"

She pushed away a sudden, wholly inappropriate yearning. "Why is it that our supposed relationship becomes more intense every time we talk about it? Next you'll have us engaged and planning our own wedding."

He grinned and Holly completely understood why so many women went out with him. That smile was lethal.

"All done, Mommy. I even have my coat," Lydia announced from the doorway, where Audrey was helping her with the sleeves. "I just need my boots."

"You do. It's cold outside. We don't want you to freeze your toes off."

Lydia giggled and the sound was a blunt reminder to Holly that her daughter was the only thing that mattered to her. Not a man with devastating good looks and a smile that made her want to fall into him and never climb back out.

———

CHAPTER TEN

NOT FOR THE FIRST TIME, HOLLY REFLECTED THAT SHE WAS probably wrong to regret losing her former in-laws more than she regretted losing her ex-husband.

Holly smiled at Stacy Pacheco, Troy and Kristine's older sister, as she grabbed another bacon-wrapped shrimp off the plate of appetizers on the table.

Her former mother-in-law really knew how to throw a party. Their large, comfortable home on the shores of Lake Haven was decorated beautifully for a holiday bridal shower, with signs that said A Merry Little Bridal Shower and Snow in Love, along with garlands and fairy lights and plenty of food.

She was especially happy that Susan had arranged care for the children of invited guests. Lydia was happily playing in the large downstairs family room with her cousins, Stacy's children, as well as children of other guests. They were all watched carefully by a couple of older ladies from Susan's church.

"It's so lovely to see you, my dear." A woman with pure white hair in an elegant style pressed Holly's shoulder then took the folding plastic chair next to her.

She smiled at Troy's grandmother, who was tiny and fierce, one of her favorites of his relatives. "Nona. Hello. It's lovely to see you as well. It's been far too long."

"I stopped by your floral shop the other day, only you weren't there. The young lady who was working behind the counter, I think she said her name was Ginger, said you were out making deliveries. Don't you have people to do that for you?"

"I'm a little shorthanded right now but we're making do.

We all take turns on the deliveries. I had a special one that day for a friend recovering from surgery so I delivered it personally."

"Oh, how nice of you. That's why your flower shop is doing so well, because you haven't forgotten how important that personal touch is."

Most of the time, she felt like Evergreen & Ivy was barely hanging on, but it was nice to believe she was making a difference and the store was gaining a positive reputation.

"I'm only sorry I missed you. Was there something special you were looking to order?"

"Not to worry, dear. I already took care of it. Your Ginger was a big help."

"I'm so glad."

Ginger might be a bit distractable but she was also caring and compassionate, as well as being creative and talented.

"I was picking up a half-dozen white roses for my friend Esther's birthday. Her husband used to give her a bouquet every year. This is her first year without him and I know how she must be missing him. It's been ten years without my Ned and I still somehow forget he won't be sending me flowers on our anniversary like he used to do."

Holly made a mental note to check with Susan about when Nona and Ned's wedding anniversary had been so she could arrange a delivery on that day.

"I know how Esther has been missing Sheldon," Nona went on, "and I thought some flowers might help her feel better, even if they're not from him."

"Flowers make everything feel better."

Nona beamed and patted her hand. "I've always thought so. Now where is that darling girl of yours?"

"She's downstairs with the other children. Last I checked, they were starting up a Christmas movie."

"I'll have to make sure I see her before the party is over. That girl is a precious angel."

"Not all the time. She can be stubborn and fiercely independent when she wants to be."

"Good. She'll need to be."

That was another reason she loved Nona. The woman understood the challenges in store for Lydia and appreciated the strength and courage Holly was trying to instill in her daughter.

"How are you enjoying living at the Shelter Inn?"

Troy's grandmother had moved into the senior apartment building in Shelter Springs over the summer. Holly and Lydia had walked over to visit her several times after she made the move but Holly was embarrassed to realize a few months had passed since they last stopped by.

She pushed away the guilt, trying to give herself a break. She was doing the best she could to juggle all the plates in her life.

Speak to yourself like someone you love, Hannah often urged her. It was advice she had been doing her best to follow.

"Those people are crazy." Nona shook her head. "They never stop moving. If they're not hiring a bus to go look at the fall colors they're playing bingo in the recreation room or having jazzercise classes in the pool. It's exhausting for an old lady like me."

Holly smiled. "They always have a stall at the Christmas market, don't they?"

"Oh yes. We've all been working like fricking elves on crack to fill our stall. If I have to stuff one more little amigurumi animal, I might poke myself in the eye with a crochet needle."

She laughed, charmed as always by the older woman.

"Oh, cut it out. You know you love it there." Nadine,

Nona's daughter and Troy's aunt, gave her mother a long-suffering look as she and her sister Nancy sat down at their table. "We all know you love nothing more than to be right in the middle of the action. You're probably running the place by now."

Nona scoffed. "Not even close. You girls know I'm just a shy, retiring, former librarian."

Nancy snorted. "And I'm a Radio City Rockette."

Like their mother, the sisters were full of personality and never afraid to speak their mind. Troy had always been a little embarrassed about his father's family. Not Holly. She adored them all.

They chatted about their plans for the upcoming holidays and about the popular Christmas market in town.

"So Holly," Stacy suddenly said during a break in the conversation, "what's this I hear about you bringing a hot date to the wedding?"

Holly froze, her fork poised halfway to her mouth. She set it down sharply, feeling her face flush. "I'm not sure. What have you heard?"

Troy's sister pressed one hand over her very pregnant belly. "Only that he's some gorgeous pilot and he's supposed to be crazy about you."

"Who told you that?" she asked, aghast.

Stacy gestured to her mother, who was deep in conversation with Kristine's future mother-in-law, a woman Holly didn't know.

"Mom couldn't stop talking about it. She said you were all hush-hush about him but she happened to talk to your sister, Hannah, at the Shelter Inn the other day and she told her all about him. Susan is over the moon that you're dating again."

"Why?"

Stacy and her aunts exchanged a look and then Nancy, the oldest, finally spoke.

"She took your breakup hard, especially since Troy was the one who walked out on you and moved in with Brittany right away."

"Mom feels guilty that any son of hers could be such a jerk," Stacy said bluntly. "You know we have all been pretty upset at Troy."

Holly set her fork down, her appetite gone. She had hoped she could come to the bridal shower and simply enjoy a pleasant time without having to exhume her failed marriage over and over.

"It's been two years," she said. "We've both moved on."

"I still think it's tough for Mom to truly embrace Brittany and their baby when we all know you were treated so poorly in the whole deal."

She hated being put in the position of a victim with his family. It wasn't fair to anybody.

"I hope that's not true," Holly said quietly. "Little Hudson is adorable and completely innocent in the whole thing."

"The important thing is, you have somebody now," Nancy said cheerfully. "When she sees you happy again with your sexy pilot, maybe Susan can finally relax and enjoy the holidays, Kristine's wedding and her newest grandbaby."

Holly shifted, mortified by this whole conversation and annoyed that everyone was putting so much emphasis on her supposed relationship. She did not need a man in her life to be happy and it frustrated her that Troy's mother seemed to think she did.

"Tell me all about him," Nona said, her wrinkled features avid with curiosity. "How did you meet? Was it love at first sight?"

She forced a smile. "Um, he's the brother of my friend Kim, who works for me."

"Oh good. So this Kim can vouch for whether he's good enough for our Holly and Lydia," Nona said, her tone completely serious.

"I suppose," she said after a moment.

This whole thing was spiraling quickly out of her control. She hated lying to Troy's family. But what would happen if she came clean and told them all she wasn't truly in a relationship with Ryan?

"We just started dating," she said. "It's still early days."

"You like him, though. That's the first step," Nona said.

She did like him. Probably too much. Earlier in the day when she had been certain he wanted to kiss her, she had felt giddy with anticipation.

"He's a pilot? Is that what you said? Who does he fly for?" Nadine asked.

"Um, he's a helicopter pilot in the navy, stationed in San Diego. Right now he's sidelined because of an injury, one of the reasons he was able to come to Shelter Springs for the holidays to spend time with his family, but he's hoping to be flying again soon."

"Oh, he has family here?" Nona asked.

She really needed to figure out how to change the subject but nothing seemed to come to her.

"Yes. His father and stepmother live here in town," she said. "Doug and Diane Caldwell."

"You remember Diane. She used to be Diane Hall before she was married," Stacy said.

"Oh, she is such a sweetie," Nadine said. "She was a year behind me in school and the nicest person."

"She's still nice," Stacy said. "She's on the library board.

She also volunteers at the kids' school and listens to them read to her several times a week."

Holly seized on the most flimsy of excuses to change the subject.

"Are your kids doing any Christmas shows this year?"

She knew Stacy's oldest, Ella, was in a children's choir that usually performed at least a few concerts every year.

"Yes. Several. Ella has to miss one the day of the wedding but she's performing this week at the Shelter Springs market."

"Oh, do let me know when and Lydia and I will try to make it."

"I'll text you the details."

To her vast relief, Nancy asked a question about Stacy's pregnancy and the conversation shifted to other topics.

By the time the shower wrapped up, Holly wasn't sure who was more exhausted, her or Lydia. Her daughter yawned as they walked to the car.

"Did you have fun with your cousins and the other children?"

Lydia nodded. "Grandma gave me treats."

She held up a gift bag that Holly could see contained small Christmas-themed party favors. "Oh, how nice. I hope you said thank you."

She nodded. "I did, Mommy. And Ella let me play with her Barbie. And we played dress-up. I was a cowgirl and Ella was a princess."

Troy's family was always so warm and inclusive to Lydia. While Holly would have preferred to maintain a little more distance between them to make things less awkward all the way around, she couldn't bring herself to do it. Lydia needed her father's family in her life, even if Troy himself had become a distant figure since he moved out of state. Maybe because of that.

A light snowfall had coated the windshield but it was easy to brush it off after she loaded Lydia into her booster seat.

Snowflakes floated through the air as she backed out of the driveway and turned toward Shelter Springs.

"Ooh. That's pretty," Lydia said as they passed a park and botanical garden a few blocks from her grandparents' house. Spruce Creek Park was decorated with vivid LED light displays as well as a huge, brightly colored tree in the center.

"I want to see the lights, Mommy. Can we?"

"Not tonight, honey. We're both tired."

"Please oh please oh please?"

She glanced in the rearview mirror and saw Lydia's face glowing with colors reflected from the display. As much as she wanted to go home and put her feet up for a few moments, she found herself pulling into the small, crowded parking area.

Stopping would only take a few moments. And wasn't this what the holidays were all about? Seizing these priceless, fleeting moments of joy to store up and cherish through the rest of the year?

"We can't stay long, since we didn't bring all our warm clothes, okay? Perhaps we can come back another time and be here longer when we're all bundled up for the cold."

"You promise?"

She kissed her daughter's forehead. "I promise."

Lydia was vibrating with excitement as Holly helped her out of her booster seat. At least Lydia had her favorite purple snow boots on so her feet would stay warm.

"I can't wait! I can't wait!"

Holly held her mittened hand, her heart awash with love as they walked through the soft snowfall along a path lit by hanging lanterns on candy canes.

Holly squeezed Lydia's hand as they stepped through a glowing archway at the park entrance, its rainbow lights casting a kaleidoscope of colors on the snow-dusted ground. Lydia's gasp of delight made Holly's heart swell, grateful she had made the effort. Her daughter's eyes were wide with wonder, her rosy cheeks flushed with the excitement that only Christmas magic could bring.

"Mommy, look! Look!" Lydia cried, tugging on Holly's hand as she pointed toward a row of trees wrapped in shimmering gold-and-silver lights. "It's sparkly!"

"It is, sweetheart," Holly replied, crouching down beside her. "And look over there!" She gestured toward an animated display of Santa and his reindeer. The lights twinkled in time with a cheerful holiday tune, and Lydia clapped her mittened hands together, hopping up and down in delight.

The two wandered farther, following a path lined with more glowing candy canes. Lydia stopped at every display, her fascination growing with each discovery.

"Look! Penguins!" she exclaimed, her breath visible in the chilly air as she pointed to an LED display of penguins skidding across a frozen pond. Holly loved seeing pure joy radiate from her daughter's face.

Then Lydia spotted the giant Christmas tree in the center of the park.

"That's big!" she whispered, her eyes shining.

She pulled Holly toward it, her boots crunching over the snow. The tree sparkled with multicolored lights that seemed to dance as they stood beneath it, the massive golden star at the top glowing like a beacon.

Holly blinked back tears, her heart full as she held her little girl close. For all the challenges they faced, moments like this reminded her of the beauty in seeing the world through Lydia's eyes—a world where wonder was everywhere and magic always felt within reach.

"I love this tree."

"It is beautiful," she agreed. "Let's take your picture."

They weren't alone in the park and other families were taking selfies around the tree. She and Lydia managed to find an empty area by the tree and she crouched down to her daughter's level, holding her phone out and smiling.

They had taken several when she heard a deep voice from nearby. "Want me to take a picture of both of you?"

She looked around and suddenly spotted a tall, dark-haired man standing a few yards away. Feeling vulnerable from her crouched position, she rose. "Ryan! What are you doing here?"

"Hi, Ry!" Lydia exclaimed, clearly thrilled to see him.

"Hi, Lydia," he said with a wide smile for her daughter that did ridiculous things to Holly's insides.

He turned back to her. "Audrey made cookies this afternoon after we finished decorating and wanted us to take some to Diane."

"Oh, how sweet."

He made a face that told her he didn't necessarily agree and hadn't wanted to deliver cookies to his stepmother. Or, more precisely, probably hadn't wanted to deliver them to his father's house. He had, though. That touched her almost as much as his clear affection for her child.

"We were heading home when we saw this place," he said. "Audrey wanted to stop and see the light display. Apparently she comes here every year with her mom. Then she found some friends and abandoned me."

He stepped closer and she was suddenly back at Kim's house with him, her heart pounding with awareness and her breath caught as she waited for a kiss that hadn't happened.

"Give me your phone and I'll take one of both you and Lydia."

She handed it to him, then returned to her daughter's side. She again bent to Lydia's level, their faces side by side. She smiled into her phone camera, oddly aware of the man on the other side of the camera.

"Beautiful," he said, handing her phone back to her.

"Thanks. We stopped on impulse, too. We're not really dressed for a big outdoor excursion but at least it's not too cold."

"Fortunately it's not a big park. It doesn't take long to see everything."

"Have you been through the entire thing? What are the highlights?"

"Audrey really liked the holiday castle toward the exit. She said that has always been her favorite."

"We'll check it out. Thanks."

"You come too, Ry." Lydia held her hand out to him. He looked a little disconcerted but after a brief hesitation he reached for her mittened fingers.

This felt entirely too domestic, Holly thought, with her holding one of Lydia's hands and him holding the other. She thought about dropping her daughter's fingers but didn't know how to do it without calling more attention to the situation.

"How's your stepmother tonight?" she asked instead.

"She seems to be okay. Like Dad said earlier today, she's using her crutches now. She can even go up and down steps with them."

"And your dad?"

His mouth tightened. "Fine."

Again, she knew whatever was between him and Doug wasn't any of her business but she sensed it was a painful topic. Something about the intimacy of the night, this magical, colorful fairyland beside the lake, made her want to help.

"Why are you so angry with him, Ryan? What did he do?"

His jaw hardened again. For a moment, she was certain he wouldn't answer her but after a long pause, he sighed. "It's not really what he did. It's what he didn't do."

———

CHAPTER ELEVEN

WHAT WAS IT ABOUT THIS WOMAN THAT MADE HIM WANT TO confide all his painful secrets to her?

Lydia bounced along between them, eyes glowing as she looked around, clearly not paying any attention to their conversation. He looked between her and her lovely mother, whose quiet calm called to him like a safe port in a blizzard.

As they neared the holiday castle at the end of the park, Lydia stopped in her tracks, her mouth forming a perfect O.

"A princess castle!" she exclaimed, pressing her hands to her cheeks in awe. The LED castle shimmered in white and gold, its turrets reaching high into the dark sky, while the "moat" of animated lights rippled and glowed beneath it. Other children were running around inside the illuminated structure and Lydia looked at her mother, as if afraid to hope.

"Can I go in there?"

"You can. We'll watch from out here," she answered, much to his relief since the interior couldn't have been taller than five feet.

Lydia raced in to join the other children. They found a bench that had a clear view of Lydia. Only then did he finally return to her question of earlier.

"My mom died when I was thirteen. Kim was two years older."

"Yes, she told me. That's a tough age to lose your mother."

"Any age is tough. But yeah. It was hard. She had been sick for about six months before she died. An inoperable brain tumor. She fought hard for six long, difficult months."

"I'm sorry."

"Yeah. It was horrible. Mom tried so hard to put on a cheerful face for us but the chemo and radiation beat her up hard." He paused. "I should say, it was horrible for Mom, Kim and me. Dad took it all in stride."

"Or at least that's what you saw," she said gently.

He frowned. "Maybe. But did my dad take emergency leave to care for her—or for us—even in her last weeks of life, when we knew the end was near? Of course not. Why would he let the inconvenience of a dying wife and two frightened, grief-stricken children interfere with his brilliant military career."

The sympathy in her expression seemed to seep through him.

"That must have been tough. But, again, that might have been what you saw from your perspective. I'm sure your father grieved in his own way."

He wasn't sure he could agree with her.

"Four months after Mom died, I was sent to military school. Kim was sent to boarding school. I gather her experience there wasn't much better than mine at military school. That's where she started drinking and dabbling in drugs, anyway."

"Poor Kim," she murmured. "And poor Ryan."

"We needed our dad—and each other—but he couldn't be bothered with either one of us. It was easier for him to send us both away."

"Were you able to still see each other during summers and school breaks?"

He studied Lydia, now twirling in a circle with her arms outstretched. Before he could answer, Audrey came by with a couple of other girls her age.

"Hi, Holly! I didn't know you were here. Is Lydia here, too?"

She nodded out to the castle. "She's over there."

Audrey looked delighted. "Can I go show her a couple of other things we found on the other side of the park?"

"We weren't planning to stay long."

"We'll be quick, I promise," Audrey said.

"Why don't you meet us in ten minutes back at the parking lot?" Ryan said.

By now, Lydia had caught sight of her friend and she hurried over to them and threw her arms around Audrey.

Chattering to each other, Audrey and her friends led Lydia down the illuminated path.

As if in tacit agreement, he and Holly rose together and walked down the path back toward the big Christmas tree in the middle of the park.

"I'm sorry for the interruption. You were telling me about your school breaks," she said.

He didn't want to talk about the past. He wanted to focus on this moment, with this lovely woman. But she had asked and he still wanted her to know the truth.

"We saw each other during the summer and over the holidays. I wouldn't call it pleasant, though. Whenever we were home, Dad would treat us like we were new recruits who needed a firm hand. I'm not sure he knew what else to do with us."

"Probably true."

"When Kim was seventeen, she refused to go back to boarding school. She ended up basically running away and moving in with her boyfriend, Audrey's father."

"From what she's told me, he didn't treat her well."

He felt again that deep resentment toward the man, all wrapped up together with his anger toward his father. "No, though she never talked about it to me. I wish she had. We were always close. We needed each other, you know?"

She nodded. "Hard times always feel easier when you have someone to share the burden with."

"If our father hadn't sent us away, we could have made it work. It's not like we were infants who needed supervision from him twenty-four-seven. We were teenagers who could have mostly fended for ourselves at home. Together. We could have leaned on each other. Grieved together. He could have still fulfilled his military obligations and Kim and I could have muddled through."

He sighed. "Instead, he took the path of least resistance, without caring whether it was the best thing for his children."

She rested her fingers on his arm. Despite the layers of cloth between them, he almost thought he could feel the warmth and sympathy of her touch. "I can see why you're angry with him," she murmured. "That must have been rough for all of you."

He wanted to kiss her. That interrupted moment earlier on Kim's porch had teased him all day with the possibility of what might have been.

The urge to pull her into his arms was as tough to ignore as the ache in his leg.

"For the record, I don't usually whine about my childhood. I know I should be over something that happened two decades ago. It happened, it's done. I've moved on."

"You still have the scars, though."

"We all have scars, don't we?" Ryan's voice softened, his gaze fixed on the lights that seemed reflected in her eyes. "Some you can see, some you can't. The ones on the outside . . . they're easy. People notice them, maybe even ask about them. But the ones inside? Sometimes they're the ones that shape you, whether you like it or not."

He looked down at her, regretting that he had said so much. "Anyway, that's the whole ugly story. I don't have much to do with the colonel now, which is better all the way around."

"Kim doesn't seem bitter about your father. She moved here to be closer to him and Diane."

He still found that baffling, as he had when Kim told him she was moving to Idaho where their father had retired.

"Maybe she's better at hiding it than I am," he said.

Even as he spoke the words, he thought of his sister escaping into a bad marriage, about her past brushes with the law and her current stint in rehab. Maybe suppressed pain and grief contributed to her struggles with substance use disorder.

Their father wasn't wholly to blame for everything, he knew. Much of their pain had probably resulted from losing the mother who had been the anchor of their family. But Doug's careful reserve and his virtual abandonment of them hadn't helped.

"For what it's worth, I like Diane," he said. "I know Kim does, too. Since the colonel married her, she's been a good influence on him. Kim was right when she told you the person you have met is not the same man my father was after my mother died."

"Time has a way of changing all of us, doesn't it? Some for the better, some not. I'm not the person I was a few years ago. And I wouldn't want to be."

She was a remarkable person.

By all rights, Holly should be the bitter one, filled with anger at her ex-husband, who had left her and her child with special needs. Instead, she was doing her best to keep her daughter in his life, to cement ties with his family.

He admired her more than any woman he had met in a long time. Maybe ever.

"I suspect you haven't changed all that much," he said, his voice low. "You were probably still a lovely person two years ago."

She met his gaze, her blue eyes startled, then she gave a husky laugh. "That shows how little you know me, Lieutenant Commander Caldwell. I'm impatient, short-tempered, cranky in the morning without my coffee. And I can be petty, too."

"I don't believe that."

"My sister could tell you stories, believe me. Sometimes when a customer is rude to me or to one of my employees, I deliberately don't give them the best flowers."

He laughed, completely charmed by her. "Okay. You've convinced me. You're a horrible, evil person who should have nothing to do with my sister or my niece."

She smiled back at him and he thought he could happily stand here all night in the lightly falling snow while the sound of children's laughter rang through the December air.

"Seriously, I appreciate the listening ear and I'm sorry if I sounded whiny."

"You didn't at all. Anyway, I asked."

"Yes, but I didn't have to answer."

She tilted her head and studied him. "Why did you?"

As he considered her question, he realized he had wanted to tell her. Something about Holly's kindness and compassion had assured him she would listen with understanding.

"I've never really had anybody else to talk to about what happened after my mom died," he admitted. "Kim only gets upset if I ever mention it."

"So you stopped saying anything and held it all inside."

"Basically. I'm a guy. A lot of us tend to do that."

"And those guys usually end up paying a steep price for burying everything."

"My relationship with my father doesn't really take up much space in my life. Most of the time our interactions are polite and cordial, if distant. I don't have much to do with him, which is fine with me."

"Until your sister asked you to come out to Shelter Springs to help her."

"Yeah. It's much harder to avoid him this year. I haven't spent this much time in the same state with him in a long time, especially not during the holiday season, which seems to heighten and exacerbate every childhood emotion."

"Understood. I live in the same town as my parents and I still revert back to a thirteen-year-old girl when I'm at their place."

He would have liked to have known her as that young girl, a reaction that unnerved him.

"Maybe you should give your dad a chance," Holly said after a moment. "From an outsider's perspective, it seemed clear this afternoon that he wants to mend the distance between you. He's making an effort, anyway. Would it hurt to meet him halfway, even if only for the sake of your stepmother and for Kim and Audrey?"

"I'll think about it," he said after a moment.

She nodded, giving him such a radiant smile that he finally gave up fighting the urge. While lights twinkled around them and snow gently brushed their skin, he leaned down and brushed his mouth against hers.

HOLLY CAUGHT HER breath as his mouth, cool and delicious, covered hers.

It wasn't a truly passionate kiss or even a long one. They were in a public park, after all, surrounded by others, though there was no one else in this particular corner of the park right now.

While their contact only lasted a few seconds, it was intense enough to stir up a vast ache of yearning.

She wanted to truly kiss him. To throw herself against that long, powerful body and let his muscled arms keep her warm all night long.

She blinked back to awareness.

"What was that all about?" she said, embarrassed at the slight wobble in her voice.

Ryan sent her a look she couldn't interpret.

"Why don't we call it practice for our big date?"

If that was practice, she wasn't sure she could withstand the real thing.

"I am really sorry to drag you into this whole fake-dating nightmare."

"I'm not. You've given me something to look forward to while I'm in town."

"You can't really be looking forward to going to a wedding."

"You know, a week ago I might have agreed with you but now I think it might be fun. I meant to try on one of my dad's suit jackets while I was over there tonight and I totally forgot."

They both continued walking and when they reached the parking lot they found Audrey taking selfies with her friends and Lydia under the archway.

Lydia skipped over to them as soon as she spotted Holly. "Guess what, Mommy? We saw a light-up snowman and a light-up Santa."

"That's fun."

"Audrey said we should go on sleds. I want to."

"That would be super fun, too."

"Tonight?"

"It's almost your bedtime, honey. We need to go home."

"I didn't mean we would go sledding tonight," Audrey told her. "But we'll take you, I promise."

"Okay," Lydia said, then gave a huge yawn.

"Let's get you to your car," Ryan said, scooping her up in his arms and earning a tired-sounding giggle.

When Holly opened the back door, he set Lydia in her booster and helped her with the seat belt.

"Good night," he told her.

"Bye, Ry. Bye, Auddy."

He smiled at her and closed the door, then turned to Holly.

"Thanks again for the listening ear," Ryan said.

"Anytime," she answered.

As she slid into her car and eased her car into reverse, her grip tightened on the wheel. How was she supposed to guard her heart against a man like Ryan, especially when a big part of her didn't want to?

CHAPTER TWELVE

—

HOLLY GLANCED AT THE FARMHOUSE CLOCK HANGING IN THE store, then at the stack of invoices for deliveries that had to be made that day, including a condolence bouquet for a viewing scheduled later that night.

How was she going to juggle everything?

She really hated to close the shop in the middle of a busy shopping day, especially since the foot traffic in town had increased exponentially since the town's annual Christmas market had opened the weekend before.

The Shelter Springs holiday market had become a tradition for people in the entire region, which was a boon to all the local small businesses. Shoppers didn't only restrict their spending to those retailers with booths at the market.

Run by her dear friend Amanda, the market featured music, food and shopping. She loved that a portion of all sales went for a charitable cause each year. This year the market was raising funds to add on to the town library and expand the children's area, a cause close to her heart.

Among the many things she had to juggle this season, Holly knew she definitely had to add a visit to the market. Lydia loved it and the market was always a great place to pick up last-minute gifts. Besides that, she loved supporting other small businesses.

As much as she wished she could spend the day wandering up and down the stalls, it wouldn't happen today.

She looked at the clock again. If she closed the shop for an hour, she could possibly finish the deliveries and take one more thing off her plate. Hopefully she wouldn't miss that many walk-in sales.

It wasn't the best solution but she didn't know what else to do.

She grabbed her Back in One Hour sign out of a drawer and headed for the front door. Before she could reach it to hang the sign, the door opened and she was astonished to see Ryan enter the store.

Her heartbeat kicked up as memories flooded her mind of his mouth on hers days earlier.

That kiss hadn't been far from her mind since it happened. She hadn't seen him since leaving the park. At times she wondered if she had imagined the whole encounter, but the memory was entirely too vivid for her to have made it up.

At stray moments, she would find herself reliving it and would have to give herself a stern lecture and jerk her mind back to the present.

It was only a kiss. Not some kind of cataclysm. Except somehow it felt earth shaking, as if her carefully constructed world had shifted half a step to the left. No matter how hard she tried, she couldn't quite manage to nudge it back into place.

"Oh. Ryan. Hello."

He gave her a brief smile and she had to wonder if he was also remembering that charged instant between them.

"Hi. You look like you're headed somewhere," he said, looking at the sign in her hand. "Are you off for lunch?"

"I wish."

If she wanted lunch, she would have to grab a protein shake out of the fridge in the break room and drink that on her way to make the deliveries. Again.

"Busy day?"

"You could say that. I'm on my own today, since both of my two current employees are out with the flu."

"Oh no. That can't be good."

"Unfortunately, there seems to be a lot of illness going around. I guess it's that time of year. I've got five deliveries and four of them are get-well bouquets."

"What's the other one?"

"Condolences, unfortunately. A ninety-year-old man who goes to church with us passed away last week. The funeral home would like all of their condolence flowers this afternoon prior to the viewing if possible. I'm closing the store for an hour so I can deliver them all."

He looked out the window at the busy downtown area.

"Is that wise? Don't you worry about losing business if you close now?"

"Sure I do. That's always a worry but even more of a concern this time of year, when we see a large percentage of our walk-in sales."

"It seems more busy than usual out there," Ryan said, gesturing out the front window. "Is something going on in town?"

"It's our annual Christmas market. It's become a huge deal in town, bringing visitors from across the area. Lucky for us downtown merchants, they don't limit their shopping to the market."

"That's right. Audrey was telling me about the market the other day. She said it's a big deal, with a fundraising component as well."

"That's right. Each year the market committee chooses a different organization to help. This year it's the library. In years past, we've helped Meals on Wheels, the local food bank and the women's shelter, to name a few recipients. Because the regular Shelter Springs businesses also benefit from the increase in traffic, those of us in the downtown Chamber of Commerce also donate a portion of our sales."

"Seems like a nice thing to do."

Why was he here at her store in the middle of the day? For the life of her, she couldn't think of a reason for his presence and he didn't seem in any hurry to tell her.

The door opened before she could ask. Two older women Holly didn't know wandered in, talking and laughing together. They greeted her cordially and she didn't miss the brief looks of appreciation they gave Ryan before they started looking at her display of flower-centered crafts.

Apparently she wouldn't be closing for a while, at least not until the women finished shopping.

Ryan must have seen some of her frustration in her gaze. "How can you close down in the middle of the day?"

"I would prefer to stay open, but in this case it's unavoidable. I have to deliver the condolence bouquet before the viewing. And since I'm already out, I should probably take care of the other deliveries. The prospect of new sales from foot traffic is always enticing, but not at the expense of people who have already paid for flowers and expect them to be delivered in a timely manner."

Ryan glanced at the women who were filling shopping baskets with some of the dried flower sachets Holly created during the summer.

A look of indecision crossed his features before he turned back to her. "Why don't I make your deliveries for you? That way, you can stay here and hold down the fort and won't miss any sales."

She stared, wholly taken off guard by his suggestion. "You?"

He shrugged. "Why not? To be honest, I'm sort of at loose ends while Audrey is in school."

"Is that why you're here? Because you were bored?"

"In a way, I guess. I was in the neighborhood, actually, shopping at the bookstore down the street. I grabbed a couple of gifts for Audrey and a new mystery by an author I enjoy.

Since I was close by, I thought I would see if I could pick you up a sandwich or something for lunch."

His unexpected thoughtfulness sent warmth seeping through her. How lovely to have someone spontaneously think of doing something nice for her.

"That is very kind of you."

He shrugged again. "It was only an idea. I'm not used to having so much free time, if you want the truth. I've already repaired everything I can find that needed it at Kim's place and have even tried out a few new recipes, with mixed success."

Oh, he was a hard man to resist.

"Even with the hour I spend every day on the treadmill trying to rehab my knee," he went on, "that still leaves me with five or six hours to fill, especially since Audrey comes here after school to help you with Lydia."

"I'm sorry."

"Don't be sorry. She loves hanging out with Lydia and is thrilled at how much you're paying her. But the bottom line is that she's pretty self-sufficient, which leaves me with huge chunks of time to fill. I can't read my book all day so why don't I make your deliveries for you?"

She couldn't deny his offer was tempting. It would be lovely to tick one more thing off her list with his help.

"You don't know your way around town, though."

"I have several navigation apps on my phone that can help. I find I'm pretty good at finding my way, which comes in quite handy when you're trying to locate your landing spot on an aircraft carrier in the middle of the ocean."

She blinked, disconcerted to imagine the risky situations he had probably navigated during his time in the military. Ryan was a hard, dangerous man, something difficult to remember when he could be so sweet with her daughter and was thoughtful enough to consider grabbing her lunch.

The front door opened before she could answer and her friend Natalie walked through, her arms loaded with packages.

"Hey, Holly!"

"Natalie. Hi."

"Are you slammed?" Nat asked. "I was hoping to order a hostess gift for a party Griffin and I are going to Friday but I can come back."

Holly looked down at the closed sign she had been about to hang on the door and then at Ryan.

She would never find it easy to accept help, but as she was shorthanded and couldn't take care of everything alone, she really would be grateful to have him handle the deliveries.

"I always have time for you, my dear. Have you met Ryan Caldwell? This is Kim's brother. Ryan, this is my dear friend Natalie Shepherd. Sorry, Natalie Taylor. She got married this summer to the brother of one of our other dear friends."

"Nice to meet you," he said.

Natalie's eyes lit up. "You're Ryan? Hannah was telling me all about you. I understand you're Holly's plus-one for Kristine Moore's wedding."

"Yes," he said after a moment. "I'm really looking forward to it."

He gave her a heated look she could only describe as smitten, obviously conjured on the spot for the benefit of curious onlookers. Holly had a sudden wild wish that he would look at her like that for real, instead of as part of an unnecessary performance.

She made a face. "No need for the besotted act," she told him. "Natalie is one of our dearest friends. I'm sure Hannah probably told her the truth, that you're only taking me as a favor. And because she asked you on my behalf."

Natalie looked startled. "Seriously? I didn't hear that part of the story. Hannah only said you were exactly the kind of guy

Holly ought to be taking to a wedding where she can't avoid seeing her jerk of an ex-husband. I definitely agree."

Ryan grinned at both of them, sending nerves fluttering through Holly. "I'm looking forward to it," he repeated. "We're going to have a great time."

A few more customers came in behind Natalie. Now Holly had five customers inside the store. She wasn't leaving anytime soon and that fact was clearly obvious to Ryan as well.

"About those deliveries," he said. "My truck is parked down the road. I'll move it closer to the back door and when you have a breather here between customers, you can show me what I'm taking where."

He turned and walked out of the shop without giving her a chance to argue. As soon as the door closed behind him, Natalie turned to her, eyes dancing with glee.

"Wow. He's gorgeous. Hannah was absolutely right."

Holly sighed. "I know."

He was entirely too gorgeous. And she was entirely too drawn to him.

"And now he's making flower deliveries for you?"

She moved toward the counter. "I'm extremely short-staffed right now, with Kim gone until after Christmas. Both Ginger and Carla are out sick today. I planned to close the store for an hour while I tried to catch up with deliveries. Ryan offered to make the deliveries for me so I don't have to lose business unnecessarily."

Natalie grinned again. "I have to say, if a guy like Ryan Caldwell showed up on my doorstep holding flowers for me, I would probably either believe he was a hitman or suspect that I was being punked."

"Or that it was the single luckiest day of my life," one of the older women said, obviously eavesdropping on their conversation as she shopped the ornaments for sale on one of the Christmas trees.

There was so much more to Ryan than his extraordinary good looks. He was kind to her daughter. He cared about his niece. He was deeply loyal to his sister.

She liked him entirely too much.

"What kind of hostess arrangement would you like?" she asked Natalie, eager to change the subject.

"I have no idea. Something festive and bright. Whatever you create will be beautiful, I know."

"Can you give me a minute to organize the deliveries for Ryan? Then we can go over some options."

"I'm in no rush at all," Nat assured her. "Take care of whatever you need to do. If you want me to, I can also ring up your customers, as long as their order isn't too complicated."

Nat had pinch-hit for her before at Evergreen & Ivy when she was in town, between her stints as a travel writer and digital nomad. She knew the drill for working the cash register and the credit card system.

"Thank you," Holly said. She was deeply grateful for all of her friends, especially the three she considered her ride-or-die team: Natalie, Amanda and, of course, Hannah.

She was in the back organizing the deliveries by address when Ryan opened the back door.

"Okay. What am I taking and where is it going?"

The deliveries were nestled together in two large cardboard boxes with dividers between them to protect the delicate arrangements from damage.

She gestured to the boxes and handed him a paper full of addresses. "These numbers I've written next to each arrangement correspond with the delivery address on this paper. I can also text it to you if that is better."

"That would probably be best. That way I can punch it right into my navigation app." He looked at the flowers. "Wow. These are all lovely. You really know what you're doing."

She smiled, gratified at the praise. She had loved working with flowers since she had taken a job during the summers here at the store, owned at the time by her father's sister.

After college, Holly still worked the occasional part-time shift for some extra spending money, arranging her schedule around her full-time job as an office manager for a medical clinic in town.

Around the time of her divorce, Aunt Mary had decided she wanted to retire and asked Holly if she might be interested in purchasing the store.

To this day, she wasn't sure if Mary really had wanted to retire or if she was only offering Holly a way to support herself and her daughter after Troy left.

Regardless, she would always be grateful for the opportunity and for Mary's willingness to carry the loan so she could afford it.

"Thank you," she answered Ryan. "Most of the time I feel like I'm winging it but I've worked here since I was a teenager so I've been able to pick up a few skills here and there."

She picked up one of the boxes and carried it outside the delivery door while he picked up the other one.

He had opened the back door of his pickup truck and she slid the box inside on the floor.

"Those boxes should be stable, as long as you don't take any wild corners."

"I'll drive like an eighty-year-old on the way to church."

"Maybe you'd better not do that," she said with a smile. "I know a few eighty-year-olds in town who drive hell-for-leather. You don't want to be on the road when any of them are heading to church."

"Thanks for the warning." He smiled and for one charged moment, he gazed down at her. Once more, she remembered being in his arms and felt breathless and tongue-tied and silly.

She turned away, closing his truck door to protect the flowers from the cold. "Thank you so much for doing this. Once more you've come to my rescue. This is becoming a habit."

"I'm glad to do it," he answered, swinging into the driver's seat. "I'll stop back in when I'm done with the deliveries to bring back the boxes and give you my report."

She should probably tell him he didn't need to return the boxes, he could simply find a recycling bin somewhere, but he closed the door and put his truck in gear before she had the chance.

She definitely needed to work harder to resist the man, she thought as she returned to the store. At this rate, she was going to end up with a broken heart, something that certainly hadn't been on her wish-list for Christmas.

CHAPTER THIRTEEN

BY THE TIME HE MADE THE FOURTH DELIVERY, RYAN FELT LIKE A
rock star.

With the exception of the subdued employees at the funeral
home where he had dropped off a striking arrangement of
white lilies and roses, as well as eucalyptus, ferns and succulents
in muted colors, everyone seemed delighted to see him. It was
kind of nice to be in the business of delivering something that
made people happy.

All of the recipients had also wanted to know who he was,
how he knew Holly and why he was helping deliver for Evergreen & Ivy.

She was clearly well-known and well-liked around town.

He checked the final address and saw it was for a resident
at the Shelter Inn, a retirement community he had seen when
driving through town. The arrangement was cheerful and
bright and also particularly fragrant.

He pulled into a visitor parking space in front of the building and picked up the final arrangement.

As soon as he walked into the main entrance, a couple of
elderly women who had been leaving what looked like a recreation room made a beeline for him.

"Ooh, flowers. Who are they for?" one of them asked, her
eyes a vibrant blue behind thick glasses.

Was that info confidential? He couldn't think of a good
reason why it might be.

"Um, Birdie Lovell," he said, looking at the careful note
Holly had written for him.

Her companion, a tall, striking woman with warm dark eyes,
beamed. "Oh good. Birdie has been so under the weather this

week, poor thing," she said. "Some gorgeous flowers will be just the ticket to brighten her day, especially since you have roses and gardenias there that will smell delicious. Birdie can't see so well."

He had no real answer to that so he only smiled politely.

"Can you tell me where to find Birdie?"

"Her apartment is down the hall. I'm sure she's there, as she's been staying mostly to herself so she doesn't spread her crud. We can show you, can't we, Florence?"

"Sure can, Arlene. Follow us."

He had the apartment number clearly written on the extremely organized list Holly had given him but he had the feeling if he told these women he didn't need their help, they wouldn't listen to him anyway.

On the short walk down the hall, they asked his name, if he was new in town and his connection to the floral shop.

"Holly is a friend," he explained, a little surprised to realize that somehow that had become true since he had arrived in town.

He liked Holly far more than he probably should.

"She was in a bind this afternoon," he explained, "so I offered to help with some of her deliveries."

"Oh, aren't you the sweetest thing," Florence said, giving him a frank, admiring look that made him squirm.

"I don't know about that. I'm glad for the chance to help out."

"That girl deserves a nice guy like you to help her out," Arlene said.

"Especially one who looks like he should be a Navy SEAL," Florence said.

"Not a SEAL, but I am in the navy. Lieutenant Commander Ryan Caldwell. I'm a helicopter pilot."

Florence chuckled. "Even better. My husband, James, used to fly helicopters in the army. One of the few Black pilots back in the day. He flew in Vietnam."

"Really? He was one of the six hundred MOL?" he asked, using the term the relatively small number of Black pilots who fought in Vietnam used to refer to themselves. He knew it stood for the six hundred *men on the line*, men whose extraordinary bravery was even more significant given the prejudice they often faced from their own side.

"He was indeed," she said, giving him an appraising look. "I'm surprised you know that term."

"I've studied the history of pilots in all branches of the military. A few months back I read a great book about the six hundred."

"Oh, you definitely need to chat with James then. He'll talk your leg off."

"I would enjoy that," he said truthfully, making a mental note to come back and find Florence's husband at some point during his stay here in town.

A moment later, they reached an apartment door that was decorated with a festive garland and wreath.

"Here you go," Arlene said.

He rang the doorbell and he and his newly acquired posse waited until an elderly woman wearing a bright pink sweater with a pompom candy cane on it opened the door. At her side was a large yellow Labrador retriever.

"Hello?" she said, looking so clearly at them that it took him a moment to remember her friends had said she had low vision.

"Birdie, it's Florence and Arlene," Arlene said. "We've brought you a surprise. A very good-looking man who comes bearing flowers for you."

"Oh, how lovely. I can smell them from here."

The bouquet was colorful and fragrant. He suddenly knew without a doubt that wasn't accidental. Holly had deliberately chosen particularly bright and odiferous flowers for Birdie's arrangement.

Her thoughtfulness and knowledge of her customers left him oddly touched.

"What is your name, young man?" Her voice sounded raspy and she coughed into a handkerchief.

"Hello, Ms. Lovell. My name is Ryan Caldwell and I'm making deliveries for Holly Moore at Evergreen and Ivy."

"That's *Lieutenant Commander* Ryan Caldwell," Florence put in. "He's a helicopter pilot, like my James."

"Hello, young man. How nice to meet you."

"Someone sent you a get-well bouquet," he said. "I'm sorry you've been feeling under the weather."

She gave a dismissive gesture. "I've had a nasty bug for the past few weeks but fortunately I'm on the mend. Who sent them? Is it that rascal Paulo? I told him I was feeling better."

"He misses you," Florence said with a smile.

"That man is crazy about you," Arlene added. "I'm sure he's upset that he wasn't able to be here when you've been feeling so poorly."

"That's what he gets for going off without you to Mexico for ten days with his daughter," Arlene said tartly.

"You should have gone with him. I know he asked you," Florence said.

Birdie made a face. "I know. I wish I had said yes but the timing wasn't the best, with the holidays and the market and everything. I'm glad I didn't go with him now. I came down with this bug the day after he left and I would have been sick with the flu the whole time and ruined it for everyone."

She made no move to take the flowers from him and Ryan wasn't quite sure how to deliver them and make his escape.

"Um, there's a card here. Would you like one of the ladies here to read it to you?"

She tilted her head and seemed to study him. He wondered how much she could see.

"No," she said with a mischievous smile. "You have a sexy deep voice. Why don't you read it?"

"If you like his voice that much, it's too bad you can't see the rest of him," Florence said with the same kind of mischievous smile.

What was it about women of a certain age that made them so uninhibited—and so eminently likable?

He pulled the card out, cleared his throat and began to read.

To my dearest love,
  Wishing you strength and sunshine to chase away the clouds.
You are always in my heart.
                    With all my love, your Paulo

"Here you go," he said, holding out the card close to her hand. She reached for it and clutched it to her heart with a happy sound.

"You need to put that poor man out of his misery and marry him already," Arlene said gruffly.

Ryan laughed. "He doesn't seem miserable to me. Seems like this Paulo is doing just fine, wearing his heart on his sleeve."

"Don't kid yourself, young man," Florence said. "True love doesn't come around often. If you're lucky enough to find it, you grab hold and don't let go. Otherwise, you blink, and life is gone."

Her words landed heavier than Ryan expected. A quiet ache stirred in his chest, a flicker of awareness he couldn't quite shake.

For so many years, he had been focused solely on his career. The idea of love, of sharing his life with someone, wasn't something he had let himself consider. But as all three of the women's gazes softened, eyes misty with a lifetime's worth of stories, he wondered if he was missing something he hadn't known to look for.

Ryan cleared his throat and smiled politely. "I'll keep that in mind."

"Thank you for delivering them. Let me find my purse so I can tip you."

"Not necessary," he assured her. "It was entirely my pleasure. It was nice to meet you all."

"Definitely." Florence beamed at him. "I would love to introduce you to my husband but he's not here right now—he's working at our booth at the Christmas market. Come back, though. I know he would love to talk to you."

"I'll do that," he said, meaning the words.

As Ryan drove back to Evergreen & Ivy, the quiet hum of the engine seemed to underscore his thoughts.

The word *community* hung in his mind, sparked by Florence's words and the way her face softened when she spoke about love. He'd never given it much thought before—not consciously, anyway—but now he couldn't ignore the weight of its absence in his life.

He definitely had a community of sorts with the other navy personnel he worked with. Nothing threw people together like a long deployment on an aircraft carrier. But it wasn't quite the same as the warmth and welcome he found here in Shelter Springs.

Growing up, his family had been in constant motion, chasing his father's next assignment from one air base to another. His mother had tried her best to make each house feel like home, putting up familiar curtains, setting out the same blue mug that held her coffee every morning. But it had never really been enough.

Ryan remembered the hesitant smile she wore when she

introduced herself to yet another neighbor, and the way her laughter never quite reached her eyes at those base gatherings.

Kim had hated it even more. The tears, the slammed doors, the way she would throw herself into a new school year with a chip on her shoulder, knowing it wouldn't last. She had longed for roots, for stability—and now, looking back, Ryan wondered if maybe she had been right to want those things.

Community mattered.

It wasn't something he fully understood when he was younger. Back then, he'd been focused on getting by, on carving out a life for himself that wasn't tied to anyone or anything. But now, as he thought about the people he had met in Shelter Springs and the way they seemed to lean on each other without hesitation, he felt the faintest pang of longing.

He was still thinking about the power of connectedness as he drove through the thriving downtown area. He found a parking spot not far from Evergreen & Ivy and pulled the cardboard boxes from the back seat of his truck.

When he walked into the store, he found Holly checking out a customer. He set the boxes in the back and lingered until she had finished.

When the store was empty again she turned her attention to him. "Thank you so much. Did you run into any problems?"

"None at all. The addresses were all easy to find and someone was home at each location to receive the delivery. Everyone was very nice and they were all thrilled to receive beautiful flowers. Except the mortuary, anyway. They were pretty matter-of-fact about it."

"That tracks," she said with a smile. "How is everyone feeling? I'm especially worried about Birdie Lovell. She would have been your final delivery of the day, if you followed the chart I gave you."

"She was. Birdie was pretty unforgettable."

"That is an understatement. I adore her. Her granddaughter Amanda is one of my closest friends and her grandson Griffin is married to my friend Natalie whom you met here in the store earlier."

"She loved the flowers. It was very thoughtful of you to pick particularly fragrant blossoms for her bouquet. She said she's feeling much better, though she didn't have much of a voice."

"She must be hating that. Birdie loves to talk."

"I did receive that impression, yes. As do her friends Arlene and Florence."

"Oh, they're wonderful, too. I want to be just like them when I'm that age. Feisty and funny and unapologetic."

He could imagine it perfectly and felt a weird little pang that he wouldn't be around to know her when she was the age of the older ladies.

"I actually live in Birdie's house," Holly told him.

He blinked at the unexpected information. "Do you?"

"She lived in Rose Cottage for years, then Amanda lived there with her for awhile and stayed after Birdie moved to the Shelter Inn. I bought the house from Amanda after she married this summer and moved to her husband's house with Rafe and his son. Rafe's grandfather Paulo is Birdie's beau, the one who sent her the flowers."

Again, he thought about that community he had never really known, entangled lives and interconnected worlds.

Before he could answer her, the door burst open and a pint-sized dynamo burst through, her cheeks flushed from the cold and her almond-shaped eyes bright and happy.

"Hi, Mommy!" Lydia said, dropping her backpack inside the door of the shop and racing to her mother with her arms out.

"Hello, my darling," Holly said, kneeling down to embrace her child. "How was your day?"

"Good. I played with Jane at recess. She pushed me on the swings. We had music and sang 'Jingle Bells.' I love 'Jingle Bells.'"

"I know you do."

"And for lunch, I had grill cheese."

"That sounds like an amazing day," she answered, as Audrey followed Lydia inside, scooping up her backpack on the way.

His niece looked surprised to see him leaning against the counter.

"Oh, hi, Uncle Ry. What are you doing here?"

For some ridiculous reason, he felt a flush of embarrassment. He certainly couldn't tell his niece that he couldn't seem to stay away from Holly Moore or that he didn't have anywhere else he would rather be right now than here in this warm, charming flower shop that smelled like pine and cinnamon and home.

"Your uncle saved the day for me. I was in a bind, on my own here, and was about to close the store to make a few deliveries when Ryan stopped by. He offered to take care of the deliveries so I didn't have to close the store and could stay here and wait on customers."

"You delivered flowers to people?" For some reason, Audrey seemed to find that both astounding and hilarious.

"I was happy to pitch in."

"I don't know what I would have done if you hadn't," Holly said. "We've been so busy today with the market in town, I've barely had time to catch my breath. I can't tell you how grateful I am."

She turned to Audrey. "And you are helping so much by being here with Lydia today."

"You know I love hanging out with the Lydi-bug."

She hugged the little girl to her and Ryan felt a burst of pride for his niece, who was learning so much compassion for others. She was a great caregiver to Lydia and should perhaps think about pursuing a career in special education.

She was only thirteen, he reminded himself. She had plenty of time to explore different interests and figure out what she wanted to do with her life.

He had never imagined he would pursue a career in the military as his father had done. He never wanted to be like the colonel in any way. After earning his pilot's license, he had considered becoming a commercial pilot, but the navy and all the opportunities it offered had appealed to him more.

He could not imagine his life unfurling any differently than it had up to now but he expected he was going to have to make some tough decisions soon about his future, especially if his knee continued to give him problems.

"Can we go to the market tonight, Uncle Ry?" Audrey asked him. "I have to finish my Christmas shopping and my friend Megan is performing with her choir at seven."

"The market? Really?" He could imagine few things he wanted to do less.

"It's really fun, I promise. Everyone in town goes. Last year Mom and I went three or four times. We haven't been once this year and it ends next week."

He glanced at Holly, who gave him a sympathetic look. "It really is fun," she said. "Definitely a highlight of the holiday season around here."

He had vowed to give his niece on unforgettable Christmas, even if that involved subjecting himself to a crowded convention hall filled with holiday shoppers snapping up things they didn't need.

"I suppose we can do that. What time is the concert? Can we go after dinner?"

"You can always go *for* dinner," Holly suggested. "They have an entire food stall area featuring local restaurants."

She was *not* being helpful. He gave her a mock frown, which she returned with her usual sunny smile.

"I suppose we could do that. What about you and Lydia?" he asked, driven by an impish whim. "Do you want to grab dinner with us over at the market?"

She looked momentarily startled by the suggestion then appeared to reconsider.

"We could do that. I owe you, after all your help today. The least I could do is buy you something to eat at the food court."

That hadn't been his intention when he made the suggestion but they could wrangle over details later. "Why don't I come back here around closing time? That way we can walk over to the market from here."

"Probably easier than trying to find a closer parking space," she agreed. "It should work, especially if Lydia takes a nap back in the break room."

"She usually does," Audrey said. "We do some yoga, put on quiet music and both close our eyes. She usually falls asleep and I do my homework."

Holly's affectionate smile at Audrey left a funny ache in his throat that he did his best to ignore.

"I'll come by a little before you close at six, unless you need me to make more deliveries this afternoon."

"You have done more than enough. I don't have any more deliveries today."

"Okay. I'll get out of your hair, then. I'll see you all in a few hours."

And in the meantime, he would do his best to remind himself of all the reasons he didn't belong here in this small town.

CHAPTER FOURTEEN

HOLLY WAS TOO BUSY THE REST OF THE AFTERNOON TO DWELL much on the prospect of spending the upcoming evening with Ryan. That's what she told herself, anyway. At random moments when the thought of him crowded into her brain—along with sparkly anticipation—she tried to quickly push it away.

She had to do something about this growing fascination she was developing for the man. She knew better than this. Any entanglement with Ryan was doomed to end with a broken heart.

She had one job right now: giving Lydia the absolute best life she could. That left no room in her life for a tall, gorgeous naval helicopter pilot who lived a thousand miles away.

Not that he wanted a relationship with her anyway. Why would he be interested in a divorced, perpetually stressed single mom trying to juggle a business, a home and a child?

Still, as the clock ticked down, she was aware that the anticipation seemed to be building inside her like the crackle of a firework before it explodes.

She was tying up her usual end-of-day routine when the door opened. Expecting Ryan, she looked up and was startled to see her mother and her sister come in, stamping off boots and shaking off snow.

She had been so busy, she hadn't noticed the winter storm forecasters had been predicting had arrived in full force.

"Oh wow. Looks like you just hiked through a blizzard. I didn't even realize it was snowing."

"It started as we left the market," Hannah said. "It's a fast-moving storm, though. I don't think we're supposed to get more than a few inches."

"Did you find anything good at the market? We're heading over as soon as the store closes."

"Oh, I wish we had known." Her mother's face dropped. "We would have coordinated with you so we could go together."

Hannah frowned. "Sorry. I thought you said you probably weren't going to make it to the market until Monday."

"My plans changed unexpectedly," she answered. Even as she spoke, the chimes on the door rang out again and Ryan walked in, snow dusting his dark hair.

He stopped when he spotted the other women. She could feel her face heat and hoped her too-observant mother and sister didn't notice.

"Am I too early? I thought you were closing the store at six."

"I am closing right now."

She moved to the door and flipped the sign.

"You two are going to the market together?" Hannah asked.

"With Audrey and Lydia," Holly said quickly. "Audrey has a friend performing tonight and I owe Ryan dinner for helping me with deliveries today when I was in a bind."

Her mother studied him with interest. "I don't think we've met."

"Sorry, Mom. This is Ryan Caldwell. Kim's brother. This is my mother, Paula Goodwin. And you already know Hannah."

Her mother's features lit up. "Lieutenant Commander Caldwell! The one who is taking Holly to Kristine Moore's wedding."

Holly could feel her face heat even more, if possible. Rudolph the Red Nosed Reindeer had nothing on her. As bright as she was sure her features were, they wouldn't even need a streetlight to find their way to the Christmas market.

Ryan looked amused. "Yes. I'm looking forward to it."

"Oh, Hannah is absolutely right. You're perfect!"

"Okay," he said slowly.

"Did you stop in for any particular reason?" Holly asked, unable to keep the note of desperation from her voice.

Her mother ignored her. "Seriously. Troy is going to *freak out* when he sees you moving on with your life. Serves him right!"

"I'm not moving on with my life. I mean, I *am* moving on with my life, of course. But not with Ryan. He's only doing me a favor by taking me to the wedding."

"That doesn't mean I'm not still looking forward to it," he said again with that same devastating smile.

She narrowed her gaze, wanting to tell him again that he didn't need to use that seductive smile on her or on her family and friends. They all knew the truth. Hannah had been the one to persuade him to go along with the whole scheme in the first place.

Before she could say anything, Lydia and Audrey came out of the break room, Lydia's hair messed from sleep.

Her daughter gasped with delight.

"Grandma!" she exclaimed, racing over to Paula, who scooped her up with a laugh.

"There's my girl. What have you been up to?"

Lydia delivered a long treatise on the many activities of her day.

"And your mom told me you're going to the market," Paula said when Lydia stopped to catch her breath. "Do you know who's there? Santa Claus!"

Lydia's mouth fell open. "He is?"

"Yes. And maybe your mom will even let you sit on his lap so you can tell him what you want him to bring you."

"Can I?" She looked at Holly with so much pleading in her

expression that Holly had to keep from rolling her eyes at her mother for backing her into this particular corner.

"We'll have to see. We might not have time, after we eat dinner and listen to Audrey's friend's concert and look through the shops a little."

"Let's go now!" Lydia exclaimed.

"Come on. I'll help you get your coat on," Paula told her.

"It's back in the break room," Audrey said.

All three of them headed in that direction while Holly went through the final steps to close the store for the night.

"So why did you guys stop by?" Holly asked.

"Do we need an excuse to say hello?"

"I suppose not."

She went to grab her own coat off the hook by the back door, where she liked to keep it in case she had to help any customers load a large purchase into their vehicle from the back.

Hannah followed her, keeping an eye on Ryan, who was checking something on his phone across the store.

"I actually did have a reason for stopping by."

"No," she said in mock surprise. Her sister was as transparent as a snow globe.

Hannah made a face but spoke in a low voice. "I wanted to give you the heads-up. McKenna Dodd told me Troy and his new family are back in town. Apparently they arrived last night. She bumped into Brittany at that cute gift store over in Haven Point."

She froze, one arm snagging inside her coat sleeve. Seriously? She wasn't upset that they were here. The wedding was in two days, so she knew they would be arriving soon.

No, she was angry that Troy apparently had been in the area nearly twenty-four hours and hadn't tried to connect with the daughter he hadn't seen in two months.

"Has he reached out to let you know he's back?" Hannah asked.

"Not yet. I'm sure he will as soon as he gets the chance."

She tried to give him the benefit of the doubt. Troy paid child support every month exactly on the first and he did call every few weeks to talk to Lydia. He would reach out soon, she was certain.

"Are you okay?"

She took her sister's hands. "Hannah. I'm fine. I wish everyone would stop treating me like I'm a victim in this situation. I'm not. I'm perfectly happy with my life right now. I am certainly not pining for my ex-husband."

No. She was pining for the man out front on his phone right now.

"Good. Because he's a sleaze bucket who was never good enough for you anyway."

"He's not a sleaze bucket. You know he's not."

Hannah narrowed her gaze. "I disagree. What else would you call a man who walks out on his amazing wife and his beautiful daughter to hook up with someone who is nearly a decade younger than he is, with fake boobs and a spray tan?"

"I don't want to talk about Troy or Brittany tonight, okay?"

"Neither do I," Hannah growled. "If I had my way, we would never talk about him again."

"Unfortunately, he will always be Lydia's father."

"Don't remind me," Hannah muttered.

She hugged her loyal sister, so very grateful for her support. "Thanks for letting me know he's in town."

"You're welcome."

Hannah looked as if she wanted to say more but their mother came out of the break room with a now adequately bundled-up Lydia.

"We do need to go. Your father is making dinner tonight and I don't want to miss his amazing lasagna."

"Is he?" Hannah said with interest. "Maybe I'll swing by for dinner."

"You're always welcome. All of you are."

Holly hugged her mother and sister one more time. When they left, Holly drew in a deep breath and faced Ryan, who was watching her with an unreadable look in his eyes.

How much of her exchange with Hannah had he heard?

"I think we're ready. I only have to arm the alarm."

"What about my backpack?" Audrey asked. "Should I take it to the market?"

"My truck is parked out front," Ryan said. "We can leave it in there on the way to the market."

She set the alarm and opened the front door for them all, then locked it behind her.

Together their little group headed toward the convention center a block away, a large, graceful building that had once been a grand hotel catering to the long-ago tourists who used to visit the area to partake of the healing waters of its namesake springs.

Audrey and Lydia walked ahead of them, holding hands.

"Are you sure you're up to this?" Ryan asked her as they approached his truck. "You've been on your feet all day and probably want to go home and collapse. I can take Audrey on my own. You and Lydia don't have to go with us, if it's too much for you."

Her day had been long and exhausting and right then she wanted to lean against him and soak up his strength.

As tempting as she found that, it wasn't necessary. Since her divorce, she had found hidden strength inside herself.

"Lydia is looking forward to it. I don't want to disappoint her."

"What about you? Everything doesn't have to be about Lydia, Holly."

She needed that reminder. "I'm looking forward to it, too," she said with honesty.

He smiled down at her and in that moment, she couldn't imagine anywhere else she would rather be.

When they walked into the convention center a few moments later, they were immediately hit from all sides by noise that echoed in the big hall.

Music, laughter, conversation. It all created a wild cacophony.

Holly glanced at Lydia and found her daughter looking around with shining eyes. Fortunately, she didn't get overstimulated easily. Lydia seemed to thrive on noise and chaos.

"My friend's group is performing at seven. Want to eat first?" Audrey asked.

"Yes. Let's do that," Ryan said.

"The food court is over there." Holly pointed to an area in the center of the cavernous convention hall set up with food booths and picnic tables. Even from here, she could pick out various delicious scents from the offerings there.

She always forgot how much she enjoyed the holiday market. Yes, it was crowded and chaotic and loud but it was also undeniably festive and exciting.

They headed together toward the food court area. As they made their way through the crowd, she said hello to several people she knew, both booth vendors and customers. That was another thing she loved: connecting with neighbors and friends here.

She introduced Ryan to a few people and couldn't help noticing that their group received more than a few speculative looks. She tried to ignore them, though she was fully aware the whole town had to be curious about the gorgeous stranger who was currently holding the hand Lydia had thrust into his.

So what? She would much rather have them look at her with speculation about a possible new love interest than with pity.

"What kind of food sounds good to you guys?" Ryan asked as they approached the food court. "Looks like our options are unlimited. Everything from pitas to curry to tacos."

"I love tacos," Lydia announced.

Holly knew that was absolutely true, though there were very few foods Lydia didn't love.

"Sounds good to me," Audrey said. "What about you, Uncle Ry?"

"I'm a big fan. Some of my favorite places to eat are the taco trucks in San Diego."

"We have some good ones here too and a couple of them have stalls here at the market. I don't think you'll be disappointed in any of them."

She was starving suddenly, Holly realized. That protein drink hadn't been nearly enough to sustain her through a long day.

She led the way to the line for a stall operated by a family she knew and liked. "I think you'll like this one. They make a fantastic carne asada."

"Works for me," Ryan said.

The line moved quickly and soon it was their turn.

"It's my treat," she said firmly as Ryan was about to order.

He frowned. "That's not necessary."

"Are you kidding? You rescued me today and Audrey has been a lifesaver for the past two weeks. The very least I can do is buy you both a taco."

While he looked like he wanted to protest, she was glad he didn't.

Their food was ready quickly and Ryan and Audrey carried their trays to an empty table.

The meal was delicious, as usual, and the conversation even more enjoyable. She was laughing at a story from Audrey about a mix-up in one of her classes when Lydia suddenly jumped up from the table.

"Daddy!" she shrieked, racing toward something behind Holly.

She whirled around to find Troy looking shocked as their daughter hurtled toward him. He managed to transfer the shopping bags he held in both hands to one so he could give Lydia an awkward hug with the other.

"There's my girl. Hi, Lydia."

"I missed you, Daddy."

"I missed you, too."

He kissed the top of her head then looked up. A weird expression crossed his handsome features as he took in their little group.

"Hi, Holly. How are you?"

"I'm good."

And wondering why you didn't bother to reach out to your child the moment you came back to town instead of waiting twenty-four hours then accidentally bumping into her.

"How was your drive from Portland?"

"We hit some snow in eastern Oregon but it wasn't too bad."

She was suddenly very conscious of Ryan watching this rather stilted interchange with interest. Troy appeared conscious of Ryan as well.

"Hi. Have we met?" Troy asked.

"Don't think so." Ryan's voice was laconic, slow and very sexy. "Ryan Caldwell. This is my niece, Audrey."

"And my friend," Lydia chirped.

Audrey gave her a warm smile. "Yep. We're best buds."

Troy had left town before Kim and Audrey moved to Shelter Springs, she remembered. He wouldn't have met either one of them.

"Are Brittany and Hudson with you?"

His features softened. "Yes. She has the baby with her. They're with her mom. I left them looking in Amanda Taylor's lotion shop when I came over in search of a Diet Coke."

Apparently his drink of choice hadn't changed.

"Daddy, guess what? I want to see Santa Claus."

Lydia's speech was always a little harder to understand when she was excited—or when someone wasn't accustomed to her cadence or patterns.

"You want what?" Troy asked, brows knit in confusion.

"She said she wants to see Santa Claus," Ryan said. "We're going to head over there as soon as we finish eating and watch one of the youth groups perform on the stage."

Holly did not miss his use of the inclusive *we*. She knew it was deliberate, connecting them all together in an exclusive club where Troy wasn't a member. She wanted to kiss him, right there in the middle of the crowded food court.

"Oh, that sounds fun. Maybe we'll find you and tag along. I'm sure Brittany would love to have a picture with Hudson and Lyd together on Santa's lap."

She instinctively wanted to protest that Lydia was more than a photo prop but she forced down the words.

"Great. I believe Amanda told me they were moving Santa's workshop back inside this year."

"We saw it when we came in. You can't miss it, with the flashing lights and the long line of kids."

"Okay. We'll find you after Audrey's friend performs."

He frowned. "Can't I just take her now, after I grab my Diet Coke?"

Lydia skipped back to their table and picked up her quesadilla again. "I want to see the singers, too. They might sing 'Jingle Bells.' I love 'Jingle Bells.'"

Troy looked as if he wanted to argue but he seemed to reconsider when Ryan gave him a cool look.

"Give us maybe forty-five minutes," Holly said. "We can meet you over by the Santa line."

He gave a reluctant nod, waved to Lydia again and then picked the shortest queue to grab his drink.

Suddenly her flavorful carne asada tasted like floral foam but she made herself nibble another bite.

"So. That's your ex." Ryan's tone was bland but she didn't miss the unimpressed look in his eyes.

After she made sure Audrey and Lydia were not paying them any attention, engaged in a discussion about whether green or red salsa tasted better, she turned back to Ryan.

"Yes. That's why my sister stopped at the store earlier, to let me know Troy was back in town."

"Lydia seems happy to see him."

"She loves her dad. I try not to do anything to stand in the way of that."

"Even when it's hard?"

"*Especially* when it's hard."

After a moment, he gave her a smile that made her feel like all the sparkly lights of the Christmas market were glowing inside her and they returned to their meal, which suddenly tasted much better.

CHAPTER FIFTEEN

—

HOW, EXACTLY, HAD HIS LIFE COME TO THIS?

He had been asking himself that same question since he arrived in Shelter Springs and had yet to find an answer.

A few short months ago he had been flying training missions miles offshore above the Pacific Ocean. Now he was sitting in a crowded Christmas market in a small Idaho town, listening to a bunch of off-key, squeaky-voiced kids sing carols.

What was he doing *here*, first of all? And what was he doing sitting next to a woman who smelled like flowers, holding an adorable little girl who had climbed into his lap and snuggled against him without waiting for any kind of invitation?

The bigger question, he supposed, was why on earth would he feel so content at the status quo?

He tried to relax into the moment. The kids really weren't that bad. They had some nice harmony and Audrey's friend Megan sang a solo in a song he had never heard before about angels and animals.

The crowd clapped with enthusiasm after their final number and Ryan set Lydia on her feet so he could stand.

"Now Santa!" she exclaimed.

Audrey made a face. "Can I go talk to Megan while you guys go do that?"

"You have to tell Santa what you want," Lydia insisted, her eyes troubled.

Audrey sent Ryan and Holly a sort of conspiratorial look before she turned back to the little girl. "I already did," she said. "I wrote him a note about it. I should be good."

Lydia appeared to find that acceptable. She clearly didn't want to wait around arguing the matter.

"Let's go!" she said, tugging Ryan's hand with one of hers and Holly's with the other.

Holly laughed, looking bright and lovely as she let her child tow them away from the stage seating area.

"This way, honey," Holly said, steering the three of them in the other direction.

"Last year they had this outside," she told Ryan as they made their way through the crowd. "But apparently some of the parents complained about having to stand out in the cold with their little kids."

"Your Idaho winters aren't for the faint of heart."

"I know. But I thought it was magical out there under the stars, next to the big colorful Christmas tree. Apparently I was in the minority. So this year Santa has moved back inside."

Her ex was right. You couldn't miss it. The line of excited children stretched about thirty feet from the cozy little structure decorated with lights and candy canes.

They found her ex-husband standing slightly outside the crowd with a tall, statuesque blonde woman who was holding a cute baby, carrying what looked like a designer diaper bag and talking with an older woman.

The younger woman's face lit up when she spotted Holly and Lydia.

"There you are! I was so happy when Troy said he bumped into the two of you. What could be more perfect than Hudson having his older sister by his side when he has his first picture with Santa?"

By her forced smile, Ryan could tell Holly could think of several answers to that, but instead she greeted the two women with a warmth he had to admire.

"Hi, Lydia," the older woman said after greeting Holly back. "Are you excited to see Santa? What are you going to ask for this year?"

Lydia's brow furrowed as she considered. "A dollhouse and some books and some dishes for a tea party."

She slanted her mother a sly look. "And a puppy."

Holly arched her eyebrows. "We talked about that, honey. Santa can't bring you a puppy this year because it would be too scared to ride in the sleigh."

"What kind of puppy do you want?" Troy Moore asked his daughter.

For some reason, Ryan could imagine the man surprising his daughter with a dog for Christmas, despite Holly's clear objection, so that he could be the hero of the hour. Troy would then take off again, leaving his ex-wife with all the responsibility.

He knew people like this in the military, who acted without thinking through the repercussions for those impacted by their shortsighted decisions.

His own father fit that description.

"A yellow one," Lydia was saying, pronouncing the word "lello." "My friend named Ty has a yellow dog named Sandy."

"I'm sorry, honey," Holly said firmly, looking at her ex as she spoke so he didn't miss the message. "We can't have a dog right now. But maybe you can ask for a puppy next year."

Lydia's pouted but with more resignation than disappointment as they all headed into the queue.

"Aren't you going to introduce us to your friend, Holly?" the older woman said, with a pointed look at Ryan.

Pink tinged her cheeks. "Of course. Ryan, this is Brittany, Troy's wife, and that little cutie is Hudson. And this is Brittany's mother, Carol Baker. This is Ryan Caldwell. Um, a friend."

He wanted to help her out so he gave her a private smile and what he hoped was an adoring look—which probably looked like he was swallowing a burp.

"Lovely to meet you all," he said. "Holly has told me a great deal about you."

Brittany gave Holly an uncertain look, as if wondering what she had said about them. She suddenly looked painfully young. She couldn't be much older than early twenties, which made her probably a decade younger than Holly and Troy.

Though tall and striking, Brittany didn't have any of Holly's grace or quiet beauty. Why would any man in his right mind choose her over Holly?

The conversation was stilted and awkward at first as the line slowly moved them closer to Santa's workshop but Holly seemed adept at keeping it flowing. He had to admire that, too. She seemed to sense Brittany felt insecure and was doing her best to put the other woman at ease.

Feeling oddly protective of both Holly and Lydia, he stepped in to help when the conversation stalled again.

"I understand you're in town for a wedding."

"That's right," Troy answered. "My little sister finally decided to tie the knot. Weddings aren't my favorite thing. Normally I would have tried to wiggle out but since it's so close to Christmas I decided we could make it work."

"Kristine was telling me how lovely the flowers are. It's so kind of you to do that for her," Brittany said. Her words sounded genuine.

"I was happy to do it. I love Kristine."

"And I understand you're going to be a flower girl," Brittany said, smiling down at Lydia, who for some reason had decided to grab Ryan's hand again.

He had to wonder why she hadn't grabbed her dad's hand instead.

"Yes. I have a pretty dress and Mommy is putting flowers in my hair."

Brittany obviously couldn't understand Lydia's words, which

were sometimes a little garbled. Admittedly, it had taken Ryan a minute to pick up her speech rhythm but now he understood her clearly.

The other woman looked to Holly for translation.

"She said she has a pretty dress and that I'm planning to weave some flowers in her hair that match the bouquet."

"She will be so adorable," Brittany said, her voice just shy of gushy. "I'm only sorry we got married in Tahoe and I couldn't have her be a flower girl for our wedding."

"Yes. Too bad she missed it." Holly spoke without a trace of dryness in her voice but he picked that up, too. "She was only three at the time, though, and probably wouldn't have been able to follow directions."

"Now I'm five," Lydia said.

"You're such a big girl," Carol said in the sort of high-pitched voice someone would use when speaking with either a baby or a puppy. It grated on him. Those protective instincts flared again and he did his best not to speak to the older woman in the same tone.

"It's too bad you're not wearing the pretty dress you'll have on for the wedding. It would look so good in the photos," Brittany said, giving Lydia's cute red Christmas sweater somewhat of a disparaging look.

"This is what she wore to school today," Holly said with a trace of defensiveness. "We weren't expecting to visit the market today. We came straight from the shop and didn't have time to go home and change."

"It's fine. She's sweet in whatever she wears," Brittany said.

When it was their turn, Brittany took charge. Though Hudson seemed not in the mood for a photo shoot, she set up the scene like she was directing a big-budget Hollywood movie.

After she had taken what had to be two dozen pictures of Lydia and Hudson together on her phone, Brittany's mother spoke.

"Why don't we take a few with just Hudson now," Carol suggested.

At her stepmother's urging, Lydia stepped down with a confused expression, returning to her mother and Ryan.

"When do I tell Santa what I want?" she asked in a low voice.

"After the photo shoot. I'm sure they'll be done soon."

By now, Hudson's whines had turned into full-fledged crying and the very patient Santa handed him back to his parents.

"We probably need to take him home," Brittany said. "He's tired and had a long day of traveling yesterday."

"I'm sure that's it," Holly said.

"It's good to see you," the other woman said. "And nice to meet you, Ryan."

"I'll see you again at the wedding." He couldn't resist taking Holly's hand in his. "I'm lucky enough to be Holly's plus-one."

He couldn't help noticing Troy didn't look particularly happy about that. Too bad.

"Is it my turn?" Lydia asked, an edge of impatience in her voice.

Holly winced. "Oh yes. Sorry," she said.

Lydia climbed back onto Santa's lap.

"I know you, Miss Lydia," he said. "I don't even need to ask if you've been good. I know the answer already. Of course you have."

Lydia beamed at him, though Ryan thought she suddenly looked a little nervous.

When Holly took some pictures with her phone, Ryan

decided to snap a few of his own. They might be nice to look at after he returned to California, so he could remember this unique Christmas.

"Tell Santa what you would like," her mother urged, when Lydia remained silent.

"A dollhouse," she whispered.

"A dollhouse," Santa repeated. "I'll see what I can do about that. Anything else?"

She went through her list quickly, then with another sidelong look at her mother, she added, "And a yellow puppy, if you can take it on the sleigh."

The guy in the Santa suit must have seen Holly's sharp head shake. "I'm not sure about that one," he said kindly. "Christmas isn't always the best time to get a new puppy. That's probably something you should ask your mommy for, not Santa Claus."

She again pouted briefly but smiled one last time before hopping down again.

"Thank you," Holly murmured to the man.

"You're welcome, Holly," he replied, confirming Ryan's suspicions that she and the man behind the beard and spectacles knew each other.

"He knows your name, Mommy," Lydia said, an expression of astonishment on her features. "Does he know yours too, Ryan?"

"Sure do," Santa said. "That's my old friend Ryan. Good to see you again."

Ryan had to admire the guy's quick thinking.

As they walked away from the grotto, Lydia seemed giddy about the interaction, chattering a mile a minute, only about half of which Ryan could follow.

"Thank you for coming with us," Holly said.

"It was fun. It's been a long time since I've seen Santa Claus."

She smiled up at him and Ryan again had to fight the urge to lean down and capture her mouth with his.

He had to get a handle on his growing attraction to Holly Moore or he was going to end up doing something stupid.

He didn't belong here in this small town filled with Christmas markets and curious neighbors. The sooner he remembered that, the better.

It was tough not to fall for Holly—or for her adorable daughter—but he needed to remind himself that his time here in Shelter Springs was temporary. As soon as Kim returned to pick up the pieces of her life again, he needed to head back to San Diego and do the same.

CHAPTER SIXTEEN

—

AS TIRED AS SHE WAS FROM HER LONG DAY, HOLLY DIDN'T want the evening to end.

She had loved every moment spent with Ryan and Audrey. For a few moments, she hadn't felt like a tired mother or a frazzled small business owner. She only felt like a woman in the company of an attractive man who made her feel like she had sparklers going off inside her.

As much as she had loved being with him and Audrey, she was aware of a little niggle of worry on the edge of her subconscious.

If she wasn't careful, she was going to make a fool of herself over him and end up finding a broken heart in her stocking this Christmas.

"I'm tired and my feet are cold," Lydia said on a whine. As Holly had feared, the excitement of the day had been too much for her daughter, even with her nap after school in the break room.

"We can't have that," Ryan said. Before Holly could respond, he swept up the girl and set her on his broad shoulders. Lydia gave a surprised shriek then giggled.

"I'm big," she said.

"You sure are, honey," Holly said. As she looked at the pair of them, she felt the ice she thought encased her heart chip away a little more.

"Did you have fun?" she asked Audrey. "Your friend's group was really good."

"It was," Audrey agreed. "I liked when they rang the bells, too. That sounded cool."

"And you found a few purchases." She nodded to the bag Audrey carefully guarded.

"Yep. I think I'm almost done with my Christmas shopping, thanks to you paying me way too much to babysit Miss Lydia."

"The paltry sum I'm paying you isn't nearly enough for the great job you do," she assured the teen.

They reached his truck first, which had a light coating of snow.

"You don't have to walk us to my car."

"Don't have to, maybe, but I'm going to," Ryan answered.

"Like Lydia, my feet are killing me, too," Audrey said. "Can I wait in your truck, Uncle Ryan? I can start it up for you."

"You know how?"

"Sure I do. I warm up my mom's car all the time."

He pulled a key ring out of his coat pocket and handed it to Audrey. Looking gleeful, she unlocked the driver's side door and climbed inside.

"I'm trusting you to lock the doors until I get back and to make sure that gearshift doesn't leave Park, even for an instant," he said sternly. "Got it?"

Audrey made a face. "I won't touch the gearshift, I promise. I'll just start it up and then look at my phone."

They walked through the alley toward Holly's parking space behind the store.

She pressed her key fob to activate the remote start in her own SUV. By the time they reached it a moment later, Lydia's chin was resting on Ryan's hair and her eyes were half-closed.

After Holly opened the rear door, Ryan lowered the girl carefully from his shoulders and set her into her booster seat.

"I think she's going to be asleep the moment I get her home."

"Or earlier," he said, his expression amused in the glow of the streetlight in the empty parking area.

While she hooked Lydia's seat belt, he grabbed her scraper without a word and went to work brushing the snow off her vehicle for her.

His thoughtful gesture meant almost as much as his offer earlier to deliver her flowers.

"Thank you," she said when he finished, after she had closed Lydia's door.

"You're welcome. Thanks for dinner," he said.

She smiled. "It was a really fun evening."

"Even seeing your ex?"

She thought about her reaction to unexpectedly encountering Troy. "It was totally fine."

She could have left things there but she decided to be honest with him. "Everyone seems to think I should be devastated by the breakup of my marriage. Maybe I was upset at first that Troy could walk away so easily, but that was mostly on Lydia's behalf. Our lives are much easier without him, which is a terrible thing to say. The only reason I would ever dare say that out loud is because the door is closed and Lydia is already asleep."

He nodded and she had to wonder what he must be thinking at her confession.

"Well, I had a great time, too," he said.

"I'm not sure I've ever enjoyed the Christmas market as much as I did tonight."

Was that too much of a confession? Had she revealed more than she intended about her growing feelings for him?

"I can honestly say it was the best Christmas market I've ever been to."

She had to smile. "Now I have to suspect you've never been to any other Christmas markets."

"True. But even if I had been to dozens, I would still have enjoyed the Shelter Springs market the most."

"I'm glad."

For a moment, they simply stood there, the silence between them stretching, yet somehow full. Then Ryan reached out, brushing a snowflake from her hair with a gentleness that stole her breath. Before she could think, his hand slid to her cheek, cradling her face with his warm hand as if she were something precious.

And then he kissed her again, as she had been dreaming about for days.

The world seemed to vanish, leaving only the snow, the moonlight and the steady strength of his arms as he pulled her closer.

Holly felt herself melt into him, her hands curling against his coat, her heart thudding like a faint echo of the Christmas music they had left behind.

She wanted to stay like this forever, to lean into him and let his warmth surround her.

He was the one who ended the kiss, easing away from her and resting his forehead against hers briefly.

"I told myself I wasn't going to do that again," he murmured.

Why not, when it's so very lovely? She wanted to ask the question but couldn't seem to form the words. She wasn't sure she wanted to hear his answer.

"Right. Probably not a good idea." Her voice sounded hoarse, ragged, and she could only hope he didn't notice.

He studied her in the moonlight then gently pushed a strand of hair away from her face.

"You're a beautiful, desirable woman, Holly. I hope the fact that your idiot ex-husband left you for someone barely out of her teens doesn't ever make you think otherwise."

She blinked at the intensity of his tone and his words. Before she could manage to gather her thoughts enough to answer, he kissed her softly one more time, then gestured to her car.

"You should go."

She nodded and slid into the driver's seat. With hands that trembled from far more than the cold temperatures, she hooked her seat belt then backed out of her parking space and headed for Rose Cottage.

She didn't need to look in her rearview mirror to know he watched to make sure she was on her way before walking back to his own truck.

THE NEXT DAY, only one more day before Kristine's wedding, passed in a blur. She would be so relieved when this weekend was over and she could be done with weddings for a while.

Fortunately, both of her ill employees assured her they were feeling better and would be more than happy to cover the store the next day so she could focus on the wedding.

She was finishing up a last-minute order for a birthday floral arrangement when her cell phone rang. After spending all day on the Evergreen & Ivy phone, she didn't really want to answer a personal call but she sighed when she recognized her former mother-in-law's name and number.

"Holly. Hello." Susan sounded exhausted in even that short greeting.

"Hi, Susan. How are you holding up?"

"One more day. We can make it through that, right? In thirty-six hours, this will all be over."

Or only beginning, really, for Kris and Matt.

"That's right. And before we know it, it will be Christmas."

"Oh, don't remind me. I haven't even given Christmas more

than a passing thought. That will have to wait until after the wedding. The next time one of my children wants a Christmas wedding, remind me to do whatever it takes to talk them out of it."

Holly didn't bother to point out that Susan's children would all be married after Saturday afternoon.

"I won't keep you," Susan went on. "I only wanted to confirm that you're still planning to take Lydia to the wedding rehearsal tonight."

"Yes. Definitely. It will be a good chance to hand out the flowers for all the bridesmaids and the groomsmen."

"Thank you. Great idea. That way you won't have a frantic scramble tomorrow trying to ensure everyone has one. Oh, I also have to give the restaurant our final total for the rehearsal dinner. Are you sure you won't join us?"

"I'm sure. Thank you again for the invitation, but you're not even planning to start until after eight. That's pretty late for Lydia."

"Are you sure? You know you're more than welcome."

"I'm sure. We had a late night last night and she was cranky this morning. I don't want that to happen tomorrow."

"That's right. Brittany said they bumped into you at the market. She said you were with your helicopter pilot, whom she described as, quote, 'fire' and 'fine AF.' Whatever that means."

While she would agree with the description of Ryan, Holly certainly couldn't tell her mother-in-law that Ryan wasn't hers, as much as some part of her might wish things could be different.

It was for the best, she tried to tell herself, as she had been doing since that stunning kiss the night before. Simply pretending to have a man in her life complicated her world enough. She could only imagine how tough it would be to juggle a real relationship with a man like Ryan right now, when she was barely keeping her head above water.

"It was fun to bump into Brittany and Troy and that cute little Hudson at the market. He's growing so fast, isn't he?"

The older woman didn't take the bait.

"Yes. He's adorable. Listen, when all this wedding craziness is behind us, I would love the chance to get to know this Ryan. I want to make sure he's good enough for you and Lydia. Maybe the three of you could come for dinner after the holidays."

After Troy and Brittany returned to Oregon. Her mother-in-law didn't say the words but Holly caught the subtext anyway.

"I hope you know we love you both, my dear," Susan went on. "Nothing will ever change that."

Holly tied a brightly colored bow on the vase and set the bouquet aside, trying to ignore her guilt.

What had her own mother always told them about the perils of dishonesty? When you tell one lie, you'll eventually have to come up with dozens more to cover it up.

She should never have told the Moore family she was dating someone. Everything would be so much easier right now if she had only kept her mouth shut.

And much more boring, she had to admit.

Ryan had brought energy and light to a world that had become consumed with work and parenting.

She would miss him when he returned to his real world.

"I appreciate that," she finally answered Susan. "But Ryan has to head back to San Diego right after Christmas. I'm not sure how much time he will have for socializing before he leaves."

"Oh, that's too bad. But the next time he's in town, we have to make sure we can arrange something ."

She hadn't given any thought to seeing Ryan again after he left town. Surely he would return to visit his family here occasionally. How could she avoid seeing him?

Great. Something new to worry about. She pushed it away for now.

"Do you have all the help you need setting up all the flowers at the church and the reception venue tomorrow?" Susan asked.

"I should be good. Thank you. Hannah and some of our friends will help me."

"Okay. See you tonight, then."

She had ended the call and returned her phone to the back pocket of her jeans when the door chimes sounded.

She looked up in time to see the man she had been talking about walk into the store.

Her heart started a steady drumbeat that she could swear matched his footsteps as he smiled and walked across the room toward her.

She could almost taste him on her lips again, feel the strength of him against her.

She drew in a steadying breath and forced a smile. "Hi."

"Um, hi." He looked around the store. "You don't look quite as busy today as you were yesterday."

"We haven't had as much foot traffic. That's actually good, since I'm busy prepping everything for the wedding tomorrow."

"Do you need any help with deliveries? I have to head over to my dad's place and thought I would ask if you need me to drop off anything on my way."

She considered her to-do list. "I have one delivery in Haven Point, actually. I planned to take it later, but if you're heading in that direction anyway, I would really appreciate it."

"No problem. Happy to do it."

"I'll get the arrangement ready for you. Can you give me five minutes to make some finishing touches?"

"Sure."

She brought the elaborate arrangement, shaped like a Christmas tree, out of the cooler in the back to her work counter. Working quickly, she added miniature red and silver ornaments to accent the large white Asiatic lilies, red miniature carnations, noble fir and Oregonia branches.

The whole time she worked, she was aware of Ryan studying her with an intensity that left her uncomfortable.

Finally, when she was nearly finished, he spoke in a low voice. "Do I owe you an apology?"

She looked up. "For what?"

"Last night. For kissing you again."

Once more, her mind carried her back to his arms, her senses flooding with the warm, familiar scent of him as she felt safe and whole and wanted.

"You owe me nothing, Ryan. I hope that's not the reason you stopped by today."

He gave her a searching look and she hoped he couldn't see any trace of her growing feelings for him. "I shouldn't have kissed you."

Why did you?

She almost blurted out the question but managed to refrain. "It's totally fine. I know it didn't mean anything. Don't worry. I'm not going to start thinking we're really in a relationship. I know exactly where we stand with each other."

"Good that one of us does," he muttered.

She wanted to ask him what he meant by that but couldn't quite find the courage.

"I know you aren't looking for a relationship," she said quickly, wondering if they would ever be able to return to the comfortable friendship that had been growing between them.

"Do you?"

She nodded. "Kim talked about her younger brother often. I told you that. She gave the impression of a man who has no interest in anything serious."

"Kim talks about me entirely too much," he said, his tone disgruntled.

"She loves you and she worries about you," Holly said. "Regardless of what Kim might have said, my point is that you don't need to be concerned that I'll start getting ideas."

"Ideas."

She wanted to add that even if he were looking for a relationship, she knew full well it wouldn't be with a frazzled single mom of a special-needs daughter, a woman with a business and a home in a little town in Idaho. Again, she chickened out.

Anyway, she should be more concerned about what *she* wanted. And that certainly wasn't a broken heart.

"I'm not looking for a relationship, either," she hastened to assure him. "Been there, done that, thanks. I spent nearly a decade with a man who was absolutely the wrong person for me. You can be sure I'm in no hurry to walk that road again."

He opened his mouth to say something but appeared to change his mind. "Okay," he said instead.

This was not going the way she intended. She released a pent-up breath. "Look, Ryan. I enjoy being with you and it's obvious Lydia adores you. As far as I'm concerned, there's no reason we can't still hang out while you're in town."

When he said nothing, she could feel herself flush.

"Unless you want to back out of the wedding, which I would completely understand. You don't have to go with me. Lydia and I will be fine."

"We're going to the wedding together," he said, his voice

firm. "I came here to clear the air and make sure we're good before tomorrow."

"We're fine," she assured him. If she told herself that often enough, she might actually begin to believe it.

"Great. Tell me what time to pick you up. What time does Lydia have to be there?"

She hadn't really thought through the logistics of traveling together to Haven Point, where all the celebrations would be.

"I have to be there all afternoon to set up. I had planned to take our wedding clothes and finish getting ready either at the church or at the Moore house. Do you want to meet me there?"

"That works. You said the wedding starts at five, right?"

"You really don't have to come to the wedding ceremony itself. Why don't you meet us at six at the reception venue? It's right next door to the church, in a beautiful historic building now used for events."

"I can do that."

She had a sudden thought that should have occurred to her before this. "What about Audrey? I didn't even consider her."

"She'll be great. She's already made arrangements to sleep over at one of her friend's houses so we can party all night if you want."

Despite all her warnings to herself about guarding against impending heartache, Holly indulged in a quick, fleeting picture of what it might be like to truly party all night with him.

"Or until Lydia drops. Whichever comes first," she said, forcing herself back to her current reality of wedding prep and customers and a to-do list that seemed to lengthen by the moment.

"Deal," he said with a smile. "Write down the address where you want me to take the flowers."

She quickly found the information for him as well as a box he could use to safely transport the arrangement.

"Thank you again for doing this."

"No problem. I'll see you tomorrow evening, if I don't talk to you before then."

Despite all her stress over the upcoming event, she felt a little thrill of anticipation. Ryan really was making it more bearable. She was actually looking forward to it, which she never would have imagined a few weeks earlier.

CHAPTER SEVENTEEN

—

A LIGHT SNOW DUSTED THE WINDSHIELD AS RYAN DROVE PAST towering spruce and fir on his way around the lake to Haven Point.

This area of the country was undeniably pretty, especially covered in a blanket of snow that glinted in the sunlight like a scatter of gems.

For a guy used to spending Christmas flying somewhere over the Pacific or heading to the beach for an early-morning surf if he was at home, this change of season held an undeniable appeal.

He could understand why Kim and his dad and Diane seemed to like it so much here. Something about the Lake Haven area sucked a person in.

It was hard for him to truly enjoy the view, though. He was still kicking himself for his actions the night before.

He should never have kissed Holly.

He might have put their first kiss down to a one-off, a momentary lapse of judgment. The night before had been different. He had thought about kissing her all evening as they walked through the market. He had been enchanted by her and by Lydia and kissing her again had seemed inevitable, especially when she had looked so soft and sweet in the moonlight.

I spent nearly a decade with a man who was absolutely the wrong person for me. You can be sure I'm in no hurry to walk that road again.

Their conversation in the store replayed through his mind. She was right. Like her ex-husband, Ryan was another man who was completely wrong for her. No question.

While he wasn't thrilled his sister apparently had talked

about him at length with Holly, he couldn't disagree with anything Kim had told her. He had no intention of developing a serious relationship with anybody. Ever.

He had figured out a long time ago that he wasn't cut out for it. The women he'd dated in the past had been quick to point it out. He had a tendency to keep his emotions locked up tight, like classified files he never gave anyone authorization to access.

They weren't wrong. He'd always assumed it was a self-protective mechanism, a scar left behind from losing his mother when he was really too young and immature to make sense of it. From those years in military school, when any hint of vulnerability, of weakness, turned someone into a victim. And from the years of navigating his father's sharp edges and colder silences.

The kind of picket-fence, happy-ever-after relationship she deserved wasn't for a man like him.

And yet, Holly.

She was different. She was warm and steady, with an internal strength that had nothing to do with stubbornness and everything to do with how fiercely she loved the people in her life.

He could see it in the way she cared for Lydia, in how she smiled even when it was clear the world had given her every reason not to. She deserved someone who could match that strength, someone who could give her all the things she gave so easily.

Someone who wasn't him.

There was also the small matter of the life he'd built for himself. All the promotional brochures were right. His career in the navy was more than a job. It was a calling. It demanded everything. His time, his focus, his freedom to move wherever the next assignment took him. Holly's life, her roots, were firmly planted in Shelter Springs. She had Lydia to think about, a home she'd worked hard to create. He couldn't ask her to leave all of that.

She deserved better. No matter how much he wanted to kiss her again, to stay lost in the warmth of her laughter, the pull of her gaze. Wanting didn't change anything.

He had to wonder why that should leave him feeling as if the sun had been swallowed by dark, ominous clouds.

He turned his attention to the task at hand, which was the way he had been taught by the colonel's example to deal with any tough emotions.

Subvert everything and do what you have to do.

The flowers were for someone named Eliza Caine. He followed the address to a huge house on a slope overlooking town. While the property looked exclusive and prosperous, there was a warm, homey feeling to it. A trio of snowmen in different sizes adorned the yard, wearing brightly colored scarves and hats. Several bird feeders hung from the trees and a couple of horses raced along a fence line as he approached the house.

After pulling the large arrangement from his truck, he carried it to the front door and rang the doorbell.

After about thirty seconds the door opened and an adorable little girl with curly blond hair gazed back at him. She held a stuffed unicorn in one hand and, oddly, an umbrella in the other. The scent of sugar cookies and pine trees and cinnamon wafted through the open door, reminding him sharply of the appealing scent at Rose Cottage.

"Hi," she chirped in a friendly voice.

"Hi there. Is your mom or dad around?"

"My mom," she said, making no move to do anything other than smile at him.

"Could you . . . get her for me?"

She appeared to consider this for a moment then nodded. As she turned to go, a woman hurried around the corner.

"I'm sorry. We've told her not to open the door by herself but she loves hearing the doorbell ring. How can I help you."

"I'm looking for Eliza Caine."

"That's me."

"Then these are for you," he said, holding out the mini-Christmas tree of flowers.

"Oh, they're lovely! Who sent them?"

"I'm not sure. I only deliver."

She took them, looking at the card with its elegant logo. "They're from Evergreen and Ivy? I love their stuff. They're gorgeous. Please tell whoever created the arrangement how grateful I am for their hard work."

"I'll do that, ma'am," he said.

"Thank you," she said, setting the arrangement on a console table in the hallway and scooping up her daughter, unicorn and all.

"You're welcome. Merry Christmas."

After refusing the tip she tried to press on him, he walked down the steps, feeling an odd ache of longing somewhere inside him.

He had only had a brief glimpse into that house. He didn't know anything about the people who lived there. For all he knew, they could be selfish, terrible people or bitterly discontented or struggling with hidden trials.

But in that one tiny fragment of time, the woman had seemed so warm and friendly and . . . happy. The little girl had been cheerful and cute. The house had radiated welcome.

He wanted that.

He thought of his condo in California, where he came

home to an emptiness each night. He had never considered himself lonely. He had plenty of close friends and could always pick up the phone and find someone to hang with.

Since coming to Idaho, he had begun to see that the emptiness of his condo mirrored the emptiness of his life. He suddenly yearned for something else.

He returned to his truck and headed back to the main road. He turned in the direction of his father's house, wishing he had another flower delivery to make.

He didn't want to talk to Doug that day but unfortunately he still needed something to wear to the wedding.

He should have driven into Boise some time over the past few weeks to pick up a new suit. It had seemed silly, though, when he had a perfectly good suit hanging in his closet back in California, as well as his dress uniforms that served for most occasions.

Good thing he and his dad were the same size, though he expected his shoulders might be a little broader than his father's.

His father opened the door before Ryan could ring the doorbell, almost as if he had been watching for him from the moment Ryan had texted as he left Shelter Springs to let him know he was on his way.

"Come in, son. Come in. We were about to have lunch. Would you care for some soup?"

He almost automatically refused but that seemed rude, especially when his father was loaning him a suit.

"Sure. Soup sounds good."

"Great. Hope you don't mind eating on a tray in the family room with Diane. The dining chairs aren't very comfortable for her so we're still eating most of our meals in there."

"I don't mind. How's she doing today?"

"She had physical therapy this morning and that's always draining."

He knew a thing or two about physical therapy. As if in sympathy, his knee began to ache and it took all his powers of concentration not to limp.

His stepmother sat in her recliner again, with a book spread out on her lap. When she saw him, her face lit up and she smiled, closing the book and setting it on the small table next to her.

"Ryan, darling. It's so good to see you."

"You are looking lovely," he told her truthfully. He leaned in and kissed her cheek, gratified to see her bruises had faded and her eyes seemed brighter, less dulled by pain.

"I've been meaning to call and check on things. How are you? How is everything going with Audrey?"

He considered it a mark of Diane's strong character that even though she was dealing with her own troubles, she was first concerned with others around her.

"She's good. I am, too."

"You're sure Audrey's all right? I've been texting with her and she assures me she's fine but I've been so worried about her. She must miss Kim desperately. They're very close."

"You don't need to worry. Yes, she misses Kim, but she understands her mother is working to get better for both their sakes."

"That's wonderful to hear. Have you talked to Kim?"

"I spoke with her a few days ago. She said she's making progress and is feeling much better, physically and mentally. Unfortunately, she's still not sure if she'll be able to come home before Christmas."

"Your father has talked to her a few times," Diane said. "I'm afraid she still blames herself for the accident, no matter how many times I tell her it wasn't her fault. The other driver ran a red light. No one could have prevented what happened except that driver who was on his cell phone."

Before he could answer, his father came in carrying a tray loaded with food, which he set down on the coffee table across from Ryan.

"You don't have to serve me," he said, his voice gruff, guiltily aware he should have offered to help him prepare the meal. "Give this one to Diane."

"Hers is in the other room. It's next."

Ryan's stepmother gave Doug a warm smile. "I can't eat carrots. I have a weird reaction to them so whenever your father makes chicken noodle soup, he pulls them out for me."

Ryan said nothing. This version of his father, caring and considerate, was so very different from the remote, distracted man Doug had been when Ryan's mother was on hospice.

Ryan waited until his father returned with another tray for his wife and then made one more trip to carry in a tray for himself before taking a spoonful of soup. It was comforting and flavorful but his lingering resentment made it tough for him to enjoy the meal.

He was grateful Diane kept the conversation going, asking about Audrey's schoolwork and her babysitting job for Holly.

"And what about Christmas?" she asked. "Are you ready with everything, in case Kim doesn't make it home in time to be with Audrey?"

"I think so. That's one of the things Kim and I talked about the other day. She had done most of the shopping for Audrey already but had a few last-minute things she asked me to pick up. I think we'll be okay, though of course it would be better for Audrey if Kim could be home for the holidays. I'm a poor substitute."

"I'm sure that's not true. From everything Audrey has told me in our text exchanges, you've done a wonderful job of caring for her. I believe she called you solid."

"I suppose that's something."

"Your father said you had Holly Moore from Evergreen and Ivy help you decorate Kim's house."

"Yes. You should see it. The place looks like something out of a magazine."

"Holly is so good at that kind of thing. Some people have that skill for taking something plain and ordinary and making it sparkle. Holly is definitely one of those people."

He could not disagree. She made each moment sparkle, too.

"And you're going with her to the wedding of Kristine Moore tomorrow."

"That's right. We made a trade. She decorated the house and I agreed to be her plus-one for the wedding."

"We're friendly with Kristine's parents and were invited to the reception. I'm so sorry we won't be able to go."

"I'm sure they understand," Doug put in.

"And how are you keeping busy while you're in town?" Diane asked.

"I've been reading a lot and working on rehabbing my knee." He paused. "Actually, yesterday I was able to deliver flowers for Holly's store, since her two other employees besides Kim both had the flu."

Both his father and stepmother looked startled at that bit of information.

"You like her, don't you?" Diane said, looking delighted.

He thought of the kiss they had shared the night before. Of her soft skin and her sweet response and how he was beginning to feel an overpowering urge to tuck her and Lydia against him and keep them safe and warm forever.

"Sure. She's great."

"I mean, really like her."

He did *not* want to be having this conversation right now with his father and his stepmother but Ryan couldn't figure out an easy way to extricate himself.

He certainly wasn't about to tell them he was very much afraid *like* wasn't the right word. His feelings were beginning to run much deeper than that.

"What does it matter whether I . . . like her or not?" he said, his tone blunt. "It's not as if I'm looking for a relationship with her."

"Why not?"

He shifted his gaze to his father, who was watching their interchange with interest.

"You're not getting any younger," Doug went on. "Life is fleeting. Before you know it, you wake up and you're my age."

"You're sixty-four years young, my dear," Diane told him.

"Yes. And I spent too many of those years focusing on the wrong things. You're mortal, like the rest of us, son. I would think your recent hard landing would remind you of that. Maybe it's time you start thinking about what you want to do with your life when you can't fly helos in the military anymore."

He frowned, that resentment swelling again. "You really think I would be happy settling down in a small town in Idaho, going to school board meetings, barbecuing on the weekend, shoveling my neighbors' walks?"

"I never thought I would be. But here I am."

Okay, the picture he painted for his father actually did sound appealing. But that wasn't the life he had created. That his father so readily agreed was only further proof that Doug obviously knew nothing about him or what he wanted.

"My life is fine the way it is," he said, his voice terse. "Exactly how I want it."

Doug studied him for a long moment and looked as if he wanted to say more. To his relief, Diane stepped in and smoothly changed the subject.

A short time later, Ryan rose. "Thank you for lunch. The soup was tasty. But I should probably grab what I came for and take off soon, as I have a few other errands before Audrey is home from school."

His father rose as well. "Come back and take a look in my closet."

Wishing again that he had come up with a better option, he followed his father to the large bedroom with big windows overlooking the lake and the mountains.

He followed Doug into the walk-in closet. As he might have expected, it was neatly organized, with items hanging by type and color on what was clearly the colonel's side. The other side was a little more messy, full of the floral prints and bright colors Diane obviously favored.

"I have three suits, charcoal, navy and black. What's your pleasure?"

He studied the options his father presented him. "Why do you have three suits?"

"I wore one of them when I married your stepmother. Diane helped me buy the other two. She likes me to dress up when we go to church or to the opera in Boise. I also have a couple of sport jackets that might work."

"I'm leaning toward the charcoal suit or one of the sport jackets."

"Why don't you try them on and see which one fits better?"

The last thing he wanted to do was to have a fashion show with his father.

"If you don't mind, I'll take the suit and a few of the jackets and decide tomorrow."

"You can take all of them, if you want. I won't be going anywhere where I need a suit until Diane is feeling better."

"Right."

"What about everything else? Shoes, ties?"

He found the colonel's eagerness to help more than a little disconcerting.

"Not necessary. I bought a shirt, shoes and a couple of ties the other day. I figured I could always use those once I'm back in San Diego. I would have bought a new suit as well but I wasn't sure if I had time for it to be altered. Anyway, it didn't really make sense since I have a perfectly good suit hanging in my closet in San Diego, plus my dress uniforms."

"Makes sense."

"I should have had one of my buddies ship my suit here but by the time I thought of it, there wasn't time."

"No need. We're a similar size. I'm sure mine will fit you."

This might be the longest almost-cordial conversation he and his father had exchanged in a long time. Maybe ever. How weird that it didn't involve flying or the military but instead was focused on fashion, of all things.

"So. About Holly Moore."

He tensed, feeling defensive all over again.

"What about her?"

His father seemed to be choosing his words carefully, which he found unusual from a man who usually plowed ahead, damn the consequences.

"If you like her, I don't think you need to rule out a relationship completely."

"We live a thousand miles apart. And I'm likely to be reassigned back east next year."

"You don't have to be. You could get out. I always have room for a good helicopter pilot at Caldwell Aviation. We get requests for heli-skiing all the time and it would be great to have you working with me."

What a nightmare that would be, working for his father.

"Besides," Doug went on, "eventually I would like to retire. When that day comes, I would love to be able to pass the torch to my son."

"We can hardly be in the same room for ten minutes without bickering. Can you imagine us trying to run a business together?"

Doug paused, his hands in his pockets. "That's my fault," he finally said, his voice low and resigned. "I'm more sorry than I can say for that. I'm trying to do better."

He stared, shocked. When was the last time he had heard his father apologize for anything? Had he *ever*?

"This accident of Diane's has been a real wake-up call. I could have lost her. I don't want to spend the rest of our time together on this planet with work as my only focus. I want to travel with her, work on our garden, enjoy our retirement together."

He had to bite his tongue to keep from asking why the death of his first wife, the mother of his children, hadn't provided the same kind of wake-up call.

Somehow he managed to hold back the words. This wasn't the time or the moment.

"Think about it," his father went on. "That's all I ask. This area is a great place to settle down, with plenty of recreational opportunities and really good people. I'm certain you would be happy here."

Once more, his father was trying to rearrange Ryan's life to suit his own purposes. He was thinking about retirement and wanted his son to uproot his life and his career plans to take over the business Doug had started here—whether that was what his son wanted or not.

If he let himself fall for Holly—okay, fall *harder* for Holly—and tried to figure out a way to mesh their lives, he would be playing right into his father's plans.

He considered that yet one more reason to make sure that didn't happen.

"I need to go," he said, grabbing hold of the suit hangers. "Thank you for the loan. Whatever jacket I end up wearing,

I'll run it to the dry cleaner on Monday and get it back to you as soon as it's done."

"It's fine. Again, I'm in no hurry."

That made one of them. Suddenly Ryan couldn't wait to get back to his carefully organized life, away from this morass of emotions every time he was with his father, away from this attraction to a woman he couldn't have, away from the seductive appeal of this area of the world.

After saying goodbye to Diane again, he hurried out of the comfortable house beside the lake, loaded the suits in the back seat of his pickup and headed back toward Shelter Springs.

CHAPTER EIGHTEEN

"OH, HOLLY. THE FLOWERS ARE STUNNING. YOU HAVE REALLY outdone yourself."

In one of the rooms of the church set aside for the wedding party to use, Holly looked up from tucking another flower into Lydia's French braid to see Brittany in the doorway, her sleeping child nestled over her shoulder.

"Thank you. I'm happy with the way everything turned out."

"Susan and Kris are thrilled. If the flowers at the reception venue are anything like these, it's going to be a gorgeous wedding. You'll have more business than you can handle."

She already had more business than she could handle but she decided not to point that out.

"And look at you, Miss Lydia." Brittany scanned the girl from the flower chain woven through her hair to the tips of her black Mary Janes. "You are the prettiest flower girl I've ever seen."

Lydia hopped down from the chair and twirled around. "I look like a princess," she declared.

"Yes, you do."

"Can I hold Hudson?" Lydia held her arms out, clearly expecting that her almost-a-princess status came with certain perks.

Brittany gave her stepdaughter an apologetic smile. "Normally he would love to have you hold him but right now he's sleeping. I'm afraid he gets really cranky when I wake him up."

Lydia's lip jutted out and she looked like she wanted to argue but Brittany gave her a one-handed hug, careful not to mess up her hair.

"After the wedding, when you're all done being the flower girl for your Aunt Kristine, you can hold him."

Lydia might have pressed the matter but her young cousins came into the room and exclaimed over her dress, distracting her from her disappointment.

While Lydia was busy chattering away with her cousins, Brittany sat down beside Holly. She looked striking, as usual, in a smart ice-blue dress that showed off her considerable assets.

On closer inspection, Holly saw she had smudges under her eyes and a general air of exhaustion about her.

"Are you okay?"

Brittany nodded with a smile that looked slightly strained. "Only tired. Hudson had a rough night so I didn't get much sleep. He's teething and isn't happy with anything I try."

"Oh, I'm sorry. I remember those days. I imagine having his schedule upended because of travel hasn't helped matters."

"No, it hasn't. I love Norm and Susan and it's very kind of them to let us stay with them but it feels like people are constantly coming and going from their house. I'm not sure we've had five minutes of quiet since we arrived."

"I'm sure things will settle down a little after today."

"But then we have Christmas and all that chaos to deal with."

"And joy," Holly pointed out.

"You're right. That's what it's about. But speaking of Christmas, I'm glad to have a minute to talk with you about that."

Holly gave a surreptitious glance at her watch. The wedding was slated to start in twenty minutes. Was this really the most convenient time to discuss holiday plans?

"To speak with me about what?"

Brittany fretted with the edge of the blanket covering her sleeping son. "I was wondering, that is, Troy and I were wondering, what you might think about Lydia staying over with us on Christmas Eve at the Moores' house."

Holly stiffened, taken completely off guard at the request. "I thought this was all settled," she said, keeping her voice as low as Brittany's so the children, chattering away, didn't overhear their conversation. "I'm planning to take her over on Christmas morning so that she can spend the entire day with you."

"I know that's what you and Troy talked about."

Brittany somehow looked nervous and determined at the same time. "But I was thinking how wonderful it would be for Lydia and Hudson to be together when they open their presents from Santa. The photos would be so priceless."

Her child was not a photo prop for her younger brother, the adorable girl with the sunny smile and the joyful heart, she thought again.

Holly swallowed hard against a host of denials crowding her throat. She wanted Lydia to have a relationship with her half brother, but not at the expense of her own relationship with her child.

"So you would have her all of Christmas Eve and Christmas Day as well?"

"No. You could pick her up Christmas morning, around ten or eleven or so. You know. After we've had time for all the things. Presents, photos, breakfast."

Holly pressed her lips together, her mind whirling with a dozen responses, all of them too heated for a conversation twenty minutes before a family wedding.

"I was just thinking," Brittany went on, "you had her all to yourself last year for all the holidays. And the year before, too. It seems only fair that Troy could have her this year, since we're in town."

She had spent the past two holiday seasons alone with her

daughter because Lydia's father hadn't bothered to show much
interest in her whatsoever until his young wife had her own
child and developed a sudden desire to be more involved in
Lydia's life.

Now Lydia's father—or at least her father's wife—wanted
to change all their careful arrangements at virtually the last
minute, days before Christmas Eve.

Brittany seemed to sense the objections Holly hadn't figured out yet how to voice. "You don't have to decide right
now," she said quickly. "You and Troy could discuss it this
evening, maybe. Or we could all talk about it together. I'm
sure we'll have a chance between now and Christmas Eve to
go over the details."

Before she could come up with an answer, Kristine's wedding planner poked her head into the room.

"We're lining up for the processional, if you want to take
your seats," Reka Bell said with a bright smile. "Is the flower
girl ready?"

"Yep!" Lydia beamed and picked up the ribbon-festooned
basket of red rose petals she would be scattering down the aisle
of the church.

"Oh, you are adorable," Reka declared. "Everyone is going
to love you."

Holly managed a polite smile, though her chest tightened
slightly. She knew people meant well, but comments like that
often focused solely on Lydia's distinctive Down syndrome
features, not the vibrant, determined little girl she knew—the
one whose strength, joy and stubborn streak brought so much
light into the world.

"I'll stay with her while she lines up," Holly said.

"I can do that," Brittany said. "Why don't you go take your
seat near the front, then she can come sit next to you as soon
as she's done with her job."

That was actually a good idea, much better than Holly trying to squeeze down the aisle toward the front while everyone in attendance looked on.

"Are you sure?"

"Yes. I meant to tell you I saw your handsome guy come in a few minutes before I came in here. It looked like he found a place for you and Lydia in the third row."

"Ryan is here?" Holly told herself the little jump in her pulse was due to maternal nerves over her child's upcoming assignment but she suspected it had more to do with knowing her date had arrived.

She hadn't expected him yet, as she thought they had agreed he would join her after the ceremony only for the wedding dinner and reception.

Soft warmth spread through her, knowing he had come early and would be waiting for her in the chapel. He must have known somehow how grateful she would be for his presence.

What a good man he was. He would never say so but she considered him one of the kindest people she had ever met.

"Are you certain you don't want to sit by Troy?" she asked Brittany.

The other woman inclined her head toward her sleeping baby. "It's probably better if I slip into a seat near the back so I can take this guy out easily if he wakes up angry."

Holly could understand the logic of that. She probably would feel the same in the other woman's strappy heels.

"Makes sense." She turned to Lydia. "Okay. Honey, I'll be up near the front, like we practiced last night. Brittany will help you know when it's your turn to go and then you can come sit by me and by Ryan."

"I like Ryan," Lydia informed her.

Yes. Holly did, too. Entirely too much.

After kissing her daughter's forehead and smoothing an

errant strand of hair back into place, Holly hurried to the chapel.

She spotted Ryan immediately. He stood a few rows from the front talking to Nadine and Nyla, Troy's aunts. He looked tall and gorgeous in a charcoal suit and red power tie and her heart seemed to skip with happiness.

Aware the whole time of the man who waited for her, she made her way toward him, stopping occasionally along the way to greet extended family members of Troy, some of whom she hadn't seen since her own wedding.

When she reached his side, Ryan gave her a devastating smile that left her breathless.

"You came to the wedding. I wasn't expecting to see you until after."

His shrug rippled the fabric of his suit. "I'm your plus-one for the entire event. It didn't seem right to enjoy the food and the party without celebrating the actual ceremony."

Oh, how was she supposed to resist him? "I'm glad you're here," she admitted.

"As am I. You look lovely," he said.

She felt flustered and in disarray after rushing around for the past few hours making sure the flowers were ready and then helping Lydia into her flower girl dress and doing her hair. She did wear one of her favorite dresses, emerald green with a rose print and a matching rose bolero jacket.

"I was going to say the same thing to you. You found a suit."

"A jacket, anyway. My dad and I are similar in size. I picked up some dress pants and borrowed a jacket of his."

His shoulders were slightly broader than Douglas Caldwell's, she couldn't help but notice, his arms more muscled. The jacket was taut in a few areas but somehow it worked.

"Thank you again for doing this." For some reason, her

throat felt tight and achy. Probably a normal wedding reaction, she told herself. Tears at the impending happy moment of someone she cared about. "I still can't believe Hannah asked you that day in the grocery store but I'm so very grateful you agreed."

His gaze met hers, an intensity in his expression. "From this point on, let's forget this was ever a bargain. I'm happy to be here, Holly. I mean it. I'm very much looking forward to spending time with you and your cute flower girl. How is she, by the way? Is she nervous?"

"Not a bit," she said with a laugh. "She's leaning hard into her princess era."

He smiled. "I can only imagine. I'm sure she'll be the best flower girl ever."

Before she could answer, the organist began playing and the reverend officiating the ceremony spoke into the microphone.

"Will the groom please come forward? And will the congregation please rise for the processional?"

Holly watched Matt Reilly and his best man move to the reverend's side, the groom trying to look solemn but unable to hide either his nerves or his obvious elation.

She and Ryan both stood and she was intensely aware of him beside her. The subtle, masculine notes of his cologne, amber and musk, teased and tantalized her.

He leaned down to murmur into her ear. "The flowers are gorgeous, by the way. I'm not an expert on flowers, as you well know, but to my untrained eye, everything looks absolutely stunning."

It was the perfect thing for him to say. Like any woman, she supposed, she appreciated a compliment about her own appearances. That he would remark about her hard work and creative effort meant even more.

The three groomsmen and bridesmaids came down the

aisle first, arm in arm, their red spray-rose boutonnieres and bouquets Holly had fashioned looking perfect. Then it was Lydia's turn, paired with one of Matt's nephews to walk down the aisle.

By the exclamations of delight, Holly knew she wasn't the only one who appreciated the cuteness overload as a beaming Lydia skipped down the aisle, tossing petals into the aisle with abandon.

"Hi, Daddy," she said in a stage whisper as she passed Troy, who was standing about three rows behind them.

Her ex-husband looked as proud as Holly felt as he smiled at their daughter and waved back.

How could she stand in the way of that relationship? If Troy and Brittany wanted Lydia to spend Christmas Eve with them, was Holly being selfish to want to hold her daughter close?

She had her daughter full-time most of the year. How could she begrudge them this time with Lydia?

When Lydia reached her side, she jumped into Holly's arms. "Hi, Mommy," she said in that same stage whisper. "Hi, Ry. Did you see me?"

"We did," Holly answered in a low voice. "You were wonderful, honey. Perfect!"

"The best flower girl I've ever seen," Ryan assured her.

"I know," Lydia said with a confidence Holly hoped she would never lose.

And then Kristine walked into the chapel on the arm of her father, the bride stunning in a simple gown of ecru satin and carrying the bouquet Holly had worked so hard to make perfect.

She turned her attention to the ceremony, determined to enjoy the moment and not worry about what the future held.

SHE OWED RYAN Caldwell far more than the paltry afternoon she had spent helping him decorate his sister's house.

He was the perfect plus-one. All afternoon, through the ceremony and the photographs and congratulations, he had chatted easily with Troy's family and friends. He was polite, interested, attentive to her and to Lydia.

She caught more than one person of her acquaintance watching them with interest. If she wasn't mistaken, a couple of Troy's younger female cousins looked almost giddy as they chatted with him.

She couldn't really blame them. Ryan was impossible to resist.

When the wedding party moved to the historic reception venue across the street from the church, he helped her move the floral sprays at the end of each pew across to the reception, where she used them to adorn the walkway into the elegant building.

And he helped her keep track of Lydia whenever Holly was distracted speaking to someone else she knew.

Now they sat at one of the tables—decorated with more of Holly's flowers—that were staged around the dance floor in the large reception hall.

"I want to dance, Mama," Lydia said as the floor began to fill up.

"Let's go." Ryan stood and reached for her hand.

As he led Lydia out to the dance floor, Holly knew she wasn't the only one sighing at the sight of the big, tough guy and the five-year-old girl in the red velvet dress and floral coronet.

"Someone seems to be having a wonderful time." Stacy, Troy's older sister, nodded her head to Ryan and Lydia as she eased her bulky frame into one of the empty seats at the table.

"Lydia loves a good party," Holly said with a smile. "I think she takes after her father in that respect."

Why wouldn't Lydia be having a wonderful time, when she currently had the full attention of a man like Ryan Caldwell? Anyone would feel the same. *Holly* felt the same. The event she had been dreading was being filled with moments she knew would become cherished memories.

"I have been nominated by the aunties to tell you they— we—all approve of your Lieutenant Commander Caldwell."

She started to automatically reply he wasn't *her* Lieutenant Commander Caldwell, then remembered she and Ryan were both pretending otherwise.

"Okay," she said instead.

"He's exactly the kind of man you deserve, Hol. Considerate, polite, attentive. And gorgeous. You really hit the jackpot."

Holly smiled, though she felt a sharp little pang somewhere in the vicinity of her heart. If only their relationship could be more than make-believe.

"Ryan is definitely all those things," she said.

"You guys are really cute together," Stacy said. "I see the way he looks at you. Reminds me of when Paul and I were falling in love."

Holly wondered if the expression she tried to don now appeared besotted or merely dyspeptic. "The early days of a relationship are exciting, aren't they?"

"With a man like that, I imagine every day of a relationship would be exciting," Stacy said.

Oh, Holly could imagine it too, entirely too clearly.

"Also, everyone is raving about the flowers. I can't tell you how many comments I've received about how beautiful they are."

"That's nice to hear."

"I've been telling anyone who will listen they should go to Evergreen and Ivy for all their floral needs."

"Thanks for the plug. I need all the business I can find."

The two of them chatted for a few more moments about the trip Stacy and her family planned between Christmas and New Year's Eve to visit family in California and, of course, hit the beach and Disneyland.

Stacy was telling her about the perfect vacation rental she had found in Anaheim when Ryan and Lydia returned to the table.

"Hi, Aunt Stacy," Lydia said cheerfully, wiping a drooping curl away from her forehead.

"Hello, darling Lydia. You've really got the moves out there on the dance floor."

"I know I do," she said with her characteristic complete lack of modesty that made all the adults at the table smile.

"I'm thirsty," Lydia said.

"You should be. Dancing is hard work," her aunt said.

Lydia nodded, picking up her glass of water with both hands and taking a long drink.

"Why don't you two go dance?" Stacy suggested. "I can keep an eye on Lydia for you. Maybe I'll drag her cousins over here and she can show them all her great dance moves."

Holly narrowed her gaze at Lydia's aunt for her not-so-subtle machinations. Stacy only gave her an innocent look in response.

"Sounds like a great idea," Ryan said. "Shall we, Holly?"

"I don't really dance," she protested.

"Yes, you do," Lydia said, calling her out without compunction. "You dance with me a lot."

Yes. Twirling around the kitchen with her daughter to some of Lydia's favorite tunes was a far cry from dancing with Ryan Caldwell, with his sexy scent and his snug suit and his devastating smile.

"Go dance, Mommy," Lydia urged.

Left with no clear reason to refuse, Holly finally stood. As Ryan reached for her hand, she could swear sparks flashed between them.

With her pulse ratcheting, she slid her fingers into his.

The band had been covering a fast song but, naturally, they switched to a Christmas love song as if on cue the moment she and Ryan hit the dance floor.

Could he feel her pulse race? She really hoped not.

As he pulled her into his arms, she felt surrounded by his strength. The warmth of his hand at the small of her back seeped through her dress, his steady presence wrapping around her like the coziest of blankets on a snowy night.

For the first time in what felt like forever, she felt safe. She met his gaze and the world outside this moment seemed to melt away. The wedding bustle faded into a blur, leaving only the two of them moving in perfect harmony beneath the twinkling fairy lights.

Her thoughts flickered to the kiss they had shared after the Christmas market, still vivid in her mind. The memory now hummed between them, a silent reminder of the connection they had found.

Dancing with him now, she could feel the echo of that kiss in every step, every slight shift of his hand, and she didn't want this moment to end. It felt too fragile, too precious, like trying to hold onto the last snowflake before it melted away.

Holly hadn't realized how much she'd missed being held like this. Not only the physical touch, but the deep, soul-nourishing sense of being seen and cherished.

She closed her eyes, letting herself sink into the music and his quiet strength.

"How are you holding up?" he asked.

"Fine, actually. Having you here helped so much."

He smiled with genuine happiness and she felt as if all the lights in the venue were twinkling inside her.

Aunt Nancy glided by on the arms of her husband. The older woman beamed at the two of them, giving Holly a meaningful wink as they moved past that made her wince.

How on earth would she be able to tell them all she and Ryan weren't "together" anymore? They would be heartbroken. She might have to string this imaginary relationship out for years.

"I like your former in-laws very much."

She gave a rueful smile. "So do I. If I hadn't liked them all so much, I might not have married Troy in the first place."

For some reason, that confession seemed to please him.

"I actually had a brief conversation with your ex too, when you took Lydia to the ladies' room earlier."

"Did you?"

"Yes. He basically asked me my intentions toward you."

She closed her eyes, mortified. "Oh no. I'm so sorry! What did you say?"

His shoulder muscles rippled beneath her hand as he shrugged. "I told him I wanted to run away with you to Tahiti but I couldn't manage to convince you yet, though I was working on it."

The mental picture he created was undeniably enticing and she wondered what Ryan would say if she told him she wouldn't need much persuading.

A few more dances and perhaps one or two more soul-stirring kisses like they had shared would probably do the trick.

"It's clear Lydia loves her dad."

She followed the direction of his gaze and found that Troy was now dancing with their daughter. Though he looked a little uncomfortable, at least he was trying.

"She really does."

His words reminded her of the conversation she had before the wedding ceremony.

"Troy and Brittany want Lydia to spend Christmas Eve with them now. They want her to open her presents from Santa at Susan and Norm's place."

A frown furrowed his forehead. "I thought you told me you would have her Christmas Eve and they would pick her up for Christmas Day."

"That was the plan. Brittany cornered me earlier today and asked if they could change the schedule. It's Hudson's first Christmas and they want his big sister to be part of it."

"How do you feel about it?"

Like she wanted Ryan to pack her and Lydia away to Tahiti so she didn't have to deal with all of this.

"All the emotions at once. I want to cry, yell and possibly throw every single flower arrangement I created for the tables against the wall."

"Understandable."

"Is it? For two years, I've been furious at Troy for walking out on his daughter. Now I'm angry that he wants to spend more time with her. Face it. I'm a hot mess, Ryan."

"You're not."

She gave a short laugh, annoyed with herself for making this harder than it had to be.

"Okay," she said, her tone almost a challenge. "What would you call it?"

CHAPTER NINETEEN

———

WHAT DID HE THINK ABOUT HOLLY MOORE?

As he held her close, moving in time to the music, her flowery vanilla scent filled his senses. She fit so perfectly in his arms, as if this was exactly where she belonged.

Her head rested below his chin, her soft curls brushing against him as they moved together, and he wished he could freeze time and keep her here with him forever.

He wasn't sure she wanted to hear the answer to her question. Would she even believe that he thought she was amazing, beautiful, gentle yet possessed of incredible strength?

Or that he thought about her entirely too often for his peace of mind?

Just now as she told him about Troy and his wife wanting Lydia to spend Christmas Eve with them, her voice had wavered and he'd felt the sharp stab of her hurt like it was his own.

His heart ached for her, knowing how fiercely she protected her daughter, how ferociously she fought for her, and how much she didn't want to let go, even a little.

He tightened his hold, letting his hand glide soothingly along her back, wishing he could take away her pain and make her believe everything would be okay.

"I think you're an incredible mom, Holly," he murmured, his voice low and meant only for her. "Lydia knows how much you love her. A few hours won't change that."

He felt her lean into him a little more, as if drawing strength from his words.

If he could, he would try to shield her from every heartache, every struggle. For now, all he could do was hold her and hope she felt how much he cared, how deeply he wanted to be there for both her and Lydia.

It wasn't his job, he reminded himself.

"You're right," she answered. "I know you're right. It's just that for the past two years—longer, even—I've done virtually everything for her alone. Even when we were together, Ryan wasn't exactly an involved father. Not like he seems to be with Hudson."

Ah. He had suspected that might be part of her frustration with her ex.

"I was the one taking Lydia to Boise for her specialist appointments, who handled all the early-intervention therapies and attended all the advocacy training. Since she entered the school system, I have done all the school individualized education plans, the consultations with her teacher and aides, the school runs. I arrange my schedule to take her to speech therapy, to occupational therapy, to recreation therapy, to play groups. I stay up with her when she's sick. I make sure she's eating a healthy diet. I sit and practice letters and math with her, even on nights when I'm exhausted from working a long day."

"You're a wonderful mother, Holly. Everyone would agree."

"Now her father, the same one who walked out on her, wants to swoop in and steal all the fun moments with her. Sledding with her, dancing at a wedding, Christmas morning."

He could feel the frustration seething beneath her skin.

"It's not fair," he agreed.

"*Fair* is a word you have to throw out of your vocabulary when you have a child with special needs. Life will never be fair. It's only a patchwork of moments—some heavy with struggle, others bright with joy—and the strength you find to keep stitching them together."

She stopped as the music changed to another slow song, one about second chances and new beginnings.

"I'm sorry. I'm getting carried away, as usual. Let's not talk about Troy or Lydia or Christmas Eve. Let's just dance for a few moments."

Sensing that was the only way he could help her for now, he pulled her closer.

As the song came to an end, Holly lifted her head from his shoulder and gazed up at him, her eyes glistening with a vulnerability that hit him square in the chest.

In that moment, Ryan recognized the truth. He was falling in love with her.

It was a quiet but undeniable realization, one that made his pulse quicken and his heart ache at the same time.

She was everything he hadn't known he was searching for. Strong, compassionate and resilient in ways that humbled him.

How could he offer her anything? He wasn't the kind of man she needed.

What a mess. How would he possibly be able to extricate her and her adorable daughter from his heart when this magical, unforgettable holiday season was over and the cold, hard reality of January cycled back around?

"Thank you," she murmured.

"For the dance? It was my pleasure," he said, with complete sincerity.

"For everything. Standing by me today. Helping me at the store this week. All of it. Your sister was exactly right. You're a hero, Ryan."

While her words touched him, he also felt a twinge of unease. He really hoped she didn't fall for him. She deserved stability, someone who could stand beside her without hesitation or compromise.

He couldn't be that man and he would hate for her to end up with a broken heart.

AN HOUR BEFORE the wedding reception was due to end, Holly decided Lydia had reached her limit. She was increasingly cranky and had rubbed her eyes at least three times in the past five minutes, a sure indication that she was tired.

"I don't want to," Lydia whined when Holly suggested they should start heading home. "I want to stay with my cousins."

"It's been a wonderful day, hasn't it?" Holly said gently. "It's always hard to see a fun day end."

Her chin started to wobble but to Holly's relief, Ryan stepped in. "Let's go find your coat and we can say goodbye to your cousins on the way. Maybe I can give you a piggyback ride to the car again."

He reached for her hand and Lydia slipped from Holly's lap.

As she watched them head to the coatroom off the reception hall, Holly sighed, already feeling the ache of impending heartbreak.

She was falling hard for Ryan and she feared Lydia was, too.

Somewhere along the way, Holly had given up trying to resist him, even though she knew nothing about the two of them together made sense.

She headed over to say goodbye to the newly married pair, who were currently giving their feet a rest, enjoying a drink at one of the tables and speaking with friends.

When Holly approached and said she would be leaving, Kristine jumped up and hugged her. If she wasn't mistaken, the bride was nearly as overstimulated as Lydia right now. Kristine seemed on the verge of tears, though perhaps that was merely the day catching up with her.

"Thank you for everything today. The flowers, letting

Lydia be in the wedding party. Everything. You made a beautiful day even better."

Holly returned her friend's hug, grateful all over again that their relationship seemed as strong as ever, despite the divorce.

"You are most welcome. Everything was lovely and I was honored to be a part of it. Congratulations again. I know you're going to live happily ever after."

"I'll reach out when we're back from Hawaii. Meantime, Merry Christmas, Holly."

"Mele Kalikimaka."

After saying a quick goodbye to Susan and Norm Moore, with more hugs all around, she joined Lydia and Ryan in the foyer.

"All set?" he asked.

She nodded, not sorry that she could now put this particular wedding in her personal rearview mirror.

They walked together outside into the December night to an unexpected discovery.

"It snowed, Mommy," Lydia exclaimed.

At least four inches of new snow had fallen in the past few hours while they had been inside the reception venue.

"I'll say," she answered with surprise as a snowplow drove past, yellow lights flashing.

Her feet in her heels were already cold and she still had to walk next door to the church, where her SUV was parked.

Ryan obviously realized the same thing.

"Why don't you hand over your keys and the two of you can go back inside and wait where it's warm. I'll bring your car over. That way we all don't have to wade through the snow."

She should argue with him but she could see Lydia was beginning to hit a wall. Being wet and cold would only make things worse.

"Are you sure?" she asked.

"Positive. Keys."

She fished in her clutch and found her fob, thinking how nice it was to have someone else to lean on, even if it was only temporarily.

"Will you be able to find my vehicle?"

"It's hard to recognize any of the cars under the snow but I can always click the key fob and see which one responds," he answered.

"Thank you."

He flashed her a quick smile then took off around the building toward the parking lot while she and Lydia went back inside. She was already grateful for the warmth and light that enveloped them again as she brushed snow off Lydia's coat and had her stomp her feet on the mat.

"I like Ry. He's nice and he's funny."

Holly could not disagree.

"He says I dance like a ballerina," Lydia declared, twirling so her skirt belled out around her.

They could still hear the music from inside so she grabbed her daughter's hands and the two of them danced a few steps together while snow fluttered down outside the windows.

A short time later, she saw headlights approach the entrance and recognized her vehicle. The two of them hurried out and she quickly put Lydia in her booster seat, double-checking the safety belts.

After she closed the door, Ryan opened the passenger door for her. "The roads are icy and your seat is set for me now. Why don't I drive you home?"

She frowned as she hurried around the vehicle to that side. "What about your truck? It's still at the church."

"I can catch a ride back to Haven Point tomorrow to pick it up."

She was a native Idahoan who had learned to drive in snowy

conditions but it still wasn't her favorite thing. She was always grateful when she didn't have to.

"Thank you, if you're sure. I can drop you off at Kim's house and also give you a ride back here tomorrow if you want."

"We'll see."

Her car was already warm and comfortable, the heater blasting, as Ryan headed toward Shelter Springs.

Lydia fell asleep in her booster seat almost before they left the parking lot.

"And . . . she's out," Ryan said with a quick glance in the rearview mirror.

With a smile, she turned to look at her daughter. "She had a wonderful day. She told me, by the way, that she likes you very much. She said you're nice and you're funny and you told her she dances like a ballerina."

His smile flashed in the darkness and there in her passenger seat as they drove around the lake on a snowy night, Holly felt the last of her defenses crumble away like a snow fort in a spring thaw.

"She's an amazing kid, Holly. It's impossible not to love her."

She swallowed a sudden ache in her throat. "I agree. Lydia is a gift to the world."

He looked in the rearview mirror again, then glanced at her briefly before turning his attention back to the road.

"When did you know she would have Down syndrome?" he asked.

"About midway through the pregnancy. After an initial ultrasound here, my ob-gyn sent me to a specialist in Boise for more intensive testing. She confirmed that it was likely and suggested we terminate the pregnancy."

"Seriously?"

"It's not uncommon. Estimates are that up to three out of four pregnancies with a Down diagnosis in this country are terminated. In Europe, that percentage is even higher, up to ninety percent. Many parents don't feel up to the challenges ahead of them or don't want to knowingly bring a child with disabilities into a world that lacks full societal support, a world that can sometimes be hard and cruel to them."

She had never, for a moment, considered it. Troy had agreed with her, but she had sensed his reservations from the beginning.

"I can't imagine a world without Lydia in it. Or one where people might be capable of treating her with anything but love."

She didn't want to shatter his faith, though she could have given him an earful about school districts that fought inclusive education or governments that didn't prioritize care and services for the most vulnerable among their populations.

"We're lucky. Most people we meet are nothing but kind to her."

"Have you decided what you're going to do about Christmas Eve?"

She pursed her lips. "I want to say no but I'm afraid I have to say yes."

"You don't *have* to do anything."

"You've obviously never been a parent. My whole life feels like one big round of things I have to do when I would rather stay in my pajamas all day and read a book."

He slowed as they approached another snowplow. "What will you do on Christmas Eve if you decide to let her stay with her father?"

"My parents always have a family party that evening. We were going to go together. My dad grills steak and we all eat too much and play board games and exchange gifts."

"That doesn't sound bad."

"It's not. It's wonderful. Lydia is usually the star of the show, of course."

"Naturally."

"She's the only grandbaby on my side so she's very spoiled by my parents, Hannah and our older brothers."

"They'll miss her this year if she stays with Troy."

"Yes. It definitely won't be the same. And when the family party is over, I'll probably go home to my empty house, sit by the Christmas tree and feel sorry for myself."

He placed a warm, strong hand over hers. Grateful for the compassion and support in his touch, she turned her hand over and twined her fingers with his.

The drive from Haven Point to Shelter Springs usually only took about ten minutes. This trip took at least twice that long because of the road conditions and overcautious drivers. As she listened to the wipers beat away the snow from the windshield and soft music on the stereo, she felt herself relax, the exhaustion of the long day catching up with her.

She must have drifted off to sleep for a few moments. She awoke when the motion stopped, opening her eyes to find they were in her driveway.

"You should have headed to Kim's place first," she said. "I could have dropped you off before driving back here."

"It's only a block. I don't mind a quick walk," he said.

"In the snow? In your dancing shoes?"

He inclined his head toward the darkness outside the window. "The snow's not as bad here. Looks like Haven Point must have had a microsquall over there. We've only had an inch or two. I'll be fine."

Sometimes that happened because of the lake effect and the wind direction. One community could be slammed while the other one barely had a trace.

"I'll help you carry Lydia to her bed," he said, hitting the remote that opened her garage door and pulling her SUV inside.

She couldn't think of a reason to argue with him. She was grateful for his help anyway. Lydia was getting bigger. In a few more years, Holly probably wouldn't be able to carry her on her own.

Her daughter hardly stirred as Holly unhooked the seat belt of her booster seat or when Ryan scooped her out and over his shoulder, where she nestled into his neck, eyes still closed.

Lucky girl, Holly thought. She would like to be snuggled in Ryan's arms right now.

"Where is her room?" he asked, voice low.

"I'll show you."

She led the way up the stairs and opened Lydia's door, across the hall from her own.

He lowered Lydia onto her bed, a low-profile twin she still called her big bed. She didn't let go, however. She held onto his neck, eyes still closed, and murmured something Holly couldn't hear.

"Shh, sweetheart," he murmured. "You're home now."

After a pause, Lydia relaxed, easing back onto the pillow.

"Thank you," Holly whispered. "I'll take it from here. I need to get her out of her fancy princess dress, since I don't think it will be very comfy to sleep in."

"Makes sense. I'll wait for you downstairs."

She nodded, though some part of her wanted to tell him to leave now before she wrapped her arms around his neck like Lydia had done and refused to let go.

Her daughter didn't awaken, even as Holly pushed her arms through the sleeves of her coat and then her dress before slipping her into a nightgown.

After all the cookies and sweets Lydia had eaten at the reception, a good mother would probably make her wake up to brush her teeth but Holly decided one night of waiting until the morning to brush probably wouldn't cause irreparable damage.

They were baby teeth anyway, a few of them already loose.

After Lydia was dressed for bed, Holly tucked the blanket around her, checked that the video monitor was on, pressed a kiss on her forehead and turned off the light.

She closed the door then stood in the darkened hallway for a long moment, her thoughts filled with the man who waited downstairs.

What was she going to do about her growing feelings, this emotional pull between them and the fierce attraction she couldn't seem to fight? She wanted to grab him by his loosened necktie and haul him into her bedroom.

She couldn't, of course. Besides the fact that her daughter slept only a few feet away, Holly knew it would be a mistake she couldn't take back. Ryan was charming, kind and impossibly good-looking, but he was also temporary.

He didn't belong in Shelter Springs and she didn't belong in his world, even if he wanted her there.

Giving her heart to him completely would only lead to a vast, deep pain. She couldn't afford the risk, not when her focus needed to be on Lydia. Her daughter deserved stability, not a mother distracted by a relationship that had no future.

But even as she told herself all the reasons why she had to keep her distance, Holly couldn't ignore the heat that flared whenever Ryan was near. His smile tugged at something deep inside her. What was she supposed to do with this growing desire, this ache that refused to be silenced?

Holly leaned her head against the door. Maybe she could bury these feelings, shove them into the same locked drawer where she kept her regrets over her broken marriage.

But even as the thought crossed her mind, she knew the truth. She was already in too deep.

When she walked down the stairs, she found Ryan standing by her Christmas tree, the colored lights playing across his features.

Everything inside her seemed to sigh.

"Did she stay asleep?"

She nodded. "Didn't even stir when I changed her clothes and tucked her in."

"Weddings are exhausting business, apparently."

"That is an understatement. At least I'll get a little break from them, since this was the last one on my schedule until February."

He smiled and she hesitated, torn between wanting him to leave for her own self-preservation and aching to prolong whatever time she had left with him.

"Would you like a drink? I don't keep much in the house but I could probably round up a glass of wine or something. Maybe even a beer at the back of the refrigerator."

"I'm fine, thanks. I was admiring your cottage again. It's so cozy and warm. A great place for a child to grow up."

She smiled, daring to take another step closer to him.

"Thanks. I feel very fortunate that my friend decided to sell right when I was looking to buy."

"You're making a great home here for Lydia. The only thing missing is that puppy."

"Ha! Don't you start in, too. It's not happening this year. Maybe in a year or two, when things are a little more settled."

She had to hope the day would eventually come when she finally felt like she had her stuff together.

"I can't thank you enough for coming to the wedding with me, Ryan," she said. "You made what could have been an awkward day actually enjoyable."

He raised an eyebrow. "I guess I'll take *actually enjoyable*. It's what I strive for on all my dates."

She laughed. "I hope it wasn't completely miserable for you."

"Not completely."

She laughed again at his dry tone. "And that's what I hope for on all *my* dates."

He smiled, though it was fleeting. "What happens now?"

She wasn't sure what he was asking. "Now I suppose we go back to our lives and enjoy the rest of the holidays. You'll be heading back to San Diego after Kim returns. I'm sure you can't wait."

He didn't look nearly as enthused by that as she might have expected.

"I meant, what are you going to tell your in-laws about us?"

She considered. "If you don't mind, I might string our relationship out a little longer, even after you go back to San Diego. You make a very good diversion."

"Good to know I can be useful for something besides flying rescue missions and landing a Seahawk on an aircraft carrier."

"I'm just saying," she said, trying for a light, easy tone, "I could always create another fictional boyfriend so everyone would back off about setting me up with someone else. But why do that when the Moore family has already met you?"

"Good point."

"Not only have they met you but they adore you. I heard from every one of Troy's aunts as well as his mother that I needed to hang on to you. I believe their exact words were that I would be a fool to let you slip away."

She found it adorable that he actually looked embarrassed about that.

"Nice to know I was a hit with the older ladies."

"With *all* the ladies," she corrected. And probably a few of the men, too.

The tips of his ears were definitely pink now.

"So you're suggesting we string this out as long as possible so people don't try to set you up with anyone else."

"Would you mind?"

"What's in it for me?" he asked in a teasing voice.

She made a face. "The knowledge that you're providing an important service for a beleaguered single mom in Idaho without having to lift a finger?"

"That sounds fine in theory but what happens when you meet someone you actually want to date? Am I supposed to disappear out of your life without a word?"

"First of all, that's not going to happen."

She suddenly knew without a doubt that was true. She didn't want to date anyone at all, if that man couldn't be Ryan Caldwell.

"Second, I'll tell them you and I reached a mutual decision that we're better off as friends."

"What if they don't buy that?"

"Fine. I'll tell them I broke up with you. I decided we weren't a good fit. You were, of course, devastated and went back to San Diego with a shattered heart. In a week or two, I will quickly find a new fake boyfriend, even hotter than you are."

As if that were possible.

He laughed and before she could guess what he intended, he reached for her hand and tugged her toward him. His mouth lowered to hers, tasting of chocolate and mint.

All the hunger that had simmered inside her all afternoon and evening seemed to explode at the touch of his mouth. Unlike their earlier kisses, this one was hot and hungry.

His arms wrapped around her, pulling her flush against him, and she surrendered to the moment, her fingers curling into the fabric of his shirt. The kiss deepened, a storm of emotions swirling between them. Desire, longing and something she didn't dare name.

Her world narrowed to the feel of him, the strength of his arms, the warmth of his body. His hand slid to her jaw, tilting her face up to his as if he couldn't bear to stop kissing her.

She felt as if she were standing on the edge of something vast and uncharted, and for once, she didn't want to step back.

When they finally broke apart, their breathing ragged, his forehead rested against hers.

"You've been driving me crazy all day in this dress. All I could think about was ripping it off you."

She swallowed hard, searching his face, her emotions in turmoil. Her hands still rested against his chest, and she felt the steady beat of his heart beneath her palms. When his lips found hers again in another searing kiss, Holly could only throw herself into the moment.

She was not sure how long they kissed. A few moments? A few hours? She only knew she never wanted it to stop. His kiss and his touch made her feel cherished, wanted, needed.

She might have done exactly what she had thought about earlier, grabbed his tie and tugged him up the stairs, if a soft cry from Lydia's room hadn't intruded on the moment like the sharp crack of a branch weighed down by snow.

She froze as reality crashed in, cold and relentless.

He pressed his forehead to hers, his expression resigned. "I guess she wasn't as exhausted as you thought."

"I . . . I have to . . . We can't . . ."

He stood up and spent a few moments rearranging her dress. "I know," he said, his voice rough. "You have to. And we can't."

"I'm sorry," she murmured.

About so many things.

"Don't be sorry. Lydia is your priority. As she should be."

"This isn't only about Lydia. I . . . I can't sleep with you, Ryan. As much as I might want to."

He released another ragged breath and nodded slowly. "I know that, too."

He pulled her close for one more embrace and kissed her forehead, much as she had kissed her sleeping child earlier.

"Go take care of your daughter. I'm going to walk home. It's not a cold shower but I guess a snowstorm is the next best thing."

She felt ridiculously close to tears as she watched him walk out into the snow, then she hurried upstairs.

WHAT A MESS he had made of everything.

Ryan made his way through the few inches of snow, grateful for those residents who had already been out with shovels and snowblowers in front of some houses. His knee ached, but that wasn't the thing bothering him the most.

How the hell was he going to be able to walk away from Holly and Lydia after Kim returned to pick up the pieces of her life?

He should never have agreed to go to that wedding. The moment he figured out how attracted he was to Holly, he should have done everything possible to keep a safe distance from her.

Women like her weren't for him. Nothing real and lasting could ever come out of a fling between them.

Holly slotted in perfectly to the cozy world of Shelter Springs. She had a thriving business here. A life. Family and friends who loved and supported her and Lydia. All he could offer her was a transient life, moving from base to base, assignment to assignment.

That would be disastrous for Lydia. He didn't need to be an expert in raising a child with special needs to know that. She required structure and consistency, not a new school in a new community every few years.

It was going to break his heart to walk away from both of them. He relived dancing with the little girl at the wedding, her features screwed up with concentration as she tried to follow his lead and not stumble.

Which one had stolen his heart first? He wasn't sure. What did it matter, anyway? He had been a goner that first day he had been in the shop and Lydia had come running in full of news and smiles to tell her mother about her day.

As soon as Kim was home and settled, he needed to pack up his gear and head back to the coast, even if walking away from them would leave him shattered.

CHAPTER TWENTY

"THANKS SO MUCH FOR WALKING LYDIA HOME, AUDREY," Holly said Monday, two days after the wedding and those hungry, heated kisses that came later. "I meant to text you and tell you I could pick her up but somehow the afternoon got away from me."

While she had expected to have a slow day on this, her last full day in the store before the holidays, instead she had received several last-minute orders for holiday centerpieces and hostess gifts. At least the store had been fully staffed so she hadn't been on her own.

"It's no problem," Audrey assured her. "I was planning on it."

"No more school for two weeks, Mommy!"

"That's what I hear."

Lydia's bubbly excitement was contagious and Holly shared a smile with Audrey.

"You don't have to stay and watch her, though. Ginger is coming back to close up after she finishes a couple of deliveries. I was thinking I would try to take off early, with the storm coming and also the party at the Shelter Inn. Are you and your uncle coming to that?"

She tried to ask the question casually, as if it didn't matter to her what Ryan did or did not do.

Ha. She hadn't stopped thinking about the man since he had walked out of her house the other night, leaving her aching and needy and hopelessly in love.

The annual holiday potluck party had begun after an emergency a few years earlier, when an intense lake-effect blizzard shut down traffic throughout the area, trapping the senior citizens who lived at the Shelter Inn away from family celebrations.

Over the past few years, it had evolved into a community event that drew more than a hundred people. More than that, counting the residents of the retirement community.

"We're probably not going to make it this year."

"Oh, that's too bad."

Holly told herself she had no reason to be disappointed. After two sleepless nights, she had determined her best course of action was to move forward with her life and put this strange chapter behind her.

"Yeah. I'll be sad to miss it." Audrey gave her a sudden impish smile. "But I'm not sure my mom will feel up to a big party."

She stared as the words sank in. "Your mom? Is she back?"

Audrey grinned. "Not yet, but she's on her way. Uncle Ryan went to pick her up in Boise. They're supposed to be here in about an hour. I was hoping I could go home early so I can try to make something for dinner. I'm sure she won't feel like going anywhere, her first night back."

Holly felt a strange mix of emotions. She was thrilled that Kim would be able to return to join her daughter for the holidays at the same time she felt a hollow ache deep inside, knowing that meant Ryan's time here in Shelter Springs would be coming to an end.

"Let me take you dinner. I made two huge slow cookers of *pasta e fagioli* soup to share at the potluck. I can easily drop some off for you on my way to the Shelter Inn tonight."

"That would be great!" Audrey exclaimed. "You know my mom loves your *pasta e fagioli* soup. She talks about it all the time. Are you sure, though? You made it for the party."

"Positive. It is the least I can do. Seriously. Your uncle was a lifesaver at the wedding on Saturday."

She didn't want to think about what had happened at her house after the reception—or what *hadn't* happened.

"Did you guys have fun? I asked Uncle Ryan but it seemed like he really didn't want to talk about it. I wondered if maybe he's not a very good dancer, especially with his bad knee."

"He's a wonderful dancer."

And kisser.

And man.

Her throat felt tight and achy as she contemplated how empty her world would feel after he left Shelter Springs, but she forced a smile.

"I'll drop off a container of soup on my way to the Shelter Inn. I even have breadsticks to go with it."

"I love breadsticks," Lydia said, pulling off her snow boots and plopping them onto the floor of the shop willy-nilly.

"I know you do, Bug. That's why I made them for you. Now move your boots and your backpack to the break room so someone doesn't trip over them, then grab a snack, okay?"

Her daughter obediently scooped everything up and trotted to the back.

"If you're sure you don't mind, soup and breadsticks sounds delicious. Thank you."

"Thank *you*, Audrey. You have been amazing this holiday season. I know our plan was for you to babysit only for a month to earn extra cash for your mom's Christmas gift, but if you want to stay on after the holidays, let me know. We could even work out a schedule for you to come one or two days a week so you don't miss out on homework time or hanging out with friends."

"I would like that."

She checked her watch. "I'm sure you're in a rush to be home, but if you want to wait for twenty minutes or so until I finish this arrangement, I can drop you off on our way to deliver it. I have to go right past your house."

"That would be great, as long as I'm there before Uncle

Ryan and Mom show up. I wanted to turn on all the tree lights and the outside decorations to welcome her home. Mom is going to be so happy with the way you helped us decorate for Christmas."

"I hope so."

She also hoped Kim had found what she needed to deal with some of her demons. She had missed the other woman's help at the store these past few weeks. More than that, she had missed her friend.

While Audrey and Lydia watched a YouTube video in the break room, Holly hurried to finish the arrangement. She was tucking in the last spray of baby's breath when Ginger walked through the employee entrance.

"How did the deliveries go?"

"Good, except I have one for someone who wasn't home. I figured I would check again on my way home after I close."

"Thanks for closing for me today."

"You've put in so many long days this month, I wish you could take the whole month of January off."

"Wouldn't that be lovely?" Holly said as she tucked the card into the arrangement.

"Are you sure you still want to close early tomorrow?"

"Yes. If people haven't purchased all the flowers they need before three p.m. on Christmas Eve, they don't deserve my flowers anyway."

With Ginger set to close the store, Holly poked her head into the break room to speak with Audrey and Lydia. "Okay. I'm ready to go."

"Guess we'll have to finish the show another time, kiddo," Audrey said.

Holly helped her daughter into her coat and boots, cleaned up the snack debris and then ushered both girls out to her SUV.

The lake gleamed in the sunshine, reflecting the majestic snow-covered mountains as she drove the short distance to Kim's house.

Audrey hopped out. "Thanks for the ride."

"No problem. I'll swing by later with dinner."

"I wonder if my mom would like some Christmas cookies."

"I'm sure she would."

"I have a pretty good peanut butter cookie recipe, the kind where you press a chocolate candy in the middle. Mom loves those. And I bet Uncle Ryan does, too."

By some miracle, Holly had spent several moments without thinking of him but now memories of their kiss crowded back.

She likely would see him later when she dropped off the food, a prospect that almost made her wish she had never suggested it.

Maybe she could drop the food off on the porch, ring the doorbell and run.

With any luck, Audrey or Kim would meet her at the door and she wouldn't even have to talk to Ryan.

Somehow she doubted the likelihood of that.

"I KNOW I already told you this but it bears repeating. You look great, Kim," Ryan commented to his sister as he drove the route from Boise to Shelter Springs.

He meant the words. She had cut her hair since he had seen her last, when she had visited him in San Diego after his accident. She had started to regain weight and no longer looked thin to the point of gaunt. Most obviously, her eyes seemed to reflect an inner light again, something he hadn't realized was missing until it was back.

She smiled, though he didn't miss the way her fingers

twisted together on her lap. "I'm not sure about looking good but I certainly *feel* better than I did a month ago."

"I'm glad."

"It's amazing how much peace you can find after a few weeks of decent food, sleep and therapy. And no booze or pills. I was more than ready for a reset—I just couldn't admit it to myself until the accident."

"Sometimes it takes something drastic to provide clarity."

"That's what my therapist said. I only wish I could have found my way to this place without Diane having to pay the price."

"How are the cravings?"

"Still there. I know they always will be. I'm an addict. I was an addict at fifteen when it was vodka I stole out of Dad's liquor cabinet and I was an addict at boarding school when I started with first marijuana and then the harder stuff. I thought I had put that world behind me after Audrey came along."

"You did."

"Not permanently, apparently. I traded one addiction for another. But I want to fix my life more than I want to take a pill and forget now."

"I'm so proud of all your hard work. I know what a huge sacrifice it's been but you've made amazing progress."

She acknowledged his words with a smile. "I only wish I could have found a way to go through the program without leaving Audrey for a month."

"I believe she will be the first to tell you it was worth it, especially if she can have her mom back."

They were silent for a few moments as the mileposts passed by. Finally, Kim spoke in a small voice. "Do you think Audrey will eventually be able to forgive me?"

He had the feeling Kim had been stewing about that question for longer than the past few moments.

"There's nothing to forgive. She knows everything you did was for her. She might be only thirteen but Audrey is remarkably wise for her age. That's because of you, sis."

She didn't look as if she completely believed him but she nodded and gazed out the windshield at the passing landscape.

"What about you? I dragged you away from everything you had going in your life so you could bail me out. Has it been horrible?"

"Not at all," he said with complete honesty. He had enjoyed his time here far more than he ever expected. "Like I said, Audrey's a great kid and very self-sufficient. She definitely has her shit together. I'm not sure she even needed me around."

"I feel that way sometimes. She's always been mature beyond her years. I didn't have much to do with that."

"I don't think you give yourself enough credit. You've been raising her alone most of her life. I don't think I fully realized what a tough road that must have been until recently."

He had experienced a tiny fraction of what it meant to be the sole responsible adult in a household. He couldn't imagine bearing that load alone for years, as Kim had managed all these years with Audrey and like Holly was doing with Lydia.

"What about Dad and Diane?" she asked. "Have you seen much of them while you've been in the area?"

He thought of his strained relationship with the colonel, their few awkward, uncomfortable interactions.

"A little, here and there."

"How is Diane? I mean, how is she *really*? I tried to talk to Dad whenever I had the chance, which wasn't often. He always assured me Diane is on the mend but I'm not sure if he was telling the truth or trying to sugarcoat it."

"She still has a long road to recovery," he admitted. "But she seems better every time I see her."

"I don't know how I'll ever make it up to her. To everyone. Dad, Diane, Audrey. You."

Ryan glanced over at Kim as they drove past snow-dusted trees that framed the landscape outside the window. He could feel the weight of her guilt like an invisible presence in the car.

"You know," he said, breaking the silence, "it takes guts to face what you've been through. Not everyone would step up and take responsibility the way you have."

Kim's gaze flickered toward him, uncertain. "It doesn't feel like enough," she murmured. "I hurt people, Ryan. Diane may never fully recover. How can that ever be enough?"

"It doesn't erase what happened. But you're doing the hard work now—the work most people would run from. You're owning it. You went to rehab, you're staying sober and you're putting one foot in front of the other. That's more than most people do. And it's the only way forward."

Tears filled her eyes, but she blinked them away. "What if I mess up again?"

"You won't," Ryan said firmly. "You've learned from this. And if you do stumble, you'll get back up. That's what matters. Diane, Dad, Audrey. They don't need you to be perfect. They only need you to keep trying. And that's exactly what you're doing."

"Thanks, Ry. I needed to hear that."

He smiled as he drove past the brick welcome sign at the Shelter Springs town boundary. "I'm glad you were able to make it home for Christmas. And Audrey is over the moon."

"I'm afraid it's going to be a bit of a ramshackle Christmas. Dad invited us for dinner tomorrow night so I don't have to worry about that part of it, but I've done nothing else to get ready. Poor Audrey won't exactly have an unforgettable Christmas."

"She will have exactly what she wants most. Her mom."

When he pulled into the driveway of her small rental house a short time later, her eyes widened.

"Oh. Someone decorated the house. Was that you?"

"With some help," he said gruffly. "Holly and Lydia Moore gave us a hand a few weeks ago. Audrey wanted to make sure you didn't have to worry about anything except enjoying the holidays when you came home."

She sniffled, wiping her eyes with a tissue she pulled from the pocket of her hoodie. "How did I ever get so lucky to have such an amazing daughter and wonderful friends like Holly?"

He only smiled in response. He had hardly put his truck in Park when Audrey flew out of the house and yanked open the passenger door.

"Mom!" she exclaimed.

Laughing and crying, Kim climbed out and wrapped her daughter in a tight embrace. "Oh baby. I missed you so much."

"I'm so glad you're home, Mom. I missed you, too."

"The house looks wonderful. And you decorated the tree!"

"Lydia and I did it," Audrey said. "Holly helped, too. And she and Uncle Ry hung all the lights out here."

"Everything is magical. Thank you for going to all that work."

She was admiring the lights in the bushes and the wreath on the door when a car pulled into the driveway behind his pickup.

Ryan stiffened when he recognized his father's Cadillac SUV. He saw his father in the driver's seat and, to his surprise, Diane in the passenger seat.

That had only begun to register when Doug climbed out and hurried up the porch toward them. To Ryan's shock, his normally stoic father wore his emotions on his features as he reached for Kim and held her in the same kind of tight, almost desperate embrace Kim herself had given Audrey.

"How wonderful that you made it home, Kimmy."

"Thanks, Dad." She hugged him back, her eyes tightly closed. The love between his father and his sister was as clear as a candle glowing in a frosty window, warm and unwavering.

Something hard inside Ryan seemed to shift and settle as he watched them. As a teenager, Kim had been as bitter as he was about the choices their father made. She had been so upset that she had run away, into the arms of a man who had dragged her further into the seedy underbelly of drugs and addiction.

Yet somehow, despite everything, the two of them had managed to heal the rift between them.

Why was it so easy for Kim to forgive? She had every reason to stay angry. More than he did, really. Their father's decisions had pushed her into a downward spiral, and yet here she was, finding solace in his embrace.

He wanted to believe it was as simple as time but he knew better. Time alone didn't heal wounds like that. Forgiveness required something deeper, something he couldn't seem to muster, no matter how hard he tried.

His father's voice, low and steady, carried through the December air as he whispered something to Kim. The sight made Ryan's chest ache. Maybe it wasn't merely time that had healed their relationship. Maybe it was something he had never let himself consider.

The possibility that their father truly *had* changed.

The thought unsettled him. How could he let go of the resentment he had clung to for so long? If he didn't, was he destined to remain on the outside, watching others find the peace he couldn't?

"We should all go in out of the cold," he said, his voice gruff.

The colonel shook his head. "I'm afraid we can't stay long. We just came from physical therapy and Diane is pooped. But we had to come and welcome home our girl."

For the first time, Kim must have realized Diane was still in the passenger seat. She froze for a moment, then made her way to the vehicle.

Diane opened the door before she reached it, holding both hands out to squeeze Kim's, even the one in the cast.

"Oh, Diane," Kim said, both her features and her voice anguished. "I am more sorry than I can ever say."

"Hush." The older woman looked uncharacteristically stern. "It was an accident. You weren't to blame—the other driver was."

"I should never have been behind the wheel. If I hadn't been impaired, I might have been able to avoid the collision."

"And if I hadn't insisted we go Black Friday shopping, we wouldn't have been on the road in the first place."

"And if I hadn't been looking at my phone, I might have done a better job as your backseat driver and warned you the other car wasn't going to stop at the red light," Audrey said, which made both of the older women laugh, defusing the charged emotion of the moment.

"I'm glad you're home, my dear."

"Are you sure you don't want to come inside?" Ryan said. "I was going to order a pizza for dinner."

"That sounds lovely but physical therapy exhausts me, I'm ashamed to say. Right now I just want to go home. We'll see you all tomorrow for Christmas Eve, though. Your dad is planning to grill steaks. I won't take no for an answer."

"Yes. Definitely," Kim said. "I'm looking forward to it."

With hugs for Kim and Audrey and a stiff nod to Ryan, Doug climbed back into the SUV and they backed out of the driveway.

As Ryan fully expected, Kim was beyond thrilled with the

interior decor. "It looks perfect. I can't believe you guys did all this."

"It was really fun, especially with Holly and Lydia helping us. I think Uncle Ry was into it, even though he pretended not to be. He and Holly took forever outside hanging the lights, anyway."

Kim gave him a surprised but speculative look. "Did you?"

"Yeah. They've spent a lot of time together, actually," his busybody niece informed her mother. "Uncle Ryan, tell Mom about your big date with her on Saturday."

He didn't want to think about her, yet he couldn't seem to help it. Their kiss seemed seared into his memory.

"We don't need to get into it now."

"What if we want to?" Kim said, giving him a teasing older-sister sort of look. "You went out with Holly?"

"He took her to a wedding she had to go to. Lydia was the flower girl. Uncle Ryan borrowed some fancy clothes from Dad and looked pretty good."

Kim's interest seemed to sharpen. "A wedding? Was it Kristine Moore's wedding?"

While he would prefer to avoid talking to his sister about Holly, he suddenly realized he needed to let her in on the truth, in case anybody happened to ask her about his supposed relationship with her employer and friend.

"We pretended to be a thing so she wouldn't have to feel awkward around Troy and his family, going to the wedding with only Lydia. We made a deal. I went with her as her plus-one to the wedding and in exchange, she helped me decorate this place for you and Audrey."

She stared at him for a long moment then she began to laugh. "Oh my word. I can't believe you did that. It's priceless!"

He couldn't tell his sister what a mess he had made of

everything. Their fake dating had begun to feel entirely too real. He was only supposed to take her to a wedding, not fall for her.

"This is delicious," Kim said, still grinning. "I can't wait to ask Holly about it when I go back to work after Christmas."

"You can ask her before that," Audrey informed her mom. "She's dropping dinner off for us on her way to that big party at the Shelter Inn tonight."

Holly was coming here? This was the first he had heard about it.

"Oh, it must be the annual potluck," Kim said.

"Right. I remember we went last year. There was so much food. I hung out with my friend Jenny, since her grandma and grandpa live at the Shelter Inn."

"Are you okay if we miss it this year? I'm not sure I'm up for a big party tonight. I'm sorry."

"Totally fine," Audrey assured her mother. "I didn't think you would want to go either, so Holly offered to drop off some of the soup and breadsticks she's taking to the dinner."

Exactly the sort of thoughtfulness he might have expected from Holly. Every day he found something else to admire about her.

"I'm making dessert," Audrey said. "Which reminds me. I have one more batch of peanut butter cookies to put in the oven."

She hurried into the kitchen, leaving him and Kim beside the cheerful Christmas tree.

"I can't believe Holly is bringing dinner. That is so sweet of her," Kim said. "I adore that woman. While I was in rehab, I had time to write down my blessings and Holly is right at the top. She's a dear friend and a wonderful boss. A truly amazing person."

Kim seemed to expect a response from him. How could he possible tell his sister about all the jumbled emotions inside him when he thought of Holly? He wasn't even ready to examine them himself.

"Yes," he finally said. "Amazing."

"It's too bad you were only pretending to be in a relationship. Holly would be perfect for you. And you would be perfect for her."

He stared at her, even as her words filled him with raw yearning. "Wow. Maybe you've been away from reality a little too long. Holly and I are completely the wrong people for each other."

"Why? You deserve someone wonderful in your life and Holly deserves a good man like you. I've been shipping the two of you since the first day I met her."

"You should know better than that," he said, his voice more curt than he intended.

"Why?"

"I really don't want to talk about this right now," he said. Somehow his words only seemed to intrigue his sister.

When the doorbell rang seconds later, his pulse kicked up like he was trying to thread his bird through the eye of a storm on a moonless night.

"I'll get it," Audrey said cheerfully. She pulled open the door where Holly stood holding a large pot of something while Lydia stood at her side cradling a bag in her arms like a baby doll.

"Hi, Holly. Hi, Lydia," Audrey said.

"Hi there. We were just talking about you." Kim sent him an impish grin.

Holly looked disconcerted. "Were you?"

"Yes," Ryan said, rather desperate to steer the conversation away from how right or wrong he and Holly were for each other. "I was telling Kim how helpful you were in decking our halls."

It wasn't a lie. Exactly. They had talked about it a few minutes earlier, before his sister made such a ridiculous claim about them being perfect for each other.

As he had hoped, his words distracted Kim. "Oh, Holly. Thank you for everything. The house is beautiful."

"You're more than welcome. I'm so glad you're home before Christmas."

"So am I. And you brought dinner, too. You're an angel."

Suddenly aware he had left her holding the pot too long, he stepped forward to take it from her. As he reached for it, his hand brushed hers and a spark leaped between them. Her gaze flashed to his and for an instant, he thought he saw an answering awareness there before she turned to hug Kim.

"I have to say, you look terrific."

Kim rolled her eyes. "You're not the only one who has told me that. I've looked in the mirror. If everyone thinks I look good now, I must really have been haggard before."

"You were beautiful then and you're beautiful now," Holly said firmly. Ryan could tell it wasn't an idle compliment, that she meant the words completely.

"I don't know what it is now," she went on. "You seem more . . . content, somehow."

Before Kim could respond, Lydia apparently felt she had been quiet long enough. She held up the bundle in her arm.

"I have breadsticks."

Kim looked at the girl with the same warm smile everyone seemed to give Lydia. "How wonderful. Breadsticks sound perfect. Thank you, Miss Lydia."

"Give them to Kim or Audrey," her mother said. "We need to go or we'll be late for the potluck."

Lydia nodded. "My friends named Hazel and Nora will be there."

"I love those girls," Kim said. "I hope you have a great time playing with them."

"I will," Lydia assured her. "You should come, too."

"Not this year, honey." Kim turned to Holly. "I am sorry to miss the potluck but I don't think I'm quite ready to face everyone yet."

Holly's lovely features softened with compassion and she gave Kim another quick hug. "I completely understand. And so will everyone else. Whenever you're ready, everyone will be thrilled to see you."

"Thanks."

"Also, I wanted to make sure you know you can take all the time off you need after Christmas. I expect that for the next month we will be slow as honey dripping on a cold morning."

"I would like to come back right after Christmas. I need to return to some kind of routine."

"Totally understandable. I'll add you back to the schedule, then. I'll be in touch with details after Christmas."

"I'm thinking about going back to school."

Kim said the words in a rush, as if afraid how they would land with her boss and employer.

"Oh, Kim. I think that's a great idea!"

"I had a lot of time to think about our future. Mine and Audrey's. I love working at Evergreen and Ivy. I hope you know how much. But I've always kind of wanted to be a nurse."

That was the first Ryan had heard that particular dream but somehow he could easily picture Kim in that profession. She was smart, caring and compassionate.

"You would make a wonderful nurse!" Holly said with enthusiasm. "What a great idea. Can you do that from here?"

"One of the counselors at rehab was telling me there's a

program where most of it is online, at least for the first year. I would go one Saturday a month to Boise for the hands-on training and also do some clinical work at the local hospital here."

"That sounds perfect. I'm so excited for you, though I'll miss you at the store when you eventually leave."

"I have a long way to go before that point," Kim said. "It's overwhelming, when I think about it."

"One day at a time," Ryan reminded her, earning a grateful smile.

"Right. I want to enjoy Christmas this year to the fullest."

Holly smiled. "I hope you have a wonderful holiday together."

"Thanks, Hol. And I hope you and Lydia do, too."

His sister's words made him wonder what Holly had decided to do about her ex-husband's request. He wanted to ask but didn't want to bring up the question now, in front of Audrey and Lydia.

It wasn't any of his business, he reminded himself. They were two people brought together by chance in one particular moment of time, whose paths soon would be diverging again. After he returned to San Diego, he likely would never see either Holly or Lydia again.

The thought of leaving Shelter Springs behind, of leaving *them* behind, settled in his chest like a weight he couldn't shake. He had grown to love the sound of Lydia's laughter ringing through a room and the way Holly's eyes lit up when she smiled.

His life without those things, without *them*, seemed suddenly colorless and bleak.

Walking away would be the right thing to do, the smart thing to do.

That didn't make it any easier.

CHAPTER TWENTY-ONE

"SO TELL US EVERYTHING. HOW WAS THE WEDDING?"

"More importantly, how was your date?" McKenna Dodd asked while juggling her two-year-old son, Austin.

Holly really did not want to talk about that night, when she had given her heart irretrievably to a certain sexy helicopter pilot.

"It was nice. Kristine made a beautiful bride, as I knew she would. She and Matt are so in love. It's wonderful to see."

"And your date?" Amanda asked, giving her a searching look.

"You know it wasn't really a date, right? He only took me as a favor."

She could only wish it had been real. Holly felt a bit like Cinderella, given one magical, unforgettable night. Now she had to face the grim reality that no one would be coming around with a glass slipper for her to try on.

"Favor or not, he still seems like a great guy to be your plus-one at a wedding for people he doesn't even know."

Oh, he was. And she had been foolish enough to fall for him.

"He's very kind."

"And gorgeous," Hannah offered. "I'm sure Lieutenant Commander Caldwell looked delicious, all dressed up."

Holly would rather talk about anything else, including the upcoming tax season, than about how gorgeous Ryan had looked at the wedding. She was trying to forget that, with abysmal results.

"Who looked delicious dressed up?" Amanda's grandmother Birdie asked as she walked past on the arm of Griffin Taylor, Amanda's brother and their friend Natalie's husband.

"Holly took a date to Kristine Moore's wedding on Saturday," Amanda said. "The brother of Kim Barnes."

"Oh, he is that lovely man who delivered flowers to me last week. He was a dear. Good for you, Holly. It's about time you put yourself out there again."

Holly had absolutely no desire to put herself *out there*, wherever *out there* was. She had created a disaster out of the single date she had gone on since her divorce, falling head over heels for the man.

"This broccoli salad is delicious," she said, trying again to steer the conversation away from herself. "Who brought it? I definitely need the recipe."

As she hoped, she succeeded in changing the subject as Natalie took credit, claiming the secret was the pepitas. Holly did her best to ignore the searching look her sister gave her. Hannah had asked her several times to spill details about the date and didn't seem content with any of her superficial answers.

The conversation shifted to a new avocado dip recipe McKenna had brought and then on to what people were making for Christmas Eve dinner the next day.

Holly thought she successfully had avoided her sister's probing—until the party was winding down and she found herself alone with her twin. The two of them sat together watching Lydia play happily with McKenna's daughters, Hazel and Nora, who always went out of their way to include Lydia.

"Okay, sis. Spill. Was your date utterly horrible? You don't seem to want to talk about it. Every time I ask, you change the subject. Don't think I haven't noticed."

"That's ridiculous. I have done nothing of the sort. How was your Christmas concert at the nursing home yesterday? I'm sorry I couldn't make it."

"It was fine. You're doing it again. I have to wonder why.

Please tell me our sexy Lieutenant Commander Caldwell wasn't a total ass to you."

"No. Not at all. He was w-wonderful."

To her horror, her voice broke on the word. Afraid that Hannah would see her tumult and insist on digging until she found out the truth, Holly jumped up.

"I think I'll grab another one of those pinwheel cookies. They were delicious. Would you like one?"

Hannah grabbed her arm and held her in place.

"No. I don't want a cookie. I want you to talk to me. What is it, Hol? You haven't been yourself all night. Was it tough to see Troy and Brittany at the wedding?"

At this, a tear did spill out as her sister's question reminded her of the other major stress in her life right now. The one she should be focusing on.

Her entire world felt like it was falling apart right now, which sounded ridiculously melodramatic.

"I'm sorry. I'm just emotional today." This part she could at least talk to her sister about. "Troy and Brittany want Lydia to spend tomorrow night with them at the Moore's."

Hannah's jaw sagged and she looked as indignant as if Holly had just told her all Christmas carols had been outlawed within the boundaries of Shelter Springs.

"No, they do not."

"I'm afraid they do."

"It's Christmas Eve! She should sleep in her own bed. I hope you told them to go straight to hell. And send us a Christmas card when they get there."

She gave a watery sniffle. "No. I texted them both today and told them yes."

Hannah stared. "Why would you do something stupid like that? Text them back right now and tell them you changed your mind. I'll do it, if you won't."

Only her twin sister would call her stupid in one breath and offer to have her back in the next.

She had wrestled with the decision for two days. She still wasn't sure she had made the right choice, but it was done now.

"It's only one night. I'll have her most of Christmas Day."

Hannah looked like she was brimming over with a million objections. She must have seen the distress in Holly's expression, though, because she snapped her mouth shut and after a pause she reached out and hugged her instead.

"Have you told Mom and Dad?" she said after a long moment. "We were all planning to head over to your place Christmas morning to watch our Lyd open her gifts."

"I haven't told them yet," she admitted. She dreaded telling their parents and their brothers. "I'll go to Mom and Dad's on Christmas Eve for dinner, as usual. And you can all still come over to Rose Cottage for breakfast. It will be just like always, except Lydia won't be there."

"What about her gifts from Santa?"

She didn't meet Hannah's gaze. "Since they weren't expecting to have her overnight until I finally agreed this afternoon, they only have a few gifts for her, so Troy asked if I could send along her gifts from Santa."

Hot color rose on Hannah's cheeks. "Let me get this straight. That man not only wants to take your child away from her mother for Christmas Eve and Christmas morning, but now he wants to give her the gifts you bought her as well."

"Not all of them. I'll keep a few so she can open them Christmas afternoon, after she comes home."

Her sister's hands curled into fists.

"That man. I would like to haul him out to the middle of Lake Haven and drop him in. Ash and Micah would help us in a heartbeat."

She had no doubt of that at all. Their older brothers had made no secret that they despised her ex-husband. The two of them were formidable. They would have no qualms enacting any kind of vengeance Holly and Hannah could devise.

She had often thought it was a good thing Troy had moved out of town after their divorce. Either or both of her brothers would probably have ended up in jail for assault, if he hadn't made himself scarce.

"Troy is her father, Han. And he wants to have more of a role in her life. I've spent two years resenting that he basically abandoned her. How can I object now, when he's trying to make amends?"

She never wanted Lydia to become a bargaining chip between them. Her daughter didn't deserve that. With all her other challenges, she had to know both of her parents loved her. Holly couldn't stand in the way of Troy's fumbling efforts to be the father he should have been all along.

That had been the deciding factor. As hard and painful as she found it, Holly knew she had to be the bigger person.

"Oh, honey."

Her sister wrapped her arms around her again and Holly, utterly miserable, despite knowing it was the right choice, choked back a sob.

"You should spend the night at Mom and Dad's," Hannah suggested. "I'll stay there, too. I had planned to stay at my place but screw that. We'll have a slumber party on Christmas Eve and stay up all night, like we used to. Maybe Ash and Micah will want to stay, too."

"That sounds fun but I'm not sure I would be very good company. I was planning to have dinner at Mom and Dad's and then go home."

"I am not going to let you sit alone in your house feeling

sorry for yourself," Hannah announced. "If you don't want to stay with the whole family, I'll stay with you at Rose Cottage. End of discussion."

Holly was so very lucky in her family. She knew without question they all loved and supported her. Unlike Ryan, who had lost his mother young and had been shut out by his grieving father. She hated even thinking about how lonely that boy must have been.

She had to stop thinking about him. Right now, her bigger concern needed to be her daughter and how she would make it through Christmas Eve without her.

"THANKS SO MUCH for this."

Troy beamed at her as he slid the large box filled with most of Lydia's Christmas gifts into the cargo area of his SUV.

It was taking every ounce of willpower she possessed not to grab her daughter, run back into Rose Cottage and lock all the doors and windows to keep him out.

She forced a smile. "You're welcome."

"I've got to tell you, Brittany is over the moon to have both kids for Christmas."

"I'm glad."

Brittany really was trying hard to make Lydia feel part of their family, something Holly could only be grateful for. The alternative would be much worse.

"Next year she can have Christmas Eve with you, for sure. And maybe the year after that, she can come spend a week or so of her holidays with us in Portland."

She would have to brace herself for the time when Troy might want Lydia to spend weeks at a time—or even months, during summer breaks—with him.

Why borrow worry? That was a problem for Future Holly to

deal with. Right now, Today Holly only had to make it through one night without her daughter. She could handle that much, couldn't she?

"I hope you have a wonderful Christmas. Your family party will be tonight, right?"

He nodded. "Kris and Matt are in Hawaii on their honeymoon but everyone else will be there. Stacy and Paul and their kids. A few of the aunts and other extended family members who are still in town from the wedding. Dad is smoking a couple of turkeys. Should be fun."

"It sounds lovely."

She tried to smile, though something in her tone must have alerted him that she was still struggling with their arrangement.

"I'm sure you could join us if you want," he said after a moment. "You know my family loves you. If you want the truth, I sometimes think they love you more than they love me."

"You know that's not true," she said, though she felt a small, petty satisfaction at his disgruntled tone.

"Well, they would welcome you with open arms for Christmas if you want to join us."

She could imagine few things she would enjoy less than Christmas Eve with her ex-husband's family, where she would definitely be out of place.

"I'll be fine," she assured him. "I'm having dinner with my folks. Hannah wants us all to have a slumber party there."

"You should. That sounds fun."

"I don't know. I haven't made up my mind yet. Whatever I decide to do, I'll be back here tomorrow when you bring her back"

"Okay. I'll be in touch with an ETA."

She nodded, then opened the rear door to smile at Lydia, who was strapped into her booster seat, playing with one of her stuffed toys she insisted on bringing along. She vibrated with excitement, though whether that was the usual anticipation of Christmas Eve or from the prospect of staying overnight with her father and stepmother and grandparents, Holly didn't know.

Her heart felt tight and achy. "Goodbye, sweetheart. I'll see you tomorrow, okay?"

Lydia beamed at her, then her brow furrowed. "And Santa will know where I am, right?"

"Definitely. But there's always a chance he might leave a few presents for you here, too. I guess we'll find out tomorrow."

Lydia's eyes almost disappeared with her bright smile. She threw her arms wide and Holly leaned down to embrace her tightly.

"Merry Christmas, Lydi-bug."

"Merry Christmas, Mommy. Love you."

"I love you, too. So much," she said, a tiny hitch in her voice.

"Are you sad?" Lydia asked, studying her carefully. Only recently had Lydia begun to become aware of other people's emotions.

She wanted to offer some glib answer but she wouldn't lie to her daughter about an honest reaction to a complicated situation.

"I'm a little sad for me," she admitted. "But mostly I'm happy that you get to spend Christmas with your daddy and Brit and baby Hudson."

She kissed the top of her head then quickly stepped away, waved one more time and closed the door.

She waited until after Troy backed out of the driveway and headed toward Haven Point before she let a tear drip down.

She quickly brushed it away.

Yes, the holidays could be tough to navigate after a divorce, especially when children were involved. But it was Christmas Eve, a time of joy and peace, and she refused to lose sight of that.

SOMEHOW SHE WAS able to put away her sadness throughout the afternoon and evening.

It simmered under the surface but it was hard to be completely down when engaged in a heated battle of Clue with her family.

"Hannah said the two of you are going to stay over tonight," her mother said during a break in the action. "I'm so glad. It will be lovely to have you. Ash is staying, too. Micah, why don't you join us?"

Her oldest brother leaned back in his chair. "You all are crazy. Why would I stay here in a tiny twin bed where my legs dangle over the edge when I have a perfectly comfortable pillow-top king bed at my place?"

"Because it will be fun! Just like old times, when you all were little and the house was filled with chaos and noise."

"You're not really selling this, Mom," Ash said with a laugh.

"Anyway, I haven't completely made up my mind," Holly said. "I don't think I'm great company right now."

"Don't be silly," Paula said loyally. "You're wonderful company, even when I can tell you're distracted, worried about your girl."

She squeezed her mom's hand. "Thanks. I'm going to make some hot cocoa. Anybody else want some?"

"I do," Micah said.

"Sure," her father said. "If it's not too much trouble."

"We'll just make hot cocoa all around," Paula said. "I'll help."

Her mother jumped up and led the way into the kitchen.

"I can do this, Mom," she said when they were alone and her mother started pulling out ingredients from the cupboard. "You could have stayed and played another game."

"You know me. I'm not a big board game fan, especially when your father and brothers get so competitive. I'd rather sit around and chat. Why don't you rest and let me make the hot cocoa?"

"Because it was my idea."

"I know that. But it's my kitchen."

"Fine. I'll help."

She busied herself pulling out mugs for all of them. When she spotted the spouted cups with the handles that her mother had bought for Lydia, the special cups she loved using at her grandparents' house, Holly had to hitch in a breath, missing her daughter with a fierce ache.

Unfortunately, her mother's hearing was far too sharp.

"Are you all right?" Paula asked gently.

For one absurd moment, Holly wanted to throw her arms around her mother and weep. She knew was being utterly ridiculous. Lydia was six miles away, not on the other side of the planet. And she would see her in less than twenty-four hours.

"I'm fine. I'm just missing my girl, you know? It doesn't really feel like Christmas without her."

"Oh yes. I know all about that." Her mother set aside the cocoa she was measuring and reached for her hand. "Being without your children this time of year can be so hard. Do you remember the first Christmas after you were married?"

"Vaguely," she said with a wry smile. "Yes, I remember. It wasn't that long ago."

"I remember it well because it was my worst Christmas ever."

"Why?"

"Everyone was gone that year. Your brothers decided to go on a backpacking trip together in Australia, remember? And Hannah was dating that dental student whose parents had a ski lodge in Utah so she decided to spend Christmas with them. And then you and Troy went on that Western Caribbean cruise with his family."

She did remember that. While she had enjoyed the cruise, it had been an odd experience to spend the holidays surrounded by a ship full of strangers—okay, and her new in-laws—instead of her own family.

"I remember."

"I have never felt so blue," Paula confided. "I was a mess. I almost didn't want to put up a Christmas tree at all. Or any other decorations, for that matter."

"Oh. I'm sorry, Mom. You should have come on the cruise with us."

"You know how seasick your father gets, even taking a little fishing boat out on calm Lake Haven. He wouldn't have enjoyed an ocean voyage at all."

That was true. Her dad suffered from terrible motion sickness. He could never take them on any amusement park rides when they were young, even the most tame merry-go-round, without being queasy.

"No, we had resolved to have a nice, quiet Christmas that year, but I was completely miserable. Your father finally sat me down and told me I was forgetting that the holidays aren't only about the parties or the big family dinners. They are about taking time to savor each moment and make cherished memories, even if you can't always be with everyone you love."

"You're right. I'm being ridiculous. I'm here with my family, all of us together. How rare is that these days, with everyone going their separate directions?"

"You're right about all of that, except one thing. You're not being ridiculous at all. I don't think that. You're a mother who misses her child. It's completely understandable. But as much as we love our children, we can't always be the center of their worlds. Lydia has a father, a stepmother and a baby brother. They love her too and need the chance to create their own memories together with her."

She squeezed her mother's hands. "You're right. As always."

Paula snorted. "I should record you saying that and play it back for your father whenever he happens to forget."

She smiled, mostly because she knew her father adored his wife. No matter what else might be going on in their lives, David Goodwin never let a day go by without making sure Paula felt cherished.

"Do you mind finishing the cocoa without me? I need to run home for a moment," she said.

Her mother looked confused and a little concerned. "Now? Why?"

"I need to grab my pajamas. I guess we're having a Christmas Eve slumber party."

CHAPTER TWENTY-TWO

RYAN COULDN'T REMEMBER THE LAST TIME HE HAD SPENT Christmas with his father.

He had visited Kim a few times over the holidays when she was still living in the Las Vegas area. If he knew Douglas would also be there, he had purposely stayed away, making some excuse about not being able to score enough leave.

He had let the colonel have far too much control over his own holiday celebrations.

Now he stood on the covered deck of his sister's house, bundled up against the cold and making stilted small talk with the man while looking out at a softly falling snow in the moonlight and the twinkling of neighboring Christmas lights reflecting on the lake.

Originally the plan had been to eat Christmas Eve dinner at his father and Diane's place in Haven Point. But Kim had been unusually obstinate about her desire to host dinner for the family at her own small—albeit beautifully decorated—house.

"I would love to have it here, if you think Diane can make it up my steps," she had told their father that morning with an unusual determination in her voice. "I don't want you to have to do anything."

She spoke to Doug by phone but had put the call on speaker, as her hands were busy rolling out sugar cookies. That meant Ryan had no choice but to hear the whole conversation.

"What about the steaks?" Doug had asked after a pause. "Can I still grill those? I've already bought them."

"Sure. That would be great and I have a grill here you can use. I want to do everything else, though. Salad, sides, dessert. All of it. I want to do this for everyone."

"I can make a salad or something," their father had said.

"I won't tell you no, but it's totally optional. You know that feeding people is my love language. The whole time I was in rehab, I kept dreaming about having Christmas Eve here in my house. I owe everyone in the family so much. I want to do this. Please, Dad."

After a quick conference with his wife in the background, their father had agreed.

Ryan had been sorely tempted to load up his gear and head back to San Diego tonight, but he knew that would have hurt his sister and niece. And, yes, maybe his father and stepmother, too.

So now he stood on the porch with Doug, talking about the weather and a TV show Doug and Diane were binging and the bowl games they each wanted to catch over the holidays.

He would rather be in the kitchen helping his sister but she had sent him out here, first to light the propane patio heater and then to help his father with the steaks.

He wasn't sure if she was trying to get rid of him so she could chat with Audrey and Diane without him or because she wanted to force him to talk to their father. He suspected the latter.

"Your sister looks good, doesn't she?" the colonel said as he turned the steaks one last time.

He was glad Kim hadn't heard their father, as she was becoming heartily sick of that observation from those who loved her.

"She really does. But then, I hadn't seen her in several months except for the occasional video call."

"I did see her regularly. I don't know how I completely missed all the signs that she was struggling with addiction again."

"Seems like she had become pretty good at masking."

The colonel sighed. "If I had been paying more attention, I might have seen that, but I thought she was doing fine. Not like she was the first time she went through rehab, after that weasel of a husband went to jail. I thought that part of her life was over. I should have paid more attention to the signs and made her get help earlier."

He could feel his jaw clench and forced his muscles to relax. "Kim is an adult," he said, his voice clipped. "You can't *make* her do anything. You couldn't do it when she was a teenager after Mom died and you certainly can't do it now."

"Let me rephrase. If I had noticed she was struggling, I could have strongly encouraged her to get help."

Ryan's nails bit into his palms as he fought to keep his temper in check. He wasn't sure why he was so angry, but it felt as if all the years of resentment and bitterness had coalesced to this moment.

"Strongly encouraged her?" he echoed, his tone sharp. "You mean the way you *strongly encouraged* both of us to bottle up our grief after Mom died?"

The colonel stiffened, a sudden bleak look in his eyes, but Ryan didn't stop. The dam had broken.

"You were so busy playing the stoic, perfect officer that you didn't see what was right in front of you. That we were broken. And now you want to act like you could have fixed everything with a few words of fatherly advice?"

"I never said that."

"You don't get to rewrite history to make yourself feel better about how you let us down. And you sure as hell don't get to stand here now and pretend this is just another problem you could have *strongly encouraged* away."

"I can't win with you," his father said, his tone resigned. "No matter what I say, it's always the wrong thing."

He glared. "You make me sound like some irrational hot-head, unreasonably angry about my childhood and ready to take offense at the slightest thing."

"I don't think you're irrational at all," Doug said quietly. "Or unreasonable, for that matter. Everything you said is absolutely true."

He stared at his father, certain he must have misheard. The colonel never admitted he was wrong about a single damn thing. He had always acted as if no other opinion mattered but his own.

"You have every right to be angry with me," Doug said softly.

"I don't need your permission for that, either."

He almost stalked into the house but that really would make him feel exactly like that moody, unreasonable teenager so he forced himself to stand on the deck, sipping his beer and gazing out at the night sky, where the clouds broke enough for a few stars to peek out.

After a long moment, his father spoke in a voice Ryan had never heard before, low and ragged and filled with pain.

"Your mother was the glue that held every piece of me together. From the moment I met her, I loved her with all my soul. When she died, I was beyond broken. I felt like I had been shattered into a hundred jagged pieces. Like somebody had just dropped a twenty-two-hundred-pound cruise missile into our world."

He swallowed. "It wasn't like it was a shock, Dad. We knew it was coming for three months, after her cancer stopped responding to treatment."

"Even until the end, I couldn't believe it would really happen. Surely God wouldn't take her away from us when we needed her so much."

"Is that why you couldn't even be bothered to take a leave of absence as she lay dying?" he asked, his voice harsh.

His father pressed his lips together, looking up at those few stars as stray snowflakes settled in his hair, on his shoulders.

"I made sure to be there the final few days. But when the doctors told her there was nothing more they could do, your mom and I talked about it. She thought it would be better for me to take my leave after she died, so I could be there for you and Kim. Among my many regrets about how I handled that time, I wish I hadn't listened to her."

He let out another ragged sigh. "I was never good at the parenting thing. That was always your mom's specialty. I knew how to manage the people under my command but a fifteen-year-old girl and thirteen-year-old boy who were grieving their mother? No. You scared the hell out of me."

"What was so scary about two children who needed the only parent they had left to step up and be a father?"

He had a hard time believing his father could ever be afraid of anything. This was a man who had been highly decorated for bravery.

"Being a single father felt completely outside my skill set. Especially when Kim was so rebellious and you basically shut down and wouldn't talk to me. I should have asked for help. Hired someone. I was too proud. Too certain that all you both needed was to get back into a solid routine."

He remembered that routine only too well. Lights out by nine, no exceptions. Up at six, chores and homework done without argument.

"We weren't new recruits, Dad. We were kids."

Doug nodded, his features solemn. "I recognize that now. At the time, I could only go by what I learned about leadership in the military. When your grades started to slip and Kim started to run wild, I did the only thing that made sense to me at the time."

"Sent me to military school and Kim to a boarding school where she was miserable. So miserable that she ran away with the first guy who came along."

Doug looked fully at him and Ryan was stunned to see his father's eyes were watery. The man who hadn't cried at his wife's graveside looked as if he was fighting back tears here on a moonlit patio on a snowy Christmas Eve, more than twenty years later.

"I am more sorry than I can ever say, son. For all of it. From the time your mom was diagnosed until she died, I made mistake after mistake. I wish I could go back and change the decisions I made back then. I can't. None of us can. I can only go forward, trying my best to be the father and grandfather now that I should have been back then."

Ryan stared at him, the words echoing in the silence between them. For years, he had clung to his anger, fed by memory after memory of his father's coldness, his inability—or refusal—to show any hint of vulnerability.

One memory surfaced now, spiky and painful. A twelve-year-old boy standing in his father's office, trying to hold back tears.

He had been desperately seeking reassurance, some acknowledgment that things would be okay after his mom's latest grim prognosis. But the colonel, seated behind his desk, had barely looked up from his paperwork.

"We don't have time to feel sorry for ourselves, Ryan. You need to be strong, for Kim and your mother."

And just like that, the conversation had ended, leaving Ryan feeling smaller than ever.

He swallowed hard, the sting of that moment still fresh after all these years. But as he looked at his father now, he didn't see the distant man behind the desk. He saw someone older, more vulnerable, trying in his own flawed way to make amends.

Maybe it wasn't enough. Maybe it never would be. But forgiveness wasn't about erasing the past. It was about choosing to stop letting it hold you captive.

"I'm not asking you to forgive me for the choices I made back then," his father said, almost as if he knew what was running through Ryan's thoughts. "I would only ask you to give me a chance to see if we can build a better relationship now, whatever that might look like."

He had no idea how to answer. A few weeks ago, he might have told his father off, expressing all the years of anger and bitterness.

Things felt . . . different now.

Being here in Shelter Springs had softened something inside Ryan.

Was it possible for them to move past the wounds of the past? Did he even want to try?

"I know I haven't said it nearly enough but I love you," the colonel said into his continued silence. "I have been proud to be your father every single day of your life."

How could he simply release all of that resentment and pain and move forward as if none of it mattered?

He thought of Holly at the wedding of her ex-husband's sister. Troy had cheated on her, had walked away from her and their gift of a child and married his mistress.

Somehow, despite everything, Holly had managed to smile and chat with his family and do her best to make Kristine's wedding joy-filled and memorable.

More than that, she had handed over her daughter to her ex-husband so that Lydia could spend Christmas with her father.

She was amazing and brave and resilient. In contrast, he felt shriveled up inside with old resentment and pain.

His father wanted to forge a new relationship. Ryan had no idea what that would look like but he suddenly realized it didn't matter. Christmas was a time of forgiveness and healing.

What had his anger accomplished anyway? *Ryan* was the

one who had suffered because of it. He was the one who had deprived himself of a closer connection with his family.

His father had moved on. He had met and married Diane, had moved here and started a flight business so that he could enjoy semiretirement with the woman he loved in a small mountain town beside a lake.

Doug had done the hard work to repair his relationship with Kim, healing it enough that Ryan's sister had moved here for a new start and to be closer to their father and stepmother.

Ryan was the one on the outside now. The one who had spent virtually every holiday of his adulthood either working or on his own.

He needed his family, with all their scars and imperfections.

These past weeks here in Shelter Springs had showed him the importance of connections. Of family. Of community.

He didn't want to be on the outside anymore.

At his continued silence, his father finally looked away. "These steaks need another five minutes. You don't have to stay out here in the cold."

"I'm not cold," he said. It was true, despite the softly falling snow and the winter wind coming off the lake. Something inside him had begun to thaw, some hard kernel of ice that had built up inside him layer by layer since his mother died.

He smiled. "How often do I get the chance to talk to my dad on a beautiful snowy Christmas Eve?"

His father gave him a long, steady look and something passed between them. Nothing more needed to be said.

Doug's smile was warm and filled with joy. His father looked happier than Ryan had seen him in years.

As he stood beside his father in the fragile peace of a snowy Christmas Eve, Ryan felt as if he had set down a heavy weight he hadn't realized he had been carrying for years.

—

CHAPTER TWENTY-THREE

THIS WAS A GOOD IDEA.

Holly actually felt happy for the first time all day as she stuffed some pajamas into her favorite tote bag.

Spending time with her family was exactly what she had needed to lift her sagging spirits, to remind her that she came from strong people who had endured things she couldn't even imagine.

Both of her parents had come from broken, abusive homes and both had managed to stop the pattern with their own family, helping their children become decent, caring humans.

Were they perfect parents? No. But she had never for one single moment doubted that she was loved and she knew each of her siblings would say the same.

She was packing a few basic toiletries when the doorbell rang.

Who would be coming for a visit on Christmas Eve? All of her neighbors had already delivered small gifts and her close friends were enjoying Christmas with their own families.

She zipped up her bag and carried it down to the living room before she looked through the window next to the door.

To her complete astonishment, Ryan stood on her porch holding a couple of gift bags.

She opened the door. "Ryan! What are you doing here?"

He held up the gift bags. "I had a few little things I wanted to give you and Lydia. It's not much. Just a couple of books I thought you both might like. I planned to leave them on your porch since I thought you would still be at your folks' place, but then I saw your light."

She was deeply touched, not only that he had bought gifts

for them but that he had traipsed through the snow to deliver them.

"I decided to stay overnight there. We're all staying, except maybe Micah. He's our oldest brother and he likes his creature comforts. I only came home to grab a few things."

She looked up and down the street in vain for a vehicle. "How did you get here? Don't tell me. You parachuted from Santa's sleigh."

He smiled and she couldn't seem to look away. Something seemed different about him. He seemed . . . lighter, somehow. She couldn't explain it.

"Nothing so exciting, I'm afraid. I needed some exercise after our huge dinner so I decided to take a walk. It's a beautiful night and you're only a few blocks from Kim's place."

It *was* a lovely night. She was ashamed that she had been so caught up in missing her daughter that she hadn't paid nearly enough attention.

Christmas lights twinkled along the eaves of neighboring houses, their warm glow reflecting off the fresh snowflakes drifting lazily from the sky. It was the kind of night that felt like magic, the kind she used to dream about as a little girl. Peaceful, perfect and full of hope.

"Come in," she said. Even as she issued the invitation she questioned the wisdom of it. She had already fallen hard for him and her feelings only deepened with every moment she spent with him.

"Kim fixed dinner? Was it only the three of you?"

He shook snow off his coat and stamped his boots. "Dad and Diane came, too."

"Is that why you felt the need to take a walk on a snowy night? You needed an excuse to escape because your dad was there?"

"Actually, no. The opposite. Things are . . . better between us."

"Oh, Ryan. I'm so glad!"

"We cleared the air a little. It's going to take me time to release all that pent-up bitterness, but I'm working on it."

She was genuinely delighted to hear that. "I'm happy for both of you. Clearly, your father wants a better relationship with you."

"We still have a lot of work to do."

"You can't expect everything to be fixed after one good, honest conversation between you."

"Exactly. But at least we are talking. That's a big step, right?"

"Huge." She smiled. "Does that mean you might be spending more time here at Lake Haven?"

He angled his head, giving her a searching look. "What would you think about that? If I were to spend more time in the area?"

She blinked. "What does it matter what I think?"

Ryan was quiet for a moment, his gaze steady. The air between them felt taut, as if the slightest movement might snap it. Then, his voice, low and rough, broke the silence. "It matters. *You* matter. I can't stop thinking about you, Holly," he said.

Her breath caught and she could feel her pulse hammering in her ears.

Before she could respond, before she could *think*, he stepped closer, his hand brushing her cheek, his touch warm against the cool air lingering in the doorway.

His lips found hers, soft and insistent, and the quiet night outside seemed to vanish, leaving only the two of them in the golden glow of the Christmas lights on her tree.

Ryan's kiss was everything she hadn't let herself admit she wanted: warm, certain and full of an aching tenderness.

Her hands found their way to his shoulders, her fingers

curling against the fabric of his shirt, holding him closer as her thoughts swirled.

A slumber party with her family might have been fun. A slumber party with *Ryan* suddenly seemed a far better way to spend Christmas Eve.

She was trying to remind herself of all the reasons that wasn't a good idea when the shrill ring of her phone cut through their embrace, its sharp tone jolting them apart.

Holly blinked, her breath unsteady, as the moment shattered around them like a glass ornament tossed at a wall.

"Can you ignore it?"

She shook her head, feeling incapable of stringing two coherent thoughts together. "That's Troy's ringtone. Lydia might be homesick."

It was all she could manage. She grabbed her phone off the table in the entryway with fingers that trembled.

"Hello?"

The voice on the other end wasn't her ex-husband or her daughter. It was Brittany and she only said Holly's name before giving a panicked-sounding sob.

Fear clutched at her. "Brittany? What is it? What's wrong?" Holly asked.

The other woman didn't answer for a long, unbearable moment as she seemed to be trying to control her sobs.

"I'm so sorry. I don't know how but . . . but Lydia is missing."

Icy fingers crawled up her spine. "Missing? What are you talking about?"

"I'm not a hundred percent sure what happened. I was feeding Hudson and putting him down to sleep."

"Tell me what you *do* know," she ordered harshly when Brittany's voice trailed off into another sob.

The other woman seemed to be trying to pull herself together. If Holly had been in the same room with her, she would have been more than happy to slap her if necessary, in order to yank her back to the moment. Instead, she could do nothing but wait in an agony of worry.

"The kids were all down watching a movie while everyone else was playing a game upstairs in the dining room," she said after a strangled pause while Holly's nerves stretched to the breaking point.

"At some point, Lydia must have . . . must have come upstairs. Nobody saw her leave but . . . somehow she did. When her cousin came up to get a drink, she was surprised to see Lydia wasn't in with the adults. That's where the other kids thought she had gone."

"But she hadn't."

"No," Brittany wailed. "Troy said he hadn't seen her since she went down to watch the movie."

Holly felt like she might be sick. How was it possible to go from the magic and wonder of Ryan's kiss to this heartrending fear in the space of a heartbeat?

"She has to be there. Have you looked in all the rooms? Maybe she's hiding."

"We've looked everywhere. Under the beds and in all the closets. The garage. Everywhere. We've all been searching for the past fifteen minutes. She's not here!"

She paused and when she spoke, her words chilled Holly to the bone. "Holly. Her coat is missing."

Dear God. It was late December, frigid, snowing. And the Moores lived on the shores of Lake Haven. If Lydia had gone outside, anything could have happened to her. A hundred horrible scenarios, each worse than the one before, played out in her mind.

How could this be happening? How could they have let

her out of their sight for an instant? Every five-year-old child needed supervision and Lydia was a five-year-old with developmental delays. She couldn't be left alone.

"Susan and Norm have called the police," Brittany went on in a rushed voice. "An officer is here now. Troy didn't want to tell you yet, not until we know more, but I . . . I thought you needed to be told."

"Thank you for that." She wasn't quite ready to completely forgive Brittany for having an affair with a married man but she was grateful for this at least, that she had gone with her instincts and reached out to Holly.

Right now, nothing else mattered but Lydia.

"I'll be there as fast as I can drive to Haven Point."

"You don't have to come. There's nothing you can do, really."

"I'll be there," she said, ending the call and rushing for her boots.

"What happened?"

She had almost forgotten Ryan's presence. "I . . . I have to go. Lydia's missing. Her coat is missing, too. I have to . . ."

Lightheaded suddenly from the shock and fear, she started to sway. He grabbed her, his strength the only solid thing in her world right now.

"I'm sure she didn't go far. We'll find her. I'll drive you to the Moore house and on the way I'll call my dad. He can meet me at his hangar and we can take his bird up to look."

She nodded, feverishly wishing this were all a bad dream and she could wake up back in his arms, worrying about nothing but a broken heart.

—

CHAPTER TWENTY-FOUR

LATER, HE HAD NO SOLID MEMORY OF THE DRIVE BETWEEN Shelter Springs and Haven Point. He knew he broke several traffic laws but he didn't give a damn.

All he could think about was that poor little girl, alone and defenseless on a snowy December night, and all the horrible things that might have happened to her.

"Where could she have gone?" Holly said as they approached the Haven Point town limits. "None of this makes sense. She's never done *anything* like this before. Why would she go out into the cold in the middle of a Christmas party?"

He had no good answer to that and could only squeeze her hand.

"We'll find her," he vowed.

"You don't know that. Children disappear all the time."

"She can't have gotten far."

"Unless someone took her."

He hadn't even made space in his thoughts for that kind of dark scenario. Holly obviously had. She hadn't stopped shaking since that damn phone call. She was falling apart and he hated that he had no way to help her through this.

"Does she know anyone else in Haven Point? Any of the Moore neighbors?"

"I don't think so." She hesitated. "She did make friends with a little boy at the wedding. Remember, she danced with him."

He vaguely recalled Lydia taking to several different children at the reception. She was a social kid, apparently, who loved to make new friends.

"Maybe she went there. Any idea where he lives?"

"No. I don't even know his name. I'm not sure Lydia does. How would she possibly know where he lives? She barely knows her own address, and only because I've drilled it into her a hundred times. It doesn't make any sense that she would leave in the middle of a family party to look for a boy she barely knows."

As he drove past the park where he had encountered Holly and Lydia and walked through the light displays, he remembered the little girl's unalloyed delight there.

He suddenly braked, filled with the unwavering conviction they should look there.

He wasn't sure where the idea came from or why it was so strong. Later, he thought perhaps Lydia had a fleet of guardian angels who had planted it in his brain.

"What about here?" He gestured toward the park as they approached the parking lot.

Holly looked at the park, the vibrant colors reflecting on her features through the window.

"She loved our visit there. On the day of the wedding we drove past during the daytime and she begged me to stop. Obviously we couldn't, as we had somewhere else to be."

"What do you think? Since we're here, should we take a look? Or would we be better off hurrying to the Moore house to join the official search? Your choice."

Her features looked taut with indecision and fear. "Let's check," she finally said. "It's not a very big park. It shouldn't take more than five minutes to cover it, with both of us looking. We might be wasting our time but I would rather look now so we can rule it out."

"I think you're right," he said. He pulled into the empty parking lot. As busy as it had been the night he and Audrey had stopped, Ryan might have expected a little more activity at the park on Christmas Eve. Hers was the only vehicle in the parking lot.

"This might be a waste of time and energy. Do you want to wait here?" he asked, though he was certain before the words were out that he knew the answer.

As he expected, she threw him a glare, already shoving open her door.

"Okay. Let's split up to cover more ground. I'll go right. You go left."

She nodded and rushed off in the opposite direction, yelling her daughter's name into the wind.

The cold bit at Ryan's face as he jogged down the path, his breath clouding in the frigid air.

How long might it take for a child to die of exposure in these weather conditions?

He didn't want to even think about it.

The park stretched out before him, silent and still, the vibrant glow of the Christmas lights casting long, lonely shadows across the snow-covered ground. The wind moaning in the treetops and the sound of his footsteps, muffled by the snow, were the only noises breaking the eerie quiet. He scanned the emptiness around him, the usual holiday cheer replaced by a gnawing sense of dread.

Where was Lydia?

She was only five. So small. Too small to be out here alone. His chest tightened as he imagined her wandering these paths. She had been mesmerized by that enormous Christmas tree. Had she come back to see it?

"Lydia!" he shouted, his voice echoing in the stillness, but there was no sound in reply but the wind.

He pushed forward, his heart thundering in his chest, the snow crunching beneath his boots. His breath burned in his throat as the worst scenarios began to claw their way into his mind. What if she'd gotten lost? What if she'd fallen into the water? What if she was hurt somewhere? What if someone had . . . ?

No. He couldn't go there.

He turned sharply toward the center of the park, where the towering tree stood like a beacon against the dark sky.

He sprinted toward it, his pulse hammering in his ears, praying with everything he had that he would find her.

As he yelled her name again, he thought he saw something move, a small pink blur.

"Lydia!" he called again, trying to sharpen his gaze. The blur moved toward him and a vast, soul-deep relief surged through him when he saw it was a small girl wearing a pink parka and a purple beanie with two little pompoms.

"Lydia!" he shouted.

"Hi, Ryan," she said as he drew closer, as if they had bumped into each other at the grocery store. He scooped her up in his arms and finally saw she had tear tracks on her cheeks.

"She's here," he yelled out in the direction where Holly had headed.

She likely wouldn't be able to hear him over the wind so he called her quickly as he carried Lydia back toward Holly's SUV.

"She's here," he said in a rush when Holly answered. "I found her by the big tree. I'm taking her to your car to warm up."

She sobbed out her relief. "Oh thank God. I'll meet you there."

"Is my mommy mad?" Lydia asked, looking confused and scared.

"Everyone has been looking for you, honey. You scared everyone," he answered. "Why did you leave the party?"

"The big tree was pretty. I wanted to see it. But then I got scared and cold and wanted my mommy."

"She's here. She'll be so happy to see you.

He emerged from the path just as Holly raced toward him from the other direction. She grabbed her daughter out of his arms and wrapped her arms tightly around her, as if afraid to let her go.

"You're here. Oh, Lydia. Thank heavens you're safe. I was so scared."

"Mommies don't get scared."

"They absolutely do," Holly said, tears rolling down her cheeks.

He hugged both of them tightly, wondering how he would possibly be able to leave them.

—

CHAPTER TWENTY-FIVE

HOLLY DIDN'T WANT TO MOVE, TO THINK. EVEN AS THE COLD seeped into her boots and snow settled on her hair, she couldn't seem to let go of Lydia.

Her gift.

She had come so close to losing her.

Lydia could have been hit by a car on the darkened streets. She could have slipped into a snowbank or fallen into the river or been attacked by a mountain lion.

Holly had always considered her child a miracle but now that word held an even deeper meaning.

She was filled with blinding joy that they had found her. *He* had found Lydia. If Ryan hadn't acted on instinct and suggested they stop here, it might have been hours before anyone thought to check the park.

"We should let Lydia's dad and his family know we found her so they can call off the search and let people go back to enjoying Christmas Eve," Ryan suggested.

Hot protests rose in her throat but she swallowed them down. He was right, though one part of her wanted Troy to suffer as long as possible. If he had been paying attention to their daughter, none of this would have happened.

That was unnecessarily cruel, though. He was no doubt as sick with fear as she had been.

"Yes. You're right."

"We should also head to your SUV so we can turn on the heater and warm her up. I'll carry her. You can call Troy on the way."

Though she didn't want to relinquish her child for a moment, she knew her daughter would be safe with Ryan.

With great reluctance, she handed Lydia over to him. Her daughter beamed her generous smile and threw her arms around his neck. He squeezed her in return, looking humbled and gratified by her trust and clear affection.

He carried her toward the vehicle, the two of them looking so right together it made her heart hurt.

Lydia would be as heartbroken as Holly when he returned to San Diego.

That was a worry for another day. Right now, she wanted to focus on the miracle of having her daughter with her, safe and whole.

With fingers that trembled from both the cold and the emotional trauma of the past half hour, she pulled out her phone and called Troy's number.

"Where are you?" he demanded. "Brittany told me she called and you were on the way. I thought you would be here by now."

He sounded as frantic as she had been.

"We're at Spruce Creek Park."

"Why?"

"Ryan had a hunch and it paid off. We found her. She's safe, Troy."

He uttered the same relieved words she did, both an exclamation of relief and a prayer of gratitude. "How did she get clear over there?"

"I guess she walked. It's only a block or so from your parents' house. She wanted to see the big Christmas tree again, apparently. Please tell everyone she's safe and we're on our way."

She heard him yell the news to his family and loud exclamation of relief from what sounded like dozens of people.

"We'll see you soon," she said, even as some part of her wanted to load up her child into her car and drive her home to Shelter Springs.

They didn't have her booster seat, as Holly had given it to Troy to use. She had to be content with securing her in the back seat with only a seat belt.

Not wanting to let her daughter out of her sight, even for a second, she slid into the back seat with her.

Moments later, before the heater even had time to warm the interior of the vehicle, Ryan was following her directions to the Moore house and pulling into their driveway.

Dozens of people—all of Troy's family—waited for them in the driveway. As soon as she unlatched her daughter's seat belt and helped her out of the vehicle, a huge resounding cheer rose from the crowd.

Lydia looked startled and more than a little confused at all the attention. Troy rushed toward them and scooped her up in his arms, much as Holly had done. He buried his face in Lydia's neck.

"I'm sorry. I'm so sorry, baby."

She blinked at him. "Why, Daddy?"

"I should have been paying more attention to where you were. But you can't run off like that. You scared everyone."

Troy was actually crying. Tears at the corner of his eyes reflected the Christmas lights from his parents' house. Seeing his reaction, Holly's anger drained away like snow melting under the first warm rays of spring.

Her ex-husband loved their child. He might not be as easy or comfortable around her as Holly would like, or as cognizant of the challenges ahead of her. He still loved her and wanted the world for her, the same as Holly did.

"You found her. Thank you. I've never been so terrified in my life. I would never have thought of the park. She asked me earlier if we could go see the big Christmas tree but I didn't know which one she meant."

He could have asked her. Lydia was very good at communicating her needs and wants, as long as someone was patient and calm.

Her grandparents hurried through the crowd of people. "Oh, honey. I'm so glad you're safe," Susan said. She was crying as well, which touched Holly.

Like Lydia's father, the Moore family didn't always know the best way to support her with all her challenges, but they loved her and were trying.

"Let's go inside where it's warm. Now that we have her back, we don't have to stand out here in the snow," Norm said gruffly.

"I don't know." Norm's sister Nadine looked up at the night sky and the softly swirling snowflakes. "Now that we know she's safe, it's kind of magical out here, isn't it? With the stars and the snow and the Christmas lights."

They all seemed to appreciate anew the beauty of this Christmas Eve. A hush fell over the family as they looked around, taking in the surrounding mountains and the tall evergreen trees.

Holly wasn't sure who started singing "Silent Night," possibly Troy's grandmother Nona. But soon everyone else joined in, a family united in gratitude that spanned generations.

Even a woman she didn't know in the Haven Point Police Department uniform sang along.

When they reached the line about "all is calm, all is bright," Holly felt more tears spill out. The words had never resonated so hard in her heart.

"Can I have some hot chocolate?" Lydia finally said when the song ended.

"You can have all the hot chocolate you want," Susan promised her. Lydia's grandfather took her hand and they led the way into their home.

Ryan, she suddenly noticed, stood nearby, slightly on the fringe of the group but still offering his silent support.

Troy pulled her aside as most of his family members returned to the house, though a few seemed to want to prolong the moment and stayed outside.

"I am so very sorry, Hol. I'm an idiot. I know Lydia needs to be watched more carefully than other children but I got distracted by the game we were playing and thought she was doing fine with her cousins. I should have made sure."

This self-flagellation seemed a huge step for a man who never liked to admit he was wrong.

"We found her. That's the important thing."

His jaw worked as he looked between her and Ryan. "Look, if you want to take her home to have Christmas Eve with you, I completely understand. All the things you sent her from Santa are still boxed up. We could load them into the back of your SUV along with her other things and you could head back to Shelter Springs. Everyone would understand."

Oh, it was tempting. Some part of her still wanted to grab Lydia, pack her into her car and never allow visitation with her father again.

She couldn't.

He had made a mistake. She certainly made plenty as Lydia's mother. She wasn't perfect. No parent was. What mattered most was that Troy was trying. After this night and the trauma of losing track of his child, somehow Holly suspected Troy would be hypervigilant now.

She shook her head and managed a smile. "No. We can stick with the plan. You're all set to have her here and she's still excited to spend the night with you and Brittany."

"Are you sure?"

She gave a short laugh. "Not really. When can we ever be

a hundred percent sure about anything? But somehow it feels right."

She certainly hadn't been sure about marrying him but she had done it anyway. That marriage might have been the biggest mistake of her life, but out of that failure had come the most priceless gift imaginable.

Yes, if she had given in to her doubts and not married him, she wouldn't have had to go through the pain and loss of their divorce.

But she also wouldn't have the indescribable joy of being Lydia's mom.

"Merry Christmas, Troy."

He hugged her. Brittany, who had remained in the background throughout their conversation, stepped forward to hug her, too.

"Thank you. We will take better care of her, I promise," she said.

"I'm sure you will. I'll just go say goodbye."

When she went inside, she found Lydia holding court in the kitchen, wrapped in a blanket and happily enjoying a sugar cookie and a mug of cocoa.

"I'm going home now, honey."

"You're not going to sleep over, too?"

She shook her head. "You will have so much fun with your daddy and Brit and Hudson. Merry Christmas, honey. I love you. Don't leave on your own like that again, okay? Promise me."

"I promise, Mommy."

She hugged her daughter tightly, said goodbye to all the Moores and walked outside.

She found Ryan still standing in the driveway, looking completely comfortable as he chatted with two of the aunts, who were bundled up against the cold.

Love for him burned through her like a crackling fire on a cold night, warming all the frozen places inside her.

"Everything good?" he asked.

Not really. You are going to leave my heart in a hundred little pieces.

She forced a smile. "Yes. I'm ready to head back to Shelter Springs whenever you are."

He looked surprised. "You're not taking Lydia home with you? I thought for sure you wouldn't want her to stay here without you, after everything that happened."

"She is still excited about spending Christmas Eve with her father and his family. I don't want to take that away from her."

She could tell he disagreed. He opened his mouth but after a long moment, he closed it again, pressing his lips together as if to hold back the words. Instead, he held open the passenger door of her SUV then went around to the driver's side.

While this was her vehicle, she didn't mind him taking charge and driving them back to Shelter Springs, as he had done on their panicked way here. She found comfort, actually, that he seemed to want to take care of her.

"You are amazing, Holly Moore," he said as he backed out of the driveway and turned onto the lakeside drive leading toward home.

"Ha. I'm not. You know I'm not. When I found out Lydia was missing, I was a complete wreck."

"So was I. And I'm not her mom."

She found comfort in that as well, in knowing he cared about her daughter—and about *her*—enough to immediately spring into action as he had.

Suddenly exhausted by the stress of the evening, she leaned back against the seat. To her shock, Ryan reached out and folded his fingers around hers. He didn't let go as he contin-ued to drive through the night while the sound of Christmas music played on the radio and a deep sense of peace settled over her like a warm quilt, soft and all-encompassing.

Somehow she must have dozed off at some point in the drive, or maybe her body only needed a reset after the stressful evening. When she sensed cessation of movement, she opened her eyes and was shocked to see they were in the driveway of Rose Cottage.

Her Christmas tree gleamed a welcome in the window.

"I can take you to Kim's so you don't have to walk home," she said, remembering she had offered the same thing the night of the wedding, which seemed a hundred years ago.

"I don't mind walking. While we were still at the Moore house, I called my dad and told him I didn't need the helo after all and that Lydia had been found. I told him to tell Kim I would be home later."

"I need to call my family, too. They didn't even know Lydia was missing. When I never came back to their house, as I promised, my mom texted me to make sure I was okay. It was right after we found her. If they had known what was going on, my brothers probably would have beaten us to Haven Point and ripped the town apart, looking for her."

He hit her garage with the remote opener and pulled inside, turned off her engine then walked around to open the passenger door for her.

"So are you heading back for your family slumber party now?"

"I don't know. I haven't decided."

She suddenly remembered where she and Ryan had been and what they had been doing when she received that fateful call from Brittany. It seemed hours ago that she had been in his arms.

"I don't know what I would have done if you hadn't been here. Thank you," she said. "You stayed calm when I was freaking out. It was your idea to check the park. I don't even want to think about the possible outcome if we hadn't."

The horrifying magnitude of what might have happened to her baby suddenly burned through her. Holly hitched in a breath that turned into one sob, then another.

Suddenly she was crying, all the emotions of the day pouring out of her. She couldn't hold back, try as she might.

In an instant, Ryan reached for her, his arms solid and dependable. "Hey. Hey. I've got you."

For how long?

She couldn't think about that now. For this moment, she only wanted to stand in the circle of his arms, where she felt safe.

Holly pressed her face into his chest, her tears soaking into his shirt, but he didn't seem to care.

She clung to him, moved beyond words at the way he held her like she was something precious.

Gradually, her sobs slowed then stilled, but she didn't step away. Christmas Eve, her family, everything else felt far away. Irrelevant in this moment.

All that mattered was Ryan. His warmth, his strength, the steady rhythm of his heart against her cheek. She pulled back just enough to meet his gaze, her fingers still clutching his shirt.

"Thank you," she whispered again, her voice trembling but full of sincerity. "I don't know how to—"

He shook his head, his eyes locked on hers. "You don't have to thank me."

The intensity in his gaze sent a shiver down her spine.

I can't stop thinking about you.

His words echoed through her memory, as tantalizing now as they had been when he murmured them to her earlier.

Without giving herself time to second-guess, Holly rose on tiptoe, her lips brushing his in a tentative, searching kiss.

For a heartbeat, he froze, as if he couldn't quite believe it. Then he responded, his arms tightening around her, the kiss deepening into something that felt as inevitable as the snowfall outside.

CHAPTER TWENTY-SIX

THIS PROBABLY WASN'T THE SMARTEST IDEA SHE'D EVER HAD.

She was feeling entirely too vulnerable right now, with her emotions raw and tangled. She couldn't move away, though. Not yet. She wanted to hold onto every possible moment with him.

He kissed her with a staggering tenderness that left her breathless, as if she were something fragile and extraordinary.

Holly's hands slid up to his shoulders, her fingers curling into the solid strength of him, grounding her in the moment. The storm of emotions that had overwhelmed her only minutes before completely ebbed away, replaced by a warmth that spread through her, chasing away every shadow.

This was safety. This was solace. And this, she realized with a trembling clarity, was something deeper.

He was the one who pulled away, resting his forehead on hers. Their ragged breathing mingled in the room and she couldn't seem to look away from the intensity of his expression.

"How the hell am I going to find the strength to leave you and Lydia?"

She blinked, stunned at the emotion in his voice.

"What?"

"The thought of it is ripping me up inside. Somehow the two of you have become . . . everything to me."

Joy exploded through her at the unexpected words and the tenderness behind them. She had no idea what to say; she could only murmur his name.

"I'm in love with you, Holly. I don't know how it happened but there it is. Somehow while we were pretending to have a relationship, I discovered how badly I wanted it all to be real.

When we lost Lydia tonight, I realized I don't want to lose her or you."

"Oh," she breathed, overwhelmed by his words and the emotion in his voice.

"You and your daughter have worked your way into my heart and I'm pretty sure you're there to stay."

This couldn't be real. Maybe she was still asleep in her car on the way home from Haven Point and she would wake up to find her subconscious had conjured up this whole exchange as a new form of torture.

No. Her fingers curled into the fabric of his shirt, feeling the hard muscles beneath. His strength was definitely real, as was the wild happiness zinging through her.

"I thought . . . you said you weren't interested in any relationship at all."

"For a guy who likes to think he's pretty smart, apparently I've said a lot of stupid stuff."

"I assumed that if you ever did change your mind, you certainly wouldn't want a relationship with someone like me."

"You mean someone amazing? A woman who has more courage than nearly everybody I've ever worked with in the navy?"

"I mean a divorced single mom in a small Idaho town who has a child with lifelong special needs."

He took her hand in his and tucked it against his heart. "I am not sure I really knew what I wanted, until I came to Shelter Springs this Christmas and met a certain lovely florist who is handling all the challenges in her life with grace and strength."

His words seemed to heal something inside she hadn't realized was broken.

Once more, he bent his head, his lips capturing hers in a soft kiss that was somehow both gentle and consuming, as if he wanted to show her everything he couldn't put into words. The aching tenderness in his touch unraveled her completely, leaving her no choice but to surrender to the moment.

She met his tenderness with her own, trying to tell him everything in her heart.

After a long, delicious moment, she eased away from him, needing to put her feelings into words.

"I've been so miserable the past few days, knowing you would be leaving soon and I would probably never see you again. I was upset about not spending Christmas Eve with Lydia but a good part of my misery was because of you."

"I'm sorry," he said, though he didn't look particularly repentant.

"I think I fell for you the very first time you came to the shop, when you met Lydia and I watched you tumble into love with her. I wasn't surprised about that part. Everyone does. They can't help it. But there was something about seeing this big, tough-looking military pilot turn to putty when he met my child. I fell hard and I've been trying to figure out what to do about it ever since."

HER WORDS SENT joy spilling through him like sunshine through a window on a stormy day.

He so easily could have missed this. It was all chance, a strange yet beautiful serendipity.

If Kim hadn't asked him for help, if he hadn't gone to pick up Audrey that day at Evergreen & Ivy, if he hadn't agreed—for reasons that still confounded him—to take her to the wedding, he wouldn't be right here in this moment, with the future stretching out ahead of them.

He had no idea what that future might look like for them.

All the reasons why this shouldn't work still held. He still had military commitments and was still stationed hundreds of miles away. Her business here in Shelter Springs was thriving and he couldn't take her away from that or from her support network of family and close friends.

They could figure all of that out. He was suddenly confident they would find a way. The important thing was that they could now figure it out together.

He kissed her again, until they were both breathing hard and she was trembling in his arms. He wanted more, so much more, though he knew this wasn't the moment.

"I have to go," she murmured against his mouth. "My family is expecting me. We're going to stay up all night and play games."

He cocked an eyebrow, heat arcing through him. "We could stay here all night and play games, just the two of us."

She swallowed hard and he saw an answering hunger in her eyes that humbled him.

"I have a feeling your games would be far more fun than Apples to Apples," she said, her voice husky.

"You can count on it."

She turned adorably pink and he had no choice but to kiss her again.

A long moment later, he set her away from him. "I won't take you away from your family on Christmas Eve, Holly."

"You could always join us."

While that idea definitely appealed, he thought they both needed a little time to come to terms with these feelings growing between them. It would be tough to hide those feelings at a party with her parents and siblings and he suspected Holly wasn't ready to explain them yet to her family.

And then there was his own family, waiting for him to spend what was left of Christmas Eve with them.

"I'm sure my dad and Diane have gone home by now but Audrey and Kim will be wondering where I am."

"I suppose you're right." She didn't bother to hide her disappointment and he had to kiss her again.

"How about we make a deal?"

She smiled. "Another one?"

"The first one worked out great for me. Agreeing to go to that wedding with you might have been the single best decision of my life."

She smiled, looking radiant and bubbling over with happiness.

"Unless you have other plans, let's spend New Year's Eve together. You, me and Lydia."

"I don't have plans. I would love that."

Her smile was so bright it outshone the twinkling lights of the Christmas tree behind her, and Ryan felt the warmth of it sink into every corner of his being. In that moment, he knew. This was what he'd been searching for, even when he didn't know he was looking.

A family, a home, a future that promised more joy than he had ever dared to imagine.

He pulled her into his arms one last time and pressed a kiss to her forehead. "Then it's a date," he murmured. "The first of many."

Holly tilted her face to his, her eyes shining with a happiness that matched his own. "Merry Christmas, Ryan."

"Merry Christmas," he said, filled with anticipation for all the holidays to come.

HOLLY CARRIED A BOWL OF SALAD TO THE DINING TABLE OF Doug and Diane's house by the lake. Looking around their warmly lit home, she was filled with a mixture of gratitude and sheer happiness.

A year ago, she could never have imagined this scene.

Lydia was sitting on the floor by the tree while Audrey read to her from a Christmas book and Lydia pointed out the words she could read herself.

Kim and Diane were in the kitchen laughing together as they worked on other preparations for the meal.

And Ryan was out on the deck with his father, the two of them engaged in the very serious business of grilling while a light snow fell around them.

The changes in their lives over the past twelve months were nothing short of extraordinary. Some had been challenging, others had been joyful, but all of them had brought her to this moment, where she was surrounded by love.

She set down the bowl and returned to the kitchen to help the two other women.

"Any idea how long on the steaks?" Kim asked. "I'm starving."

"How would Holly know? She's been in here helping us," Diane said with a laugh.

"You're right, I have no idea. But I'm happy to go ask."

She grabbed her coat and walked out to the deck, enjoying the cold night air and the moonlight gleaming on the lake.

Ryan smiled in welcome and held a hand out. She went to him, thinking she would never get tired of the way he always acted as if she and Lydia were the very best Christmas gifts he had ever received.

He put an arm around her and she settled against him. "Your sister is wondering how long on the steaks. She's apparently starving."

"Not long. Maybe seven or eight more minutes," her father-in-law said. "The grilled vegetables are done, though. Do you mind carrying them inside?"

"Not at all."

"I'll help you," Ryan said.

She suspected he wanted to steal a kiss more than he wanted to help her carry in a tray of veggies, but she wasn't about to complain.

As she suspected, the moment they were out of his father's view and inside the house, he captured her mouth with his and she glowed with happiness.

She loved being with him, probably because these moments felt rare and precious. Since their lovely lakeside wedding in September and the incredible honeymoon they had taken to Tahiti—where else?—she and Ryan had only been together for stretches of three or four days at a time every few weeks, when she and Lydia could fly to San Diego for a long weekend or he could travel to Idaho on leave.

It hadn't been the best arrangement, but he had to serve another six months before fulfilling his military obligation. Neither of them had wanted to wait that long before marrying and starting their life together, as complicated as it made things.

In six months, he would be moving to Shelter Springs permanently. She didn't know who was more excited at the prospect—her, Lydia or Doug.

Making plans to leave the military career he loved had been

tough for Ryan, but after two more surgeries on his knee and another infection in the past year, he knew he would never be able to meet the navy's stringent physical requirements.

He could, however, meet every requirement to fly commercial. That was his plan, though he had decided working with his father wasn't the right fit for now, much to Doug's disappointment. Ryan already had a position lined up flying air rescue helicopters in the region. It would allow him to still serve, only in a different capacity.

After setting the vegetables on the table, Ryan tugged her into the hallway, out of sight of everyone. He kissed her again, his mouth warm and delicious and now dearly familiar to her.

"You okay?" he asked. "I know you're missing your family party this year."

"More than okay," she murmured. "We'll see them tomorrow when they come for breakfast and to watch Lydia unwrap presents. And next year, we can swap and spend Christmas Eve with them."

"But Lydia won't be there next year. She'll be with Troy."

That thought actually didn't bother her as much as she might have expected a year earlier. Troy was working hard to build a stronger relationship with Lydia. He flew out to visit her every few months and Lydia had gone to stay with him and Brittany for a week after the wedding so that Holly and Ryan could enjoy their honeymoon.

Her daughter had come home bubbling over with how much fun she had and how cute her brother was and how her daddy was teaching her how to ride a bike.

Somehow they were all making it work.

"I'm fine with that. For now, we have this Christmas. Every moment has been wonderful. Not because everything has been perfect but because we're together."

Ryan smiled against her mouth. "Here's to many more Christmases together."

Holly's gaze drifting to the other room, where Lydia and Audrey were laughing about something and Diane and Kim bustled in and out.

"To many more," she echoed, knowing with absolute certainty that their best days were still ahead.

★ ★ ★ ★ ★

Turn the page for a sneak peek at
New York Times *bestselling author RaeAnne Thayne's next*
novel, The Sunny Day Bookshop, *coming this summer!*

CHAPTER ONE

—

Rosie

"WHO'S READY TO TAKE A TRIP TO THE MAGICAL LAND OF books?" Rosie Lucas asked as she set a plate of pancakes down in front of her granddaughter.

"I am!"

Olive's smile lit up every single inch of Rosie's heart.

The three-year-old girl and her mother, Rosie's daughter Emma, had been back in Oregon for less than twelve hours but Rosie already knew she never wanted them to leave again.

"Can I get a new book there?" Olive asked. She sent a sideways hopeful look to her grandmother that Rosie found impossible to resist.

"I believe that can probably be arranged."

Rosie still owned Wood Briar Bookshop after all, though she hadn't handled the day-to-day operations in years.

But what was the fun of owning a bookstore if a woman couldn't spoil her only granddaughter by letting her choose a picture book to bring home if she wanted?

The two of them chattered about some of Olive's favorite stories and television shows while the preschooler ate her breakfast. It was a thoroughly enjoyable time. Olive had nearly finished with her plate of pancakes when her mother rushed into the kitchen, her T-shirt still untucked and her hair slightly messy.

"Sorry," Emma said, sounding frazzled. "I know we talked about trying to get there before the store opens in—" she looked at her watch "—five minutes. I must have overslept. I don't know what happened. I never sleep through my alarm."

"I turned your phone off," Olive informed her with a cheerful smile. "It was too loud. I didn't want it to wake you up."

Emma gave her daughter a frustrated look, even as she leaned down and kissed the top of her head. "That's kind of the point of an alarm clock, honey."

"Don't worry about it," Rosie assured her. "I know we said nine but nothing is written in stone. There's no reason we have to leave at nine on the dot. We have all day. I only suggested it when you said you wanted an early start."

"Right. I do. I need to know what I'm up against. From everything you've said, it sounds like I'm going to have my work cut out for me."

Had Rosie given her daughter a task beyond her abilities? She really hoped not. She wanted to challenge Emma, not scare her away.

Ever since she and her daughter had reconnected after years of estrangement when Olive was six months old, Rosie felt as if she constantly walked a tightrope suspended two hundred feet in the air. A thin wire covered in baby oil. One misstep would ruin all their hard work toward healing the rift between them.

She didn't want to do anything to drive her daughter away again.

"You don't have to fix everything wrong with the bookstore in one day," she said carefully. "I hope I didn't give you that impression."

Emma poured herself some coffee. "I don't know. You were giving off some solid desperation vibes on the phone."

Rosie could not disagree. She did need Emma's help. More than that, though, she had been desperate to earn more of a role in the lives of her daughter and granddaughter. Despite their wary reconciliation a few years ago, Emma still lived near Seattle, hundreds of miles away from their town on the Oregon coast.

"You really are saving the day. I hated the idea of having to close the store for several weeks while your grandmother recovers from her accident, especially right as we're heading into the busy tourist season. The bookstore has barely covered its operating costs for years. I don't have time to run it myself and I don't really have time to train someone else to manage it. Not someone with your level of skill anyway."

"You do know I have zero experience at this, right?"

"You managed a restaurant, though."

She made a face. "Not a restaurant. A Starbucks. That's not the same as handling the day-to-day operations of a busy bookstore."

"First of all, Wood Briar Bookshop is not that busy, unfortunately. Mom hasn't exactly made drawing in crowds a priority."

"I'm fully aware of Grandma's philosophy. Books are meant to be enjoyed. Throwing in silly concepts like profit and loss ruins the experience."

Rosie's mother loved running the bookstore. Ordering books, talking with customers, helping a reader find the perfect selection. All the things Rosie had loved when she ran the bookstore herself.

Sylvia did not, however, enjoy having to reconcile the budget or focus on the bottom line. As a result, the bookstore wasn't exactly a profitable enterprise.

Over the years, many people had asked Rosie why she hadn't sold it after Gary's death. She never had a good answer for them, mostly because she didn't really know the reason. It made no business sense whatsoever. Her focus for years had been Lucas Construction, the company she and Gary had started together that she had muscled back out of near bankruptcy. She really didn't have time to focus on the bookstore she had owned for only a few months when her husband died and her life fell apart.

But every time she was tempted to sell, something held her back. How could she explain her love for books and her determination to keep the bookstore's doors open in a town that otherwise wouldn't have access to one?

"She hasn't changed," Rosie admitted. "If anything, her time running the store has only reinforced her beliefs. I actually heard her say to a customer once that they were free to spend as much time as they wanted browsing, reading the books, admiring the dust, and that buying was optional."

Emma laughed. "Sounds like Grandma."

Rosie gave a rueful smile in response. She loved her mother dearly. For all her quirks, Sylvia was kind, compassionate, fierce. She couldn't help that the bottom line wasn't her priority.

Emma, on the other hand, would be brilliant.

"You have a business degree and plenty of experience managing people. As far as I'm concerned, you're perfect. I'm so grateful you agreed to help."

Rosie had no idea why Emma had finally acquiesced this time. She suspected her daughter had been ready for a change, especially as the lease on the apartment she shared with two other single moms had been ending soon.

"I won't be perfect for anything if I can't wake up in time for work." Emma turned to her daughter with a chiding look. "New rule, kid. You can't turn off my phone alarm when it goes off, okay?"

"Okay," Olive said cheerfully, taking another bite of pancakes.

"Looks like Grandma made you breakfast."

"Mickey pancakes. Except I already ate the ears."

"I hope that's okay." Rosie tried to keep the anxious note from her voice but was afraid it filtered through anyway. Perhaps after Emma and Olive had settled in and been here a few weeks, Rosie might relax a little, lose some of this fear of making a wrong move and sending her daughter away again.

"Why wouldn't it be okay? I always eat the ears first. I always figured that way Mickey can't hear me chewing the rest of him."

"I meant the pancakes. I know you're vegetarian."

Emma lifted an eyebrow, the metal post piercing there reflecting sunlight. "Unless you have a special recipe these days that uses beef tallow or pork drippings to make your pancakes, they should be fine."

"No beef or pork. Just plain old pancake mix."

"Then we're good. I appreciate you feeding her."

"It was my pleasure." Rosie hoped her daughter knew she was determined to do everything possible to make sure the two of them were comfortable in her home.

"I tried to pick up things at the grocery store I thought you might like. I even bought a vegetarian cookbook and I've been looking up recipes online."

"Thank you. I really appreciate that," Emma said. She looked a little less frazzled now as she settled into a chair across from her daughter, sipping her coffee.

"Is your room comfortable? I did my best to update it. I've been slowly working on it since Christmas but after I talked to you last week, I had Bryce put a few other projects on the back burner to finish up here."

Emma's mouth tightened momentarily, then she smiled. What had Rosie said?

"It's nice," Emma assured her. "I really appreciate having two connected bedrooms and the Jack-and-Jill bathroom in between them. The rooms are perfect for now. If I end up staying in town longer than a few months while Grandma recovers, I'll probably look for my own place."

So many ifs. Rosie could only keep her fingers and toes crossed and do all she could to keep her daughter comfortable.

"You know there's no need for that. I have plenty of room, especially with Mom insisting on staying in her own place."

Rosie was not sure who was more stubborn, her daughter or her mother. Sylvia had lived in the tiny self-contained guest cottage in Rosie's backyard for ten years, ever since she'd uprooted her life in Portland after Gary's death and moved here to help them through their grief.

Her mother was stubborn, opinionated and fierce. She did her own thing and always had. Why else would she be currently recovering from a broken ankle sustained while Rollerblading at seventy-two years old?

"I'll be ready in a minute," Emma said.

"Are you sure you wouldn't like a pancake?"

"No. Coffee usually does it for me in the mornings."

This was yet another thing Rosie did not know about her daughter these days. This adult version of Emma was a virtual stranger.

The last time they had lived together, when Emma was seventeen, her daughter had loved a big breakfast. Bacon, hashbrowns, pancakes. The whole thing. Now she was a vegetarian who apparently fueled up with coffee in the mornings.

She would figure all of those things out. They had time now. Emma was here for at least a few months. If Rosie had anything to say about it, she could be here longer.

Her thoughts were interrupted by the back door opening. She looked over in surprise and found her mother peering at the three of them seated at the table.

Rosie jumped up and rushed to Sylvia. "Mom! What are you doing here? I can't believe you made your way all the way up here on your own. Why didn't you call me?"

Her mother was on crutches and she wore sleep pants that had monkey face emojis on them. Her dyed magenta hair was crumpled on one side, as if she had forgotten to comb it out after she awoke.

"I'm hungry, if you want the truth. I was out refilling my bird feeders and thought I smelled pancakes coming from this direction."

"I wish you would let me refill your bird feeders. The doctor says no weight bearing. You're supposed to be taking it easy."

"The doctor doesn't know what she's talking about," her mother grumbled. "I'm fine."

Sylvia was not fine. She had a compound ankle fracture that had already required one surgery and might possibly need another.

"I planned to drop some pancakes off before we head to the bookstore."

"Now you don't have to, since I'm here." She moved into the room, maneuvering carefully on her crutches.

"Hi, Granny Sylvie!" Olive beamed at her great-grandmother, her face sticky with syrup.

Sylvia grinned back at her. "Olive, darling. How wonderful to see you this beautiful morning. How did I get so lucky to see you two days in a row?"

"Guess what? You can see me every day."

"Aren't I truly a lucky duck, then?"

"You're not a duck." Olive chortled. "You're a grandma."

"A grandma who needs to sit down," Emma said. Rosie's daughter pulled out a chair at the kitchen table for her grandmother. "Here you go."

The older woman settled heavily into the chair, her leg outstretched on front of her.

"That's better. Who would have guessed one silly moment out of your life could have such lasting consequences?"

Anyone with a shred of common sense could have guessed. A seventy-two-year-old woman with mild osteoporosis had no business even being near Rollerblades, forget about putting them on.

But Sylvia didn't ask her. Her mother never asked advice before embarking on her escapades; she simply plowed forward. Or skated forward, in this case.

"Here you are, Mom," she said, putting a plate stacked with three fluffy blueberry pancakes in front of her. "And here's the syrup. What can I get you to drink?"

"Water is fine," Sylvia said, then sent her a hopeful look. "I don't suppose you have any bacon to go with this, do you?"

"I do, but I would rather not cook it right now."

"Why not? Bacon goes perfectly with pancakes on a beautiful Sunday morning."

Rosie sighed. "Emma and Olive are vegetarians, remember?"

Emma rolled her eyes, almost as if she were fifteen years old again. "You can eat meat in front of me, Mom."

"I don't need bacon." Sylvia looked contrite. "I'll be fine. If I need more protein, I'll have a yogurt or something."

All of them were dancing around each other like boats navigating through a foggy harbor.

"What about eggs?"

"Eggs are fine," Emma assured them. "I eat eggs. So does Olive. But bacon is fine for you, too. I'm not offended by other people eating meat just because I've chosen a mostly plant-based diet."

Rosie would figure out this new reality of having them live with her. She needed to sit down with Emma and have a good talk about her and Olive's dietary preferences—and anything else they needed to figure out so they could make this arrangement as comfortable as possible.

She had so much to learn about her daughter and her granddaughter. She and Emma hadn't lived together in eight years. Hadn't spoken for five of those.

Those years had been a terrifying time for Rosie, as she had no idea even where her daughter was or what she might be going through. Her only comfort had come from knowing Emma had stayed in touch with her grandmother and always assured Sylvia she was fine. Sylvia, in turn, had passed that information to Rosie.

How fine was up for debate. Rosie suspected the full truth would devastate her if she ever learned all the details. Emma had been a seventeen-year-old girl, living with a man nearly a decade older who had dragged her into a life of drug and alcohol abuse.

She was here now. And doing incredibly well, all things considered. Clean and sober since before Olive was born, Emma had a college degree she had worked hard to earn on her own and she had left a decent job to come back to Wood Briar and help out at the bookshop.

The two of them were working to repair their fractured relationship, but the occasional phone call, text messages and rare short visits could only go so far.

Having both her daughter and her granddaughter in her home at last—the two people she loved most in the world—felt like a priceless gift and she was terrified she would screw it up.

"We always have eggs, thanks to our girls," she said, grateful for the five little Rhode Island Reds who provided a steady supply.

When Sylvia first came to her during the Covid pandemic

and said she wanted to pick up some chicks, Rosie had been reluctant. She adored them now. Together with her two cats, one adorable little dog, a giant tortoise and the opinionated parrot she considered Sylvia's spirit animal, her house didn't lack for creatures for Olive to love.

As she cracked several eggs and scrambled them together, she listened to the hum of conversation between the three women of multiple generations.

Emma and Sylvia chattered away with a familiarity that sent a little twinge of jealousy through Rosie, though she knew she had no right to it.

She was happy her mother and her daughter got along so well. It had been a deep comfort during their years of separation to know Emma had someone reliable in her life to count on.

She couldn't help it that she wanted Emma to confide in her instead of Sylvia.

After she finished the eggs, she plated them and took a seat at the table across from her mother.

"So what's on the docket for you ladies today?" Sylvia asked.

"We're going to the book place," Olive announced happily. "Grandma says I can have a new book."

"Are you?"

Emma nodded. "I want to take a look at things and start figuring out your system."

"What time are you leaving? I only need a few minutes to get dressed and do something with this hair."

"Are you sure, Mom?" Rosie said. "We might be there for a few hours."

"I won't do a single thing that takes more effort than lifting a pencil. We can't just toss the girl into the deep end."

"You don't have to come with us if you're not up to it," Emma assured her. "We can always FaceTime you if we have questions."

Annoyance creased Sylvia's forehead. "I have a broken ankle. I'm not dying. I can handle a little trip to the bookstore."

"Are you sure?" Rosie asked.

"Positive. I don't know why your mother felt the need to drag you down here. I'm still perfectly capable of running the bookstore. I don't mean to imply I'm not happy you're here. I'm over the moon about that part. But it all feels like a lot of fuss for nothing."

Rosie squelched her guilt. This was the right decision for her mother, even if Sylvia didn't want to admit it.

"Dr. Peterson is the one who said you should take several weeks off. You have to stay off your ankle as much as possible. How can you do that when you're trying to take inventory or wait on customers?"

"I can sit on a rolling chair or something. And why are you paying our people so much, if not to wait on customers and handle inventory?"

"We've talked about this, Mom." Rosie fought down her frustration. "Listen to the doctor. Take a vacation for a month. Let your ankle heal as long as possible, and then we'll see how you are after the doctor says you can put weight on it again."

She sincerely hoped her mother would decide that with the bookstore in the very capable hands of Emma, she could relax a little and enjoy her retirement. She could sleep in all morning, go thrift shopping with her girlfriends in the afternoon— once her ankle healed, anyway—and even catch the party bus to the nearest casino to play the slots.

Sylvia made a face. "It sucks getting old, little girl," she said to Olive, who giggled as she continued eating her scrambled eggs.

To Rosie's relief, her mother let the matter slide.

They could do this, Rosie thought as she finished her eggs.

Juggling four generations in one house—okay, one house and a mother-in-law cottage in the backyard—would be a challenge but Rosie would make any sacrifice necessary to protect her mother's health, heal the rift with her daughter and have an active role in her granddaughter's life.

It wouldn't be easy, but Rosie had been dealing with hard things for a decade. Compared to everything else they had endured as a family, this should be a piece of cake.

CHAPTER TWO

—

Emma

AN HOUR AFTER THAT PANICKY WAKE-UP SCRAMBLE, EMMA was still feeling frazzled as she and her mother loaded her grandmother into the passenger seat of her beat-up third-hand Honda Accord.

"It will be better to take your car than your mother's," Sylvia had said in her no-nonsense tone.

"Why?" Rosie had asked, looking almost hurt, as if Grandma Syl had said her car smelled like a dead mouse.

"Because it makes the most sense. Emma already has a car seat for Miss Olive. And you know how hard it's been for me to boost my fat tuchas into your SUV."

So there Emma was, embarrassed about her junk-heap car. When she paid cash for it a year ago, depleting what was left of her savings after tuition, the car had represented all her hard-earned progress. She had a job. An apartment. And now a car of her own so she wouldn't have to spend an extra hour a day catching public transportation to take Olive to day care before heading to work.

They settled Sylvia into the passenger seat, carefully adjusting her cast and her crutches, then her mother walked around to open the rear passenger door next to Olive.

"You can sit by me, Grandma," Olive chirped, looking delighted at the prospect of a bookstore outing with her grandmother and great-grandmother.

Emma climbed in and backed slowly out of her mom's driveway. She was fully aware she was a ridiculously cautious driver. She rarely exceeded the speed limit and always looked both ways twice before entering any intersection.

She guessed killing her father while learning to drive could probably scar a person.

Funny, that she was so careful behind the wheel when she'd certainly specialized in every other kind of risky behavior over the past ten years.

Mindful that she was carrying three people she loved, she drove slowly through Wood Briar. The town had changed since she last lived here. New businesses had popped up here and there and a few others had closed. The pizza place where she and her friends liked to hang out now seemed to be a bakery, and the bike shop seemed to now sell tourist supplies like beach chairs, kites and towels, at least judging by the window display.

The town had added hanging baskets from the old-style streetlights, and their colorful blossoms spilled over in wild abundance.

The bookstore looked the same, taking up a prime corner of real estate only a block from the seawall.

"You can park in the back now," her mother said. "A few years ago, the downtown alliance bought up the inner block area and made a parking terrace."

That was new. Parking had always been a problem in downtown Wood Briar, especially in the summertime when tourists flocked to these small Oregon beach towns.

The tourist madness apparently hadn't kicked in yet. On that early June Sunday morning, she could easily find a space close to the back entrance of the Wood Briar Bookshop.

Olive unhooked her car seat, a relatively new skill Emma wasn't all that thrilled about. "Stay there," she ordered her. "We need to help Grandma Sylvia first."

Her daughter gave a pout but picked up her favorite doll

she had named Penelope for some reason and began chattering to her as Emma opened her trunk and pulled out the collapsible wheelchair her mother had insisted they bring for Grandma.

"I don't need this stupid thing. I've got crutches and a knee scooter. They're perfectly fine." Sylvia's wrinkled features wore a disgruntled frown as she looked at the chair.

Rosie sighed, looking weary. Emma might have expected Sylvia wouldn't be a very easy patient. When had she ever taken the easy route? Her grandmother loved causing trouble, which was one of the many reasons Emma adored her.

"You know you'll heal better if you take it easy," her mother said in an ultra-patient tone. "You're great at the crutches, but why use them when you don't have to? We rented the wheelchair. We might as well use it."

"Fine," Sylvia grumbled. "But this thing makes me feel like an old lady."

"You are kind of an old lady," Olive piped up from the back seat.

Yeah. Olive basically had no filter whatsoever. Kind of like her great-grandmother. Maybe that was why the two of them seemed to get along so well.

"Thank you for the reminder, my dear," Sylvia said, sounding amused rather than annoyed. "I'm definitely not as young as I once was. I suppose it's fine this once."

Emma and her mother helped her grandmother from the car to the wheelchair. It didn't really take both of them, but Rosie seemed happy for Emma's assistance.

"Want me to push her in?" Emma asked.

Rosie shook her head. "I've got it. Go ahead and help Olive."

She pushed Sylvia to the rear entrance of the bookshop while Emma opened the door for Olive and helped her out of the car.

"I love love love bookstores," her daughter announced, her voice bubbling over with joy as she skipped to the door.

Same, girl. Emma smiled at her, grabbing her hand as anticipation curled through her. This place would be her project for the next few months—assuming Rosie could convince Sylvia to step back, which seemed a formidable task right then.

And speaking of formidable tasks.

Emma walked inside the bookstore and was momentarily speechless. All she could think was "ew."

The bookstore seemed trapped in another era, with fluorescent lights, dingy paint and crowded aisles stacked with dusty books.

Olive looked around. "This place is messy."

That was one word for it. Emma could think of several others, none of which were appropriate to say in the presence of her three-year-old child.

"We're back here," Rosie called out.

Still holding Olive's hand, Emma made her way to the office that ran along the back wall. Dust motes floated like tiny shards of gold in the light coming through the front windows. She might think them pretty under other circumstances. Circumstances where she had not found herself suddenly responsible for turning a profit out of that cluttered, disorganized pit of despair.

Inside the office, she found her mother trying to move a chair so Sylvia's wheelchair could fit at the computer desk.

"Did you see the play area when you came in?" Sylvia asked. "I keep old books I find at Goodwill and yard sales for kids to read and take home if they want."

"That's nice," Emma said as she exchanged a look with her mother. Wasn't a bookstore supposed to sell books, though? "A play area is a good idea."

"It gives the children somewhere to hang out in the store so they don't pull everything off the shelves, plus keeps them occupied while their parents shop for books," Sylvia said. "The toys are a little outdated. I only have a play kitchen, some blocks and a couple of trucks. The kids seem to enjoy it anyway."

"Maybe Olive can play there sometimes while you're working," Rosie said, that anxious note in her voice again.

Her mother was trying so hard to make sure Emma was comfortable. Her eagerness made Emma's throat feel tight and achy.

"That will be great," she said, meaning the words.

Olive was the main reason she was there. For her daughter's first three years, she had spent more time in day care than with her own mother. Emma had been busy working or going to school, though she tried her best to work around her daughter's schedule and take mostly online classes, so she could do the schoolwork while Olive was in bed.

Her daughter was smart, healthy, well-adjusted. But in three years, she had already been through eight day care situations.

In two years, she would be heading to kindergarten, then grade school. She was growing up far too fast. Emma wanted the chance to spend more quality time with her—and to have her spend as much time as possible with her grandmother and great-grandmother.

Finding good quality childcare was the single hardest thing Emma had to do as a single mother. Harder than staying up all night with Olive when she was ill, harder than the constant grinding worry about finances, harder than the equally grinding effort to stay sober so she could be the mother her daughter deserved.

Depending on her mood, Emma found her situation either far easier or much more complicated because Olive's father was not in the picture whatsoever. Most of the time, she thanked her lucky stars that she didn't have to deal with Kevin Hollis on the daily.

Sometimes, though, she couldn't help thinking how much easier her life would be if she had someone else to help carry the relentless parenting load.

Kevin would have been a lousy father. She knew that. Emma hadn't wanted to let her child anywhere near him and she'd been relieved when he had signed away his parental rights, even when it complicated things for her.

Day care shouldn't be as much of a problem in Wood Briar, especially if she could bring Olive along with her sometimes while she worked. Besides her mother and grandmother to help out on occasion, she still had friends in town, including her best friend, Josie. She was a trad wife, a stay-at-home mom with a daughter Olive's age as well as a baby boy. When Emma told her she was coming home for the summer, she immediately offered her babysitting services. Yes, it would still be day care but in a homier environment.

Somehow, the office was even less appealing than the rest of the bookstore—windowless, cluttered, with dingy carpet and acres of dark paneling.

Emma pulled out her phone, opening a new note she labeled Possible Changes.

Beneath that, she wrote in big letters, Redecorate.

The place needed new lighting, new carpet, new paint and a whole hell of a lot of elbow grease. She definitely had her work cut out for her.

You're going to screw this up, like you screw up everything else.

She tried to push away the negative voice in her head. She didn't screw up everything. She had already accomplished far more than she ever expected during those hard years when she only cared about her next fix.

"Ready for a tour?" Rosie asked.

Emma smiled, filled with renewed resolve. Her mother was counting on her to do a good job. More than that, Olive was. Her daughter deserved a better life than the one they left behind. If she could prove herself at the bookstore, perhaps she could figure out a way to convince her mother she was capable of more.

She simply had to use the same stubborn determination she inherited from both her mother and grandmother, the grit that had pushed her this far.

Grandma opted to stay near Olive in the play area, so Emma followed her mother through the crowded aisles, jotting copious notes as they went.

The store was mostly empty except for a few customers and two employees, one at the checkout counter and one stocking books. She saw a customer looking at magazines and a couple of teenage girls giggling over what looked like a paltry collection of romantasy titles.

The comforting, familiar smell of ink and paper surrounded them, along with something musty and old.

"As you can see, your grandmother has let a few things go," her mom whispered.

Had it been hard for Rosie to turn over the operations of the bookstore to Sylvia, who obviously wasn't all that concerned about profit and loss?

At one time, owning a small-town bookstore had been Rosie's biggest dream. When she wasn't helping Emma's father at Lucas Construction, she had worked there part-time for the previous owner, a crusty man who had been certain the future lay in renting out videotapes and CDs.

With big dreams and bigger ideas, Rosie had purchased it from him only a few months before the accident. When everything had changed for all of them.

Now her mother ran the construction company alone and Grandma Sylvia dabbled in managing a floundering bookstore, between juggling her active social life and apparently Rollerblading.

Her mother was introducing Emma to the employee shelving books, a studious-looking boy with shy dark eyes and a nervous tic, when Olive's voice drifted to them from one aisle over.

"My name is Olive. What's yours?"

A deep male voice answered something she couldn't hear. It was possible Emma listened to far too many true-crime podcasts, but her mind immediately went on stranger-danger alert.

In mid-conversation, she walked away from her mother and the employee, whose name was apparently Lance, to hurry around the endcap to the next aisle.

There, she found her daughter chattering away to a gorgeous guy in a snug T-shirt and jeans.

Unlike Emma, her three-year-old seemed to excel at finding hot guys.

"Olive, honey, I thought you were sitting with your grandmother in the play area. She was reading to you."

Olive shrugged. "She fell asleep. I wanted another book. One about dogs."

"Hi, Emma. Great to see you!"

At the voice coming from the hot stranger, she looked up. He was tall, lanky, with work-rough hands and long eyelashes. She had the disconcerting thought that she should know him but couldn't quite place him.

She narrowed her gaze. "I'm sorry. I've been gone from town for a few years. Do I know you?"

"Bryce!" Her mother's voice from behind her drew the guy's attention and he straightened, smiling broadly. She suddenly knew exactly who he was.

Bryce Kendall.

The man who currently had everything she wanted.

Rosie hurried forward, her features bright with pleasure. "Oh, Bryce. I didn't know you were coming into the bookstore today. I'm so happy to see you. This is my granddaughter."

"Of course she is. I immediately recognized her from the many, many, many pictures you have on your desk. Hi Olive. I'm Bryce and I work with your grandmother."

"My grandma builds houses."

"I know. So do I. And schools and stores and restaurants sometimes."

Her mother wore a proud smile but Emma couldn't tell if it was directed at Olive or Bryce.

"I guess you know Emma," she said. "You graduated the same year, didn't you?"

"Only because I graduated a year early and Bryce was held back a year."

As soon as Emma said the words, she regretted them. They made her sound like a first-class b-word. Like a spoiled, surly child in the playground kicking sand all over someone else's bigger and better sandcastle.

"Sorry," she muttered.

He shrugged with a smile that didn't quite hide the tiny glimmer of hurt in eyes the color of new aspen leaves.

She couldn't tell Bryce or her mother the reason for her pettiness. That she was fiercely jealous of his role as her mother's trusted second-in-command at Lucas Construction.

How had that happened anyway? It still made no sense to her.

Bryce had been the class clown, always causing trouble. Though mostly annoying, he used to make her laugh the way no one else ever could.

Yet now, at twenty-seven, he was a respected builder whom her mother seemed to trust above all others.

Grandma Sylvia had mentioned to her a few months ago that she expected Bryce to one day take over running the company.

Not if Emma could help it.

Lucas Construction was her family's legacy. Not Bryce's.

Her father had fought hard to build it from the ground up to the well-respected business it was today. Going on job sites with him had been her favorite thing in the world. She used to love handing him nails, helping him clean up the site or simply sitting beside him chattering away about whatever came to mind.

She wanted in at Lucas Construction. While running the bookstore would do in the short term, eventually she wanted to prove to her mother she was capable of handling the responsibilities of a huge operation like Lucas Construction.

"What brings you to the bookstore?" Rosie asked Bryce, her features bright with affection. At forty-five, she was still as lovely as ever, Emma realized with some degree of shock.

"You know me. I love to check out the new releases and sometimes Sundays are my only chance."

"I wouldn't have taken you for much of a reader," Emma said. "We had English together both our junior and senior year and if I'm remembering correctly, it wasn't your favorite subject."

"I love books, but not really reading them."

"Oh, just looking at the pictures?"

The words spilled out, despite Emma's best intentions to be civil. What was wrong with her?

"I'm an audiobook listener. I go through two or three a week while I'm working or driving from job site to job site."

"Listening to audiobooks still counts as reading," Rosie said, a sliver of censure toward Emma threading through her voice.

"I agree," Emma said. "But does Wood Briar Bookshop sell audiobooks?"

"Not very many," she admitted. "We have a few old CDs, but that's it."

"I'm actually here to buy a gift for a friend. But I like to come in regularly and see what's new and what looks good," Bryce said. "If I find something that appeals to me, I'll listen on audio. When I find a book I love, I like to buy a copy of the physical book here for my own collection or to donate to the town library."

"I love books!" Olive announced, her features wide with delight. "Grandma Rosie said I can have one. Will you help me pick it?"

Emma thought at first her daughter was speaking to her but then realized her smile was only aimed at Bryce.

He seemed disconcerted at her friendliness. "I don't know much about kids' books, I'm afraid. We didn't have many at my house when I was growing up."

Emma couldn't even imagine that. Books had been an integral part of her childhood. Both her parents had been avid readers and she picked up her love of stories from them.

During the long, hard years in Seattle, public libraries had saved her. They had been shelter, sanctuary, a place of safety and peace.

"You don't need to bother Mr. Kendall," Emma said.

"Come with me, darling," her mother said, holding out her hand to Olive. "We'll go look at the books. I'll help you choose a good one."

"Okay." Olive stuck her hand in her grandmother's, and the two of them headed for the children's section. Emma was left with Bryce and her wholly unreasonable resentment toward him.

"Your mom tells me you're going to be running the bookstore until Sylvia is back on her feet," he said. Emma noticed his long eyelashes fringing green eyes and that he had a farmer's tan, visible when his T-shirt sleeve rode up a little, exposing a strip of paler skin that contrasted with his darker forearms.

Emma swallowed a sigh, trying to tell herself it was only a reaction to the sheer scope of the challenge ahead of her, not any quiver of awareness.

"That's right. The bookstore hasn't exactly been profitable for a few years." Or ever. "I'm hoping to use this summer as a chance to chart a different path. I would like to turn things around."

He looked around. "You have your work cut out for you."

"I'm fully aware."

"Any initial ideas?"

She looked at the note on her phone, up to multiple screens of to-do items now. "Too many," she admitted. "I don't know where to start first."

He looked around. "What this place needs is something besides books to bring people in."

"This is a bookstore, Bryce. It's right there in the name."

"Ha. Yeah, I'm aware. But you want something that would pull someone in who might not necessarily be in the market for books. They walk in for something else, something irresistible, then see a cover that speaks to them and before they know it, they have a whole stack of new titles in their basket and you have instant sales."

Emma had been thinking along those exact same lines, and it irked her that Bryce and she were apparently on the same page. "I wrote down What about a small coffee bar?" she admitted.

She wasn't sure if that was a valid idea or simply a kneejerk reaction, coming from someone who, until recently, had managed a coffee shop.

"That would be perfect! Maybe you could even work out a

cooperative arrangement with one of the local coffee places to provide staff and product. We have some great ones in town. And you could sell pastries from Coastal Crumb, the bakery down the street. Their cinnamon rolls are as addictive as books."

She could put the café set-up near the front window facing Front Street to bring in more foot traffic. They could start genre book clubs that could meet there over coffee and pastries.

The store could even host silent reading book clubs, where people sat together, drank their coffee and enjoyed their latest read.

Her mind filled with possibilities, each more exciting than the one before. Then she took in her surroundings once more, and she fell back to earth with a hard thud.

"I think I need to focus on more basic renovations first before I think about expanding. Brighten things up a little. New paint, maybe, and clear out some of the inventory so it doesn't feel as cluttered in here."

"Not a bad idea. If you need help, let me know."

"I can't believe my mother hasn't put more energy and resources into freshening up the place. She owns a construction company, for heaven's sake."

His mouth tightened, as if he was annoyed at her for daring to voice anything resembling criticism of her mother. It was another unwanted reminder of their close working relationship.

"She's been a little busy the past few years, trying to keep Lucas Construction going. That's why she brought in your grandmother to help with the bookstore in the first place."

Emma glanced over at him, surprised. "Lucas is doing great, isn't it? I mean, the town has grown so much. I see construction projects everywhere."

"Wood Briar is definitely growing, but Lucas isn't the only game in town. It takes a lot of work to stay relevant, with all the competitors. It's not easy to pay a living wage and also turn a profit. Your mom has really turned things around the past few years, but it's been a rough road."

Her parents had both worked hard to build the company. Emma remembered many hours spent hanging out in the office when she was a kid, while her mom did payroll and accounting. That was when the company was a little two-person operation and her dad mostly worked with subcontractors to build maybe three or four homes a year.

Then Lucas had branched out to commercial real estate and started working with property developers, and the business exploded. They had taken on more employees: project supervisors, designers, office staff. By the time she left town, Lucas Construction had a payroll of nearly a hundred people.

Including Pam Clarke, the office manager.

Her stomach clenched at the thought of the woman, who was about a decade older than her. From what Emma had heard, Pam still lived in town, still worked for the company. Emma would have to see her at some point, and the thought made her feel vaguely ill.

"I really would be happy to help you," Bryce said. "I'm sure your mom would be fine with it. If not, I can help during my free time. Just let me know."

Emma probably would not be doing that. "Thanks," she said.

"It really is good to see you again, Emma. I know Rosie is thrilled to have you home."

"Right. Good to see you too," she lied.

Okay, it wasn't completely a lie. What woman didn't appreciate a hot, ripped guy who loved books? But that wasn't why she had returned to Oregon. She didn't want to mess this up.

She had a job to do at the Wood Briar Bookshop. Her mother was counting on her . . . and her daughter needed the stability and connection to her grandmother and great-grandmother she was already finding here.

Emma couldn't afford to ruin everything by letting herself become distracted by a man who stood in the way of everything she wanted.

Don't miss RaeAnne Thayne's new book,
The Sunny Day Bookshop, *available soon!*